Murder
in an
English Glade

Books by Jessica Ellicott

MURDER IN AN ENGLISH VILLAGE

MURDER FLIES THE COOP

MURDER CUTS THE MUSTARD

MURDER COMES TO CALL

MURDER IN AN ENGLISH GLADE

Published by Kensington Publishing Corp.

Murder
in an
English Glade

Jessica Ellicott

KENSINGTON
PUBLISHING CORP.

www.kensingtonbooks.com

KENSINGTON BOOKS are published by

Kensington Publishing Corp.
119 West 40th Street
New York, NY 10018

All Kensington titles, imprints, and distributed lines are available at special quantity discounts for bulk purchases for sales promotion, premiums, fund-raising, educational, or institutional use. Special book excerpts or customized printings can also be created to fit specific needs. For details, write or phone the office of the Kensington Special Sales Manager: Attn. Special Sales Department. Kensington Publishing Corp, 119 West 40th Street, New York, NY 10018. Phone: 1-800-221-2647.

Library of Congress Card Catalogue Number: 2021938935

ISBN-13: 978-1-4967-2485-4
ISBN-10: 1-4967-2485-2
First Kensington Hardcover Edition: November 2021

ISBN-13: 978-1-4967-2491-5 (ebook)
ISBN-10: 1-4967-2491-7 (ebook)

10 9 8 7 6 5 4 3 2 1

Printed in the United States of America

Murder
in an
English Glade

Chapter 1

Edwina should have known that there would be trouble when Beryl had asked if she did not feel guilty about lazing around the house while her housekeeper, Beddoes, slaved away. Her friend simply could not understand the relationship between household members and domestic servants. It wasn't her fault. After all, Beryl was an American, and as such could not be expected to comprehend the nuances of such time-honored arrangements in England. Still, even with that sort of warning, Edwina had not anticipated the uproar the second day of cleaning had entailed.

When Edwina's jobbing gardener, Simpkins, had come into an enormous fortune only a few weeks previously, he had generously gone to the extortionate expense of acquiring a member of household staff. In fact, he had arranged the entire affair with the assistance of his elderly aunt before Edwina even knew he was planning such a thing. She had been shocked by his thoughtfulness, as well as his generosity.

And as much as Simpkins was an entirely inferior gardener himself, he did know just what made for a proper, old-fashioned sort of servant. There was no denying that Beddoes was exactly that. In fact, if Edwina had been in a position to secure a house-keeper on her own, she would have offered the post to Beddoes without a moment's hesitation.

What she could not have foreseen was how her years without the ability to pay for household help had changed her. She had become quite used to not needing to soothe the servants' ruffled feathers or to think about their pride. She prized Beddoes's work ethic and understood her fierce devotion to her domain, but she did not in any way enjoy the thickly churlish atmosphere filling the home any time that superior woman felt her toes being the least bit trod upon. Regrettably, Beryl had a maddening way of doing just that, several times each day.

Recently, there had been a palpable uptick in tensions between the two. The week before, Beddoes had announced her intention to give Edwina's home, the Beeches, a good bottoming out. She had gone so far as to remark that the large house did none of them the least bit of credit in its current state, and that she did not consider it in any condition to receive visitors.

Beddoes did not request permission to embark on the project, of course, and Edwina would not have thought to disagree with her. She knew her place in their arrangement and was perfectly happy to allow Beddoes her head in all such matters. Edwina had asked if hiring on a charwoman from the village to assist with the heavier duties would be welcome. When Beddoes had arched her eyebrows in disapproval at the suggestion, Edwina knew to drop the matter entirely.

Between Beddoes making pointed comments intended to encourage Beryl to desist her interfering and the ruckus caused by the turning out of every cupboard, closet, and drawer in the house, Edwina had not had a moment's peace since dawn had broken. Edwina did not like to think of herself as an artistic diva. Not in the least. But she did need a semblance of quiet in order to work on the novel she was secretly writing.

Even if she were so inclined, she could not very well stomp

around and demand peace and quiet while she worked since she had not made anyone besides Beryl aware that she was working on anything other than the odd invoice or advertising notices for the fledgling private enquiry business. Still, it would be almost worth exposing her closely held secret in order to have the other members of the household quiet down.

She pushed back from the typewriter with a wistful look and gave the whole thing up for the day. She secreted her manuscript into a locked drawer and pocketed the key before whistling for her little dog, Crumpet. He raced into the hallway to meet her just as she plucked her third-best hat from the hall tree and adjusted it on her head in front of the glass. She retrieved her beloved camera from the hall table and looped the strap over her neck. If she could not work on her novel, perhaps she might encounter something interesting to photograph.

"Let's leave all this fuss behind and have a good ramble instead," she said to him as she bent down and snapped on his lead. He capered about her feet as they struck off for the rolling fields and hedgerows just beyond the gates at the end of the drive.

There were few things Edwina liked more than a jaunt through the English countryside. The winding lanes and leafy trees and the hotchpotch of greenery all filled her with a sense of well-being with each step she took. Crumpet paused now and again to sniff extravagantly at both herbaceous undergrowth and irregular patches on the road itself. Edwina didn't care in the least as she had no particular destination in mind and no schedule to keep.

In fact, considering the state of the household at present, the longer she stayed out-of-doors, the better. She would consider the time well spent no matter where they roamed. During such walks her thoughts tended to wander down even more paths than her feet, and she always returned home bursting with ideas and notions.

Edwina's mind turned to the present difficulty in her novel.

She had trapped her hero, Bart Dalton, in a canyon blocked by a gang of bandits with no water and very few bullets left in his gun. She had delighted in getting him into that bit of bother, but she was having rather more trouble figuring out how to get him out of it again.

She was vaguely aware of Crumpet digging away enthusiastically at the base of a filbert hedge, but the larger part of her mind was busy picturing the dusty pass facing her hero rather than the country lane in front of her. She could hear the sound of the bandit gang's taunting jeers and the whinnying of her hero's valiant steed in her imagination even more clearly than she could the birds twittering in the treetops above her head.

Suddenly, though, a very real, very nearby roar jostled her from her musings. She barely had time to jump from the edge of the road onto the overgrown grassy verge before a motorcycle tore down the lane, spewing gravel, and passed her in a swirl of dust. Her heart raced in her chest as she stared after it. Even though she could see his face clearly, she did not recognize the man driving the motorcycle. The brilliant red hair of the woman riding in the sidecar flapped wildly in the wind. The woman turned and looked at her, perhaps to assess if she was injured. She lifted her arm and waved in what might have been meant as an inadequate apology.

Edwina felt well and truly rattled. She supposed that she ought to be grateful that her beloved Walmsley Parva had not yet turned into one of those pitiable villages overrun by weekenders. Lamentably, there were a few cottages routinely let by outsiders who thought nothing of careening about the highways and byways at rates of speed no sensible person would attempt. Edwina looked down at Crumpet, who had dismissed the entire incident from his mind and returned to his investigation of the hole in the ground. She stepped back up onto the road and gave his lead a gentle tug. If there was to be any peace for her today, she would have to get right away from civilization. Crumpet followed her into the field across the lane with a sad backwards glance at the hole.

Beryl had made a botched job of things from the start. She had waited until Edwina and Crumpet were safely out of sight before launching into her plan to help with the cleaning. Edwina had proved surprisingly unsupportive and disapproving of her suggestion that Beddoes could use some assistance considering the size of the undertaking. Beryl decided it would be far more productive to surreptitiously offer to pitch in after doing everything in her power to drive Edwina away from the Beeches, at least until she had softened Beddoes towards her scheme.

Her biggest mistake, she could see that clearly now, was to seek out Beddoes in her private sanctuary. Not being encumbered by the same sense of social strata as the rest of the household, Beryl thought nothing whatsoever of attempting a chatty and informal relationship with any member of domestic staff. Beddoes, inexplicably, did not share her sense of egalitarianism and had, in fact, rebuffed her every overture of camaraderie. She had acted as if Beryl had breached some sort of invisible threshold by mounting the staircase to the third floor, where the servants at the Beeches had made their homes for decades.

Her expression had been so forbidding that Beryl wished she could have bottled the look on Beddoes's face to use as an insect repellent for some future trek into a dense jungle. She retreated with haste, calling out that she would join Beddoes on the main floor of the Beeches when they were both dressed for the tasks at hand.

But, as Beryl was never one to allow a bad start to guarantee a bad end, she pushed on. Beryl had decided she would treat the whole endeavor as a new spot of adventure, albeit one for which she was particularly ill prepared. In all her years of rattling around the globe, besting land speed records or tracking wild beasts, she had always believed in having the right gear for the job. She could hardly credit the notion that she had nothing in her wardrobe that seemed the right sort of thing for a vigorous bout of housekeeping. After many clothing changes, she stood in front of the glass and observed her final ensemble.

Although it was an unconventional one, it would have to do. She had discovered a man's shirt in the back of the wardrobe and had been gratified that it had fit. Truth be told, she had been rather worried she had grown somewhat stout since arriving in Walmsley Parva. In the last few weeks she had reduced her consumption of starches and had even cut back on her imbibing ever so slightly. As she rolled up the sleeves on the shirt, she congratulated herself on a job well done.

She stepped into a pair of khaki trousers from her last trip to South America and slipped her feet into a pair of sturdy boots. She wound a scarf over her hair to keep the dust from clinging to her platinum bob and added a kerchief round her neck for good measure. The judicious use of a kerchief had stood her in good stead many times over the years whether on safari or careening about in an aeroplane. There was every possibility that it would be equally of use in whatever rigors Beddoes had in mind.

Beryl descended the stairs and cocked her ear to listen for the elusive housekeeper. While she considered herself to be a dab hand at tracking, she had always found well-trained servants to be the most elusive of quarry. A bird in the wild or a shy gazelle had nothing on an old-school parlormaid when it came to blending into the surroundings. As a woman who had spent her life making a living by standing out from the crowd, Beryl found it completely befuddling.

A low but persistent rustling noise floated towards her as she reached the bottom stair. She followed the sound to the dining room, where Beddoes stood draping the furniture with lengths of white sheeting. The table and chairs had been pushed to the sides of the room, and a ladder with a bucket of steaming water stood in readiness beneath an ornate chandelier whose sparkle was dulled by several years' worth of dust.

Beryl stepped into the room and flashed Beddoes one of her justifiably famous smiles. Beryl felt her smile fade as the house-keeper continued about her business as though she were still alone in the room. It was a rare thing for Beryl to find herself ignored and not an experience she ever enjoyed. She noisily cleared her throat. Beddoes did not even deign to shoot a with-ering glance in her direction.

"Beddoes, I am ready and willing to be of service," Beryl said when it became obvious that Beddoes was determined to ignore her presence. No matter how much she might wish not to interact with her, no servant of Beddoes's caliber would allow herself to ignore a direct address from someone she served.

"Whatever can you mean, miss?" Beddoes asked.

Beryl stepped forward and lifted one of the folded sheets from a pile atop the dining room table. "I mean, I am able-bodied and full of pep. You cannot possibly be expected to clean the entirety of this house all on your own."

"Really, miss, I would prefer that you let me get on with things on my own. I've just given the floor in here a thorough scrubbing, and cleaning the chandelier is a one-woman job."

Beddoes reached out and attempted to relieve Beryl of the length of cloth. But Beryl held firm.

"I am more than happy to help. Just tell me what to do and I will get on with it."

"It is not for me to tell you what you should be doing, miss," Beddoes said.

"But you are the one with the skills here, Beddoes. I am not able to assist if you give me no instruction," Beryl said.

"Just as you say, miss," Beddoes said, arching an eyebrow ever so loftily and giving the sheeting a hard tug.

Beryl knew a challenge when she heard one. She yanked on

the sheet with all her might. Beddoes staggered backwards and careened into the ladder. Before either of them could do a thing to stop it, the pail of water overturned, spilling its warm, sudsy contents down over the length of Beddoes and across the freshly cleaned dining room floor. The housekeeper drew in an exaggerated breath and released it with excruciating slowness. Beryl unknotted the kerchief from around her neck and attempted to use it to sop up a rivulet of soapy water running down Beddoes's cheek. Beddoes flinched and staggered back once more.

"Beddoes, I could not be sorrier. What can I do to help make this up to you?" Beryl asked, trying to keep a note of mirth from her voice. She did not think Beddoes was inclined to find the situation amusing in the least.

"You have done more than enough already, miss," Beddoes said, condescending to accept the kerchief Beryl thrust towards her.

With that she turned and strode out of the room, swinging the dining room door shut firmly behind her.

Beryl stood there with a folded white sheet in her arms, wondering what she ought to do with it. She never had been one to manage the servants. Errand boys, mechanics, newspaper reporters, and even Hollywood leading men had been easy enough for her to charm, but domestic staff had always been completely beyond her.

It had been one of the chief reasons for the breakup of her second marriage. It likely would have ruined her first as well had her husband not dropped dead of a heart attack during their extended honeymoon trip. She had been forgiven anything, at least for a while, by the servants, when she arrived at their estate as a solitary young widow rather than a new bride with a husband in tow.

She was still standing there thinking of the past and the baffling machinations of domestic politics when Simpkins pushed open the dining room door and stepped inside. Generally, Simpkins could be relied upon to offer up some good-natured guff, but as he stood there Beryl could clearly see that there was something off-kilter in his demeanor. If she didn't know better, she would have said he looked nervous, and the Simpkins she knew never looked the least bit uncomfortable.

He cleared his throat and shot a look up at the ceiling as though the resolution to his problem could be found amongst the cobwebs and ornate crown molding.

"Miss Beryl, I'm afraid I'm going to have to ask you to leave off with your offers to assist Beddoes in her duties," he said, twisting his well-worn tweed cap around and around in his gnarled hands.

"Leave off helping? But Beddoes hasn't even begun to allow me to help."

"That's as it should be. Beddoes prefers to be left on her own to get on with things. She's very particular."

"But that's just ridiculous. There is far too much for her to do here all on her own. She needs someone to give her a hand."

"Not to put too fine point on it, miss, but Beddoes feels your sort of help is perhaps a bit more of a hindrance."

"That cannot be so. I dressed for the part, I asked what needed doing, and I awaited instruction. I don't mind telling you, Beddoes was not the least forthcoming with any sort of direction," Beryl said.

Simpkins shifted from one hobnailed boot-clad foot to the other before sighing deeply. "It isn't her place to instruct a lady of the house on how to help clean it. Either you give the directions, or you stay out of the way. That is how things work in these situations, miss."

Beryl was flummoxed. Whenever she spotted a breech where she could be of assistance, she prided herself in throwing herself into it. She had to wonder if she had been a bit high-handed at other times as well. Could it be that there were plenty of other people who had not desired her help, but that she had simply not noticed their resistance to it? She gave her head a slight shake. Surely not.

"I am certain that if I simply explained my willingness to be of use, she would be glad of my help. Where is she?" Beryl took a step towards the dining room door before Simpkins laid a restraining hand on her arm.

"That won't do, miss. Beddoes told me that if you are determined to act as the housekeeper here at the Beeches, she will hand in her notice and seek a position elsewhere. She made sure to mention that she has had a number of plum offers recently and that although it would grieve her to leave Miss Edwina in the lurch, she could be convinced to do so. You wouldn't want to be the one to explain to Miss Edwina why she left, now would you?" Simpkins asked, removing his hand from her arm.

A cold wave of dread washed over Beryl. While she prided herself on her nerves of steel, she could not imagine causing Edwina to lose her household help. It had been a total and unexpected coup to have secured any help, let alone someone as competent as Beddoes, in the first place.

Every day that Beddoes was in residence, Edwina seemed to have grown more and more like her prewar self. She invited friends to tea, offered the Beeches as a meeting place for the various committees upon which she served, threw herself into their new business venture, and even devoted large amounts of time to surreptitiously work on her novel.

While Simpkins and Beddoes gave no indication they knew what Edwina was up to, Beryl had been aware that the steady stream of tapping on the Remington Portable in the library was more about creating fiction than typing up correspondence for their handful of clients. She certainly did not want to do anything to disrupt the glow Edwina had on her face at the end of a morning spent secreted away at the desk.

If Beddoes were to leave, Edwina would feel compelled to

head back to the scullery and to all that entailed. Beryl could not imagine being responsible for that, especially considering how much better a private enquiry agent than a housekeeper her dear friend had proved to be.

"Tell me the truth. Is Beddoes really as upset as all that?"

"She is all het up. As a matter of fact, I think it would be best if you cleared out of the house altogether. Why don't you come with me to the potting shed, and we'll see if we can't find something more interesting to amuse ourselves with than pinnies and dust rags."

Simpkins reached once more for Beryl's arm and with his other hand slipped a flask from his trouser pocket and waggled it at her.

Although it was always her preference to stand her ground and see an adventure through to the end, she also knew when to acquiesce to local custom with good grace. She unwound the scarf covering her head and tossed it onto the dining room table. With her head held high, she allowed Simpkins to lead her out through the side door and into the garden.

Chapter 2

Edwina had just managed to catch her breath and to steady her nerves after her brush with disaster when she spotted a figure hurrying across the fields towards her. She shielded her eyes with her small hand and squinted. Her friend, local solicitor, Charles Jarvis, waved and made his way towards her with his usual long-legged, loping stride. She paused in the shade of a broad chestnut tree and waited for him to join her.

"I was just on my way to the Beeches to speak with you," he said. "Both you and Beryl, that is."

"Are you looking for a game of bridge?" Edwina asked. Charles was very fond of bridge and was often interested in setting up an evening party to indulge in his pastime. Unlike Beryl, Charles's behavior most often tended towards the predictable.

"While a night of bridge sounds lovely, I am actually here at the request of another. I've brought you a note from Constance Maitland. From the furtive way she waylaid me on my way into the breakfast room this morning, I shouldn't be at all surprised if she wished to hire you."

"Whatever were you doing breakfasting at Maitland Park?" Edwina asked.

Maitland Park was one of the stately homes on the outskirts of Walmsley Parva. While Charles was a well-respected member of the community, Edwina had never known him to be on terms of such intimacy with the Maitland family. She could imagine he might have procured an invitation to dinner or even for an evening of his beloved bridge if they needed to make up a fourth. But breakfast was another matter entirely. Breakfasting implied an overnight stay and unless there was a domestic difficulty of which she was not aware, Edwina could think of no reason for him to sleep in a strange bed while remaining so close to home.

"I was invited to attend an artists' colony that Ursula Maitland is hosting there," Charles said.

Edwina's mind reeled. While Charles had done several things since Beryl's arrival that had surprised her, she would never have expected him to participate in something that sounded so unbridledly bohemian as an artists' colony. The idea of someone as unswervingly staid and sensible as Charles throwing himself into the undoubtably debauched environment of an artists' colony was unthinkable. She glanced at his face to ascertain if he were having a bit of fun at her expense. But no, he seemed perfectly sincere in his remarks.

Edwina was filled with the sense that she had never really seen Charles before that very moment. Beryl had often mentioned that there were hidden depths to him, but she had thought her friend was indulging in flights of fancy. Beryl imagined hidden depths in a filet of sole. Now, it seemed, Beryl just might have been right all along.

"And you agreed to attend?" Edwina asked, finding it difficult to voice a coherent thought.

She kept imagining Charles seated cross-legged on a jewel-toned satin pillow smoking a hookah while models in period costumes moved languidly around a room littered with easels and redolent with the heady scent of turpentine. It gave her chills. And as much as she would never admit it aloud, it also piqued her interest.

"It seemed too good an opportunity to refuse. I would have told you all about it before I set off for the colony, but I was invited at the last minute by a new acquaintance. I decided to throw caution to the wind and indulge in a spot of spontaneity," Charles said.

Edwina had often wondered if Beryl had been exerting an influence, and not necessarily a good one, on Charles. Here, it seemed, was the proof.

"How did you come to be invited?" Edwina asked, not entirely sure she wanted to know.

"I met one of the participants whilst I was out painting late last week. He stopped and looked at my watercolor in progress and suggested I would be a valuable addition to the colony," Charles said.

Edwina thought she detected a faint blush spreading up from beneath Charles's collar. He was never one to boast, and the mere act of telling her he had been praised by another, especially for his art, clearly left him ill at ease. Given her own reticence to discuss her novel, Edwina felt her heart go out to him. She would not have admitted she was writing one at all if Beryl had not uncovered her secret. And there was Charles exposing himself to prying eyes and judgment every time he took his easel and pans of paints to the river's edge to improve in his craft. She quite admired him and had never bothered to let him know. The least she could do was to congratulate him on his invitation.

"Was the man who invited you someone whose opinion you value?"

"He has quickly become just such a person. Truly, he has taken me under his wing and provided me with no end of encouragement," Charles said. Edwina noted the blush had spread to his lean cheeks and he kept looking at his feet like a small boy who was being taken to task by the headmaster.

"I am simply delighted for you, Charles. I am so impressed by your willingness to try something new," Edwina said, a little surprised to find how heartfelt her comment truly was.

"I have found your own boldness of late very inspiring," Charles said, taking a step closer and bringing his gaze to meet hers. "The way you have launched yourself into your business venture has made me open my eyes to life's greater possibilities."

She felt a stab of uncertainty. Beryl made repeated mention of the notion that she believed Charles to have a romantic interest in her. For her part, she had never considered Charles in that way and did not think that she wished to encourage him. She hastily changed the subject.

"You said you had a note for me from Constance Maitland," she reminded him.

He nodded, reached into his pocket, and withdrew an envelope, which he handed to her. The paper was thick and smooth. With their long-standing position in the community, the Maitland family appeared to have money, but considering the current economic situation, appearances were often at odds with reality. If their stationery told the truth, the Maitlands were amongst the lucky ones. Edwina turned over the envelope and pried open the flap, held down by a blob of blue wax embossed with an ornate letter *M*.

She read the brief note requesting a meeting for the next day at a time convenient to herself and Beryl. Constance mentioned she was interested in procuring their services, but that she would prefer to discuss the matter in person and as discreetly as possible. She requested a reply be sent verbally through Charles.

"This is very hush-hush," Edwina said, slipping the note into her own pocket for safekeeping. She wondered if she ought to burn it once she returned to the Beeches but decided it would be better to add it to the growing number of case files. There was no sense in agitating Beddoes by lighting a fire. She might resign her post.

"She did insist I not discuss the nature of my errand with anyone but the two of you," he said.

"She asks that I send a verbal reply through you. Will you tell her Beryl and I would be happy to receive her tomorrow morning at ten o'clock?"

"It would be my pleasure. I hope we can set a time for bridge once I return from my stay at the artists' colony," Charles said.

"How long do you anticipate remaining at Maitland Park?" Edwina asked.

"The colony has no fixed length of time to run as far as I can tell. I thought I would remain as long as I am enjoying it. I'll be sure to let you know when I decide to return home." With that, he lifted his hat and turned back in the direction of Maitland Park.

Edwina watched his retreating back with a mixture of astonishment and admiration. She had never been spontaneous and, if the truth were told, slightly envied those people like Beryl to whom such things came naturally. She had never considered it was a skill one could develop. As she stood watching Charles's figure disappear behind a winding hedgerow, she wondered if there was any hope that she might become a little more flexible, too.

Beryl had sought refuge in the summerhouse. Although she had appreciated Simpkins's offer to share his potting shed, she was disinclined to spend the rest of her day hunkered down on a sack of peat moss surrounded by bins of bone meal and arsenic of lead. As much as she was loath to admit it, her best days of crouching uncomfortably for hours on end were likely behind her.

She wondered, too, if Simpkins's occasional bouts of forgetfulness could be attributed as much to his frequent inhalation of such noxious materials as it could to his inclination to tipple rather more than he ought. As Beryl had no intention of reducing her own fondness for strong spirits, she thought it best not to expose herself in any prolonged way to an atmosphere so filled with potential toxins.

She had always valued her relationship with her mind, but she had come to rely on it even more since she and Edwina had taken on the role of private enquiry agents. So, she withdrew to the greater comfort of the summerhouse and settled herself in a basket chair, where she allowed her thoughts to roam freely. She and Edwina had not had a case to look into in a fortnight, and she felt undeniably at loose ends. Perhaps that explained her unprecedented interest in pitching in with the housekeeping.

Before she could consider the matter further, she heard barking, and Crumpet, Edwina's faithful Norwich terrier, raced towards her and sprang into the chair opposite. Edwina followed at an only slightly more sedate pace.

"Beddoes met me at the door and, in not so many words, asked me to keep you out here. What new mischief have you gotten up to whilst I was out to cause her to be so out of sorts?" Edwina asked, lowering herself onto the wicker settee placed in the shade of a sprawling, leafy vine.

"I merely made the mistake of offering to help with the housekeeping tasks," Beryl said.

"You've been making noises to that effect for the past few days. Surely there is more to her current fit of pique than that," Edwina said.

Beryl knew that telling Edwina less than the truth would only delay the ordeal.

"I may have tracked her to the third floor thinking I would

put her on her ease by approaching her in her lair. Rather than appreciating my overtures, she gave me a look the likes of which I have only seen from my former mothers-in-law," Beryl said.

"But you mustn't ever take it upon yourself to disturb her in her rooms unless there is some sort of dire emergency. Something akin to the house being engulfed in flames or possibly an overseas telephone call for her. Surely you knew that," Edwina said, her voice trembling.

"Apparently I did not. I wish I could say the matter ended there, but I am afraid I only went and made things worse," Beryl said.

"Please tell me you didn't complain about her cooking."

"You know I never complain about food, not even when served things with names like bubble and squeak," Beryl said. She might have made a mess of things, but surely Edwina could not think her capable of being unappreciative of someone else doing the cooking.

"What then?"

"I may have gotten into a bit of a tussle with her over some drop cloths she was draping round the dining room. To tell the truth, it ended badly."

The color drained from Edwina's face.

"Badly how?"

"Somehow a pail of water toppled over and drenched her through and through. It made rather a mess of the freshly scrubbed floor, too," Beryl said, taking a sip from the flask she had lifted from Simpkins before she left him.

"No wonder you have taken to drink so early in the day. I am surprised she is still here after weathering such an insult."

Edwina tsk-tsked in that particularly British way. She held out her hand for the flask and, after wiping its rim with the hem of her sleeve, lifted it to her lips and took a large gulp and then a second. She dabbed at the corner of her mouth delicately with a slim finger before handing the flask back to Beryl.

"Simpkins said much the same, which is why I am out here staying safely away from Beddoes and her efforts. Since we haven't any client business at present, I've been considering making myself scarce by going on a short trip, perhaps to the seaside. You could join me," Beryl said, pulling herself to the edge of her seat. "If we both just threw some things in a bag, we could be on the road in under an hour."

Edwina shook her head. She pulled an envelope from her pocket and held it out to Beryl.

"I think we may have a new case before long," Edwina said.

Beryl drew a piece of high-quality paper from the envelope and quickly read the words penned upon it in an old-fashioned but elegantly rendered hand.

"Who is Constance Maitland?" Beryl asked. "The surname is tickling something in my memory, but I cannot place it."

Her thoughts flitted once more to the chemicals in the shed, and she congratulated herself on her decision to retreat to the comfort of the summerhouse. Perhaps she ought to encourage Simpkins to do the same.

"She is the sister of Hubert Maitland of Maitland Cigarettes fame," Edwina said.

"That's it," Beryl said. "I suppose if I smoked it might have come to me sooner." Beryl decided that while she preferred not to keep secrets from Edwina, it would be best not to reveal any connection she had with Maitland Cigarettes until it became unavoidable not to do so.

"That is one vice I am delighted you have refrained from indulging in," Edwina said, waving at the flask in Beryl's hand.

Beryl ignored the comment. So often her notion of what constituted a vice and that of others did not concur. It was not that she thought of smoking as a vice per se. She had tried a cigarette a few times in her youth and had found she did not care in the least for the experience. There was no moral component to it. She simply found the experience unappealing.

"What do you think this Constance wants to consult us about?" Beryl asked.

"I haven't the least idea. Perhaps it has something to do with the artists' colony being held at Maitland Park."

"An artists' colony?" Beryl leaned forward. She generally approved of artists, and the idea of a bunch of them gathered in Walmsley Parva was a bright spot in an otherwise disheartening day. "I wonder if anyone I know is in attendance."

"Charles is attending. In fact, he hand-delivered the note from Constance to me while I was out walking with Crumpet," Edwina said.

Beryl thought she heard a note of disapproval from Edwina. Was it a lack of enthusiasm for artists, or was it that Charles was associating with them that disquieted her friend?

"Good for Charles," Beryl said. "I assume you sent back word that we are free to meet with her very soon."

"I asked Charles to invite her to meet us here at ten o'clock tomorrow morning."

"If we hurry, we could still fit in a very short trip to the seaside," Beryl said. "Listening to the waves is very soothing, and the fresh air would do us both a world of good."

"I am sure at the rate of speed with which you drive that is factually correct. But I have no interest in rabbiting about in your motorcar. Especially not after I was nearly run down while I was out on my walk." Edwina pursed her lips at the memory. "If I wanted to embark on a soothing trip to the seaside, I would take a train."

Beryl knew better than to argue with Edwina when she had such a determined set to her jaw. Besides, considering her own part in causing trouble in the household, she did not feel she ought to create any additional strain by insisting. "Then we shall content ourselves with an afternoon of leisurely lounging here in the summerhouse. I would ask Beddoes to prepare us a picnic for supper, but I do not think she would take kindly to any requests from me for some time."

Edwina shot her a vinegary look. "Considering the day Beddoes has had, you had better allow any such requests to come from me. I am quite sure if you asked, she would be far too tempted to lace the sandwich fillings with poison."

Chapter 3

Edwina felt sorry for the woman seated in front of her, truly she did. A woman such as Constance Maitland rarely asked strangers for assistance. At least not assistance that was composed of more than help finding an item in a shop or directions to a location. Constance's posture was as erect as one would expect from a lady of her standing, but her hands fidgeted ceaselessly in her lap, adjusting and readjusting the fit of her gloves, plucking imaginary stray bits of lint from her tweed skirt. As she observed her, Edwina wondered what extraordinary circumstance could have brought such a lady to see them.

She had attempted to put Constance at ease by calling for a tea tray. Edwina had noticed a look of worry cross Beryl's face as she did so. Edwina was surprised to see such an emotion from her friend, who never seemed to let much of anything worry her. It occurred to her that Beryl was much more concerned with unnecessarily provoking Beddoes than she had previously revealed.

Edwina did not expect that Beryl would ever come to understand the best way to deal with servants. Beddoes would have been deeply offended if Edwina had refrained from requesting tea on account of her preoccupation with the cleaning. To do so would have implied that Edwina did not feel Beddoes competent to perform all parts of her job.

Constance Maitland was exactly the sort of woman who would have understood all the nuances of such things practically before she left the cradle. The Maitlands were an old, highly respected family in the district. They were not gentry but were in fact the next best thing. And frankly, since the economic downturn after the Great War, perhaps not even second best. After all, everyone knew the Maitland family were far more economically viable than most of the families in the area bestowed with titles. Unlike so many of the gentry, Constance was exactly the sort of client who Edwina suspected could afford the bill for their services.

The need for paying clients, or payments of any sort for that matter, had become a far less troubling concern of late than it had been for many years. When Simpkins had come into his fortune a few weeks earlier, he had not only gone to the trouble and expense of hiring Beddoes and setting about paying to put the garden to rights but also had offered to invest in the Davenport and Helliwell Private Enquiry Agency.

His role was that of a silent partner, and so far the arrangement had worked well for all involved. Still, however much she appreciated Simpkins's generosity, she did wish for their business to make a go of things without requiring any manner of subsidy. Clients like Constance Maitland were just the sort to make that possible.

Edwina lifted her teacup to her lips and took a slow sip, eyeing their potential client covertly over the rim. Constance seemed to be coming to a decision. She gave her gloves a final fidgety tug and cleared her throat gently.

"May I have your complete assurance that whatever I share with you will be held in total confidence?" Constance asked.

"All of our clients are assured of that," Beryl said.

Edwina noticed that while Constance looked at Beryl when she spoke, she flicked her gaze back over towards Edwina for confirmation. Edwina slowly nodded.

"A business like ours does not flourish if we are not known for our discretion. Nothing that you say here will leave this room without your expressed permission," Edwina said.

"Very well, then. I should like to engage you to undertake an investigation on my behalf. Or rather, the pretense of an investigation," Constance said.

Beryl and Edwina exchanged glances. Whatever was a pretense of an investigation?

"What an intriguing request," Beryl said. "Do go on."

"I would like you to pretend to be investigating the possibility of an illicit affair between my sister-in-law, Ursula Maitland, and one of the guests attending the artists' colony at Maitland Park," Constance said.

Edwina hoped her face did not betray the shock she felt at the request. To investigate an illicit affair was already a distasteful business to be sure. But to pretend to investigate one somehow seemed rather worse. She had half a mind to refuse the assignment regardless of the social standing of the client. As she opened her mouth to make an excuse, she noticed out of the corner of her eye that Beryl gave just the slightest shake of her head.

"I see from the look passing between you that you consider this assignment to be somehow outside of your purview. I should have thought such cases were exactly what private enquiry agents routinely undertook." Constance plucked at her gloves once more.

"You are correct that agencies such as ours are often engaged to get to the bottom of extramarital entanglements. It's the pretend part that is unusual. Would you care to explain further?" Beryl said.

"I take your point and can understand why this is not a typical request. Let me state unequivocally at the outset that I suspect absolutely no wrongdoing on the part of my sister-in-law. Although I am well aware that there has been pernicious gossip in the village about my brother's choice of bride, I have nothing but admiration and fondness for Ursula. She's done Hubert a world of good," Constance said.

Constance was right to say there had been much talk in the village when Hubert Maitland had married a far younger woman. Malicious gossips had immediately called Ursula a gold digger. Other people took particular delight in imagining how much being dethroned from her place as the lady of the household would have bothered Constance.

As Edwina was not acquainted with any of the parties to any degree of intimacy, she had held her tongue whenever the topic had been introduced at the Women's Institute or over hands of bridge at card parties. In Edwina's eyes, it did Constance credit to claim that she did not suspect her sister-in-law of breaking her marital vows. Somehow it made the whole matter feel less grubby.

"If you do not suspect anything untoward going on, why would you like us to pretend to investigate?" Edwina asked.

"Do you know my cousin Cressida?" Constance asked.

"I have not had the pleasure of making her acquaintance, but I do know her by her appearance," Edwina said. Beryl simply shook her head.

"Cressida is a distant cousin and has for some years lived with us at Maitland Park. The story we give out publicly is that she is a valued member of the family and provides me with an agreeable level of companionship. The reality is rather far removed from the story. Most unfortunately, Cressida has always been an unbalanced sort of a person, and she is inclined to persistent flights of fancy that one might say border on unhealthy obsessions. Both Hubert and I feel a certain responsibility to keep an eye on her, as she is family and has no other relatives either willing or able to do so. Her doctors assured us that she is not really a dangerous person, but she is perhaps not someone who ought to live entirely without some form of oversight," Constance said.

"That's very kind of you, I'm sure," Edwina said. "Should we understand that Cressida is at the heart of this unusual request?"

"That's it exactly. Cressida has always been very protective of both Hubert and me. She took a strong dislike to Ursula from the moment Hubert first introduced her to the family. Once they married, she became even more vocal concerning her feelings," Constance said.

"I seem to recall it has been more than a year since your brother wed. What has brought you to seek our assistance now?" Edwina asked.

"It is the artists' colony that has caused the problem. She has been making very pointed remarks to all and sundry about her suspicions that Ursula is romantically linked with one of the artists attending the colony. Frankly, she is causing a great deal of discomfort to the attendees. Not to mention Ursula, Hubert, and myself," Constance said. "Of even greater concern is the fact that this is the week when I host the Girl Guides campout on the property at Maitland Park. I'm sorry to say that Cressida is not above mentioning such an indelicate allegation in front of impressionable young girls. Her accusations are proving extremely disruptive."

"Is it really necessary to hire us? Would it not be possible to simply tell your cousin that you have already hired someone to look into her concerns and that the investigators assure you that they are baseless?" Edwina asked.

As eager as she was to take on a new case, she could not feel that this charade could qualify as one. It could even be construed as an insult. To think one could hire a pair of professional investigators when actors would have sufficed seemed to her as if it could tarnish their reputation. Not only that, she would feel uncomfortable accepting payment for a job they would not actually be doing.

Beryl gave her a quelling look, but before Edwina had time to wonder if she should have held her tongue, Constance replied.

"I agree that it would seem quite an elaborate ruse, but I assure you I would not have made the decision to expose Cressida's fragile condition to those outside the family if I were not convinced it necessary to do so. My cousin may be someone who suffers from delusions and tends towards paranoia, but she is also intelligent and well informed. If I were to tell her I hired someone to look into her suspicions, she would ask for proof," Constance said. "I am sorry to say she would not be likely to take me at my word, and of course, since I would be lying to her, she would be right not to believe me without evidence."

"And you think that if she sees us actively involved in a pretense at an investigation this will help to quiet her concerns and halt her unwanted behavior?" Edwina asked.

"That's exactly what I'm hoping will happen. Cressida will be soothed by feeling as though she is being taken seriously on this matter. She is also, unfortunately, the sort who delights in the secretive side of things. I'm quite certain she would be convinced to hold her tongue if she felt that her accusations were jeopardizing a sincere investigation into any wrongdoing on Ursula's part," Constance said.

"Do you have any suggestion as to how we could go about conducting this investigation?" Beryl asked. "And will Ursula know that we are not in fact looking to discredit her?"

"Ursula has quite enough on her plate to deal with at present. She is the one in charge of the artists' colony, and it involves an enormous amount of work to keep so many flamboyant temperaments on an even keel. I thought it would be best to come up with a cover story, so to speak, to explain your interest in the occupants of Maitland Park. I have no wish for any of them to know that I have hired you," Constance said. "That said, I had not given a great deal of thought to what that might involve."

The sound of sloshing and banging reached them from somewhere along the hallway outside the library. Edwina noticed Beryl's face take on an eager expression. Clearly, she had come up with an idea.

"Girl Guides, you say," Beryl said. "What if Edwina and I were to come to stay at Maitland Park as visiting experts, at least as far as the Girl Guides are concerned?"

A small smile lifted the corners of Constance's lips. "I think that's an excellent idea. We have plenty of room at the house, and staying there would give you every opportunity to be convincing, at least as far as Cressida is concerned," Constance said.

Edwina had no idea whatsoever of the sort of thing she could be expected to teach a group of Girl Guides. She had not even been one herself in her youth. In fact, she had rather prided herself on never being roped into facilitating a Girl Guides group despite considerable pressure from members of the community, who thought it no more than her duty to be involved.

"I'm sure you would be marvelous at demonstrating campfire building or the tying of knots," Edwina said, turning to Beryl. "As for me, I doubt I have any expertise to offer to the Girl Guides."

"Perhaps you should attend as an artist," Constance said. "That would provide the perfect excuse for your presence at Maitland Park."

"But I have absolutely no artistic ability," Edwina said.

"That's hardly true," Beryl said. "What about your photography?"

"As far as I'm able to ascertain, the claim to being an artist does not seem to require one to have any sort of artistic ability whatsoever. You should see some of the things splashed about on canvases," Constance said. She tipped her head to one side and peered at a wall lined with overloaded bookcases, then moved her gaze to take in a towering stack of books perched precariously on the table at Edwina's side. "You obviously have at least a nodding acquaintance with books. Surely you could pose as a poet."

Edwina felt her stomach grow cold. While she did not wish to appear disobliging towards a client, posing as a poet struck rather too close to home. While she had gotten used to the idea that Beryl was aware that she was writing a novel, she was not yet ready to make her private pursuit a matter of general knowledge.

"While I am an avid reader, I doubt I would be able to play the role of a poet convincingly," Edwina said, straightening her posture to an even stiffer degree. She hoped she appeared far too straitlaced and conventional for Constance's suggestion.

Constance looked her up and down. "Perhaps that would not be the wisest course. After all, Ursula is herself a poet and might see through your subterfuge with ease," she said. She squinted at Edwina. "I know, you could attend as an artist's model."

Edwina grasped the suggestion with an overwhelming sense of relief. "I could pose for Charles. I am sure he would be more than happy for me to do so."

Edwina felt Beryl stiffen slightly beside her. "Don't you think you would prefer to teach the Girl Guides something?"

Edwina was surprised. Beryl was always pushing her to try new things and to be more spontaneous. She had even been known to orchestrate situations to throw Charles and Edwina together. Why would she suddenly try to convince her to use the Girl Guides as a cover story? Edwina knew full well that

Beryl was not in the least enamored with children. That must be the reason. Beryl did not want to have to face a whole group of girls on her own. Perhaps it was finally time for Edwina to encourage Beryl to be a bit more courageous instead of the other way round.

"I'm quite sure that one of us being embedded in the artists' colony makes the most sense. After all, what better way to appear to be investigating any shenanigans between Ursula and an artist than for one of us to be a part of the colony?" Edwina asked.

"I believe that would be the course most convincing for Cressida," Constance said.

"I'll just write a short note to Charles asking him to support my story in front of the other attendees," Edwina said, rising from her chair and crossing the room to a small desk for a pen and notepaper. She dashed off a few lines promising to fill him in more completely as soon as she saw him, then handed it to Constance.

"That's settled, then. I would very much like for you to come as soon as possible. There are already rooms prepared for guests so the sooner you can arrive, the better," Constance said.

"We could be there as early as this afternoon," Beryl said. "Couldn't we, Edwina?"

Constance got to her feet without awaiting a reply. "Shall we say sometime after luncheon?"

"You can expect us by teatime," Edwina said. "We do need to set our affairs in order here and do a bit of packing."

"Excellent. I will alert Ursula to expect you at the artists' colony, Miss Davenport. And I will tell Cressida the two of you are attending undercover. The Girl Guides will be simply thrilled to know that you will be a guest speaker, Miss Helliwell. Until this afternoon," Constance said. She gave them each a brief nod and swept out of the room with a far greater air of confidence than she had entered it.

As soon as Edwina had pressed the front door firmly behind Constance's retreating back, she turned to Beryl.

"How extraordinary. I should never have imagined we would be hired to pretend to investigate a case. Would you?" she asked.

"No, I don't suppose I would have. Even so, I am delighted Constance has engaged our services," Beryl said.

"You seem particularly eager to take this case on. You didn't even broach the subject of our fee, like you usually do," Edwina said. "You cannot possibly be looking forward to spending time with a group of Girl Guides, can you?"

"Perish the thought. However, I would take on any case that would get us out from under Beddoes's wrathsome glare," Beryl said. "In fact, I would take this case on for free."

Chapter 4

The drive over to Maitland Park had taken far less time than had been required for Edwina to pack. Beryl had forgotten how arduous Edwina had found the task of preparing her trunks in order to return home from Miss Dupont's Finishing School for Young Ladies. At the time, Beryl had simply thought her friend was in no greater hurry to leave the school than was she. But, from the way Edwina placed things in her valise and then lifted them out only to return them a few moments later, Beryl realized she had finally discovered something about which her friend was uncharacteristically indecisive.

Beryl, in contrast, had her own bag packed within minutes of their new client's departure. After years of traveling almost nonstop, she had become adept at throwing a few things in a bag with every confidence that they would suit her needs. She had long ago discovered that there were few situations in life to be faced that could not be competently met if one possessed a pair of well-fitted shoes and a flamboyant scarf.

Edwina refused to be convinced that packing could prove so simple and made much of the fact that making a good impression on members of the Maitland family would do their fledgling business no end of good. It was not until Beryl reminded her that artists were an unorthodox lot and that she was unlikely to commit any faux pas no matter what she chose to wear that they were able to make any headway at all. Beryl finally left Edwina to fuss over her choices and took herself off to the morning room, where the Remington Portable typewriter sat in the center of a desk near a set of French doors overlooking the garden and the goldfish pond.

Although she did not like to make mention of it, Edwina had spent a portion of every day over the last few weeks tapping away at a novel. Although Edwina had thought she had kept her creative endeavor a secret, Beryl had discovered, quite by accident, what she had been up to early on in the process. Beryl had been just the slightest bit hurt by Edwina's reticence to share her aspiration of becoming a novelist with her.

When she had informed Edwina that she knew her secret and thought it a good idea, her friend was still reluctant to discuss it openly with anyone at all. Beryl could not understand it in the least. Every time she developed a new interest or set a goal, she preferred to chat about it with anyone within earshot. Keeping such a thing to oneself made no sense to her whatsoever. But Edwina had steadfastly refused to mention it to anyone besides Beryl, and even between the two of them the matter was not to be remarked upon.

Still, she wanted to do all that was within her power to support Edwina's dream. With that in mind, she gathered up the pages of manuscript from their hiding place in a locked drawer of the desk and tucked them into an attaché case. She fetched the typewriter case from its place in a nearby closet and secured the machine snuggly inside it.

She managed to settle it into the back of the motorcar and to cover it with her own single piece of luggage before Edwina had even finished her packing. Beryl was certain Edwina would not think to take it with her and was equally certain that the atmosphere of an artists' colony would prove to be inspirational, and that her friend would have come to regret not having thought to bring the typewriter.

Although they took off far later than Beryl would have done if left to depart on her own, it was still possible to arrive by teatime. Maitland Park was located on the outskirts of the village, and the journey promised to be of short duration. The route took them along the road towards the market town of Pershing Magna. After driving along for about three miles, Edwina indicated Beryl should turn off the road at an imposing iron gate flanked by towering stone pillars so commonly found guarding the entrance to stately English homes.

A long, crushed stone drive wound through a rolling green lawn dotted with lushly leafed trees and mounding shrubberies. At the far end of the lawn Beryl could just barely make out the flashing blue glint of a pond or perhaps, given the grand scale of the property, a lake. The vast open lawn was bordered by a dense wood, giving the property an air of seclusion. At the center of it all sat the Maitland family home.

She slowed the motorcar to a crawl in order to allow them both to fully take in the view. The house rose up before them, a massive structure made of red brick. Generously proportioned bow windows ran the length of the façade, interrupted only by a grand front door.

Beryl pulled to a stop directly in front of the house. Before they could exit the motorcar, a doddering white-haired man in a black suit opened the door and motioned for a pair of younger men to remove Edwina's luggage from where it was securely strapped to the boot. With few words he ushered the sleuths withindoors.

Maitland Park was just as imposing on the inside as it was from a distance. Even in the heat of summer, the great hallway in which they stood put Beryl very much in mind of a crypt in which she had once sought shelter during a severe autumn downpour. As much as she enjoyed many things about England, she could not say that the chilly conditions in many of the houses, even during the summer, were amongst them.

Fortunately, her lifetime of adventurous expeditions had taught her to prepare for any number of weather conditions. While her silk duster and matching scarf had been a bit too warm for the drive over, she was grateful for both of them once inside. She wished she had thought to follow Edwina's lead and to add a warm hat to her ensemble. A footman had whisked away their luggage as soon as they stepped to the door so Beryl would have to content herself with those things she already wore.

The atmosphere was not warmed by the faces glowering down at them from the gloomy oil paintings hung on the walls. They put her very much in mind of portraits that greeted her when she visited at her first husband's home before they were married. One of the very first things she had done when she returned there as a widow straight from her honeymoon voyage was to remove them to a series of rooms she made sure never to frequent and replaced them with some jewel-toned landscapes instead.

The butler, a stooped and wizened man who had introduced himself as Dillings, informed them in a voice as melodious as a rusty hinge that Constance had requested they be brought to her as soon as they arrived. He instructed a pert young housemaid to show the two of them to the room where Constance awaited their arrival.

The maid chattered breathlessly with them as she led them down a long, darkly paneled hallway. She turned round again and again as she escorted them as if she did not want to allow them out of her sight. She made much of having seen film reels and newspaper articles detailing Beryl's exploits and said she would be sure to mention meeting her when she next wrote home.

In light of her dismal interactions with Beddoes, Beryl felt inordinately cheered by the positive attention. She could not help but think that the girl was the sort who would have gladly accepted the offer of help with her work rather than taking offense. With each step Beryl took down the plushly carpeted corridor, the memory of the calamitous morning with Beddoes seemed to grow fainter.

The maid stopped abruptly and opened a door halfway along the hallway. The room they entered was bathed in warm afternoon light. Constance sat at a writing desk positioned in front of an open window facing a long, herbaceous border. She glanced at a clock on the mantelpiece with a nod of approval. She got to her feet and smoothed her tweed skirt.

"Welcome to Maitland Park. Since you were able to arrive so promptly I think we should have sufficient time to introduce you to the other guests before tea. It is no use hoping that they will all conveniently assemble for a meal so that you may meet them all at once. These artists seem to have no concept of time when they are working," Constance said.

"That must be trying for you as a hostess," Edwina said.

"I don't mind so very much, but I am concerned that Cook feels ill-used by their behavior. I've tried to explain that their absence from the table in no way reflects on her abilities in the kitchen, but she does not seem convinced. I am not sure what we will do should she decide to leave us over it," Constance said.

Edwina started to make a *tsk-tsk* sort of a noise that Beryl felt certain would lead to a prolonged discussion concerning the current crisis with domestic staff. After her own recent troubles with Beddoes, she was in no frame of mind to endure such a conversation. A change of topic was definitely in order.

"Constance, which of these starving artists is the one with whom your cousin believes Ursula to be conducting the affair?" she asked.

"Of course, I should have given you that information straightaway. He's an artist by the name of Louis Langdon Beck. Apparently, he is quite well known. At least I'm told that he is," Constance said. "Frankly, I don't bother myself about such matters in the least." Constance gestured towards the door and with an energetic stride led them out of the room.

She turned down the hallway in the opposite direction to the one they had previously come and on through a large portrait gallery, the walls of which were covered by more paintings, similar to those in the entry. Every inch of wall space was filled with paintings of heavily jowled men and pinched-looking women. Now and again Beryl noticed a portrait of a child. One of them looked just like Constance with its upright posture and slight lift to her chin. Beryl slowed as she passed it to read the nameplate attached to the work. It seemed Constance had an ancestress born in the mideighteenth century named Perdita whose looks she surprisingly favored despite the years that elapsed between their lifetimes.

"From the age of the paintings hanging here it seems that the Maitland family has long patronized the arts," Beryl said.

"I suppose you could say that. Even the cigarette company has a strong art component to it," Constance said. "My brother was one of the earliest cigarette manufacturers to hire artists on full-time for his company's advertising campaigns. He has artists on staff that create original works for the cigarette cards included in each pack."

Constance led them back down a set of stairs and out into the open lawn. The rays of the afternoon sun felt luxurious on Beryl's shoulders. They crossed the lawn to a summerhouse built on a far grander scale than the one at the Beeches. As they approached Constance called out to the figure seated inside.

"Ursula, these are the new guests I was telling you about at luncheon. May I present Beryl Helliwell and Edwina Davenport," Constance said.

Seated in a basket chair was an attractive young woman

Beryl guessed could not be older than thirty. Waves of flaming red hair tumbled down over her shoulders, and a charming smattering of freckles dusted her nose and cheeks.

Beryl felt Edwina stiffen slightly beside her. She wondered what it was about the young woman that could have caused such a reaction.

"I'm so glad that you could join us," Ursula said, getting to her feet. "The more the merrier, I always say."

"We are delighted to be included," Beryl said.

She wondered if Edwina was suddenly filled with even more trepidation at the deceit this case required of them. Her friend was far less flexible in her stance concerning the truth than she was herself. Beryl simply could not understand what the fuss was about when it came to veracity. Truthfulness had never struck her as a particularly virtuous quality. In fact, she had as often seen the truth used as a cudgel as she had a comfort.

In their brief time since opening the private enquiry agency, she had been pleased to note that Edwina was softening her opinion on the subject of truth telling. Still, white lies and exaggerations did not come as naturally to her as they did to Beryl. She would just have to throw herself into any conversational breaches during their stay should Edwina's conscience threaten to get the better of her.

"Do you know where the artists can be found?" Constance asked. "I was hoping to introduce Beryl and Edwina to them before it was time for tea."

"I think you'll find Louis and probably Tuva down in the glade in the wood. He has rather claimed that spot for himself and I know that he mentioned an intention to work on some preliminary sketches there this afternoon," Ursula said. "As to the whereabouts of the others, I haven't a clue." Ursula gave them all a smile and returned to her chair in the shade of the summerhouse.

Constance took a few steps ahead in the direction of a dense copse of trees. Edwina leaned in and squeezed Beryl's arm.

"I'm quite sure that's the young woman who was in the side car attached to the motorcycle that nearly ran me down yesterday afternoon," Edwina said. "I didn't recognize her at the time, but seeing her again jogged my memory."

"I'm sure it was quite a shock, but does it matter now?" Beryl asked.

"I suppose that the only reason that it would was that perhaps Cressida has reason to wonder about Ursula's activities. The man driving the motorcycle was definitely not Hubert Maitland."

Chapter 5

As Constance led them towards the grove of trees on the far side of a sweeping lawn, Edwina cast an admiring glance around the property. Surely, the Maitland family had not had to make do during the war years with the inadequate ministrations of an elderly jobbing gardener like her own Simpkins. She found it hard to imagine that even a small army of far more dedicated gardeners than her own could keep up with such extensive landscaping.

She noticed with approval that the edges of the flower borders were sharply delineated, and that there was something in bloom everywhere she turned her gaze. The beds were neatly mulched with what appeared to be a thick layer of rich compost. Edwina felt a pang of regret as the scent of stocks filled her nostrils. Her own bed of that same perennial had succumbed to powdery mildew, an unprecedented loss that she attributed to her newfound busyness with her career.

In years past, Edwina would have been far more involved with her gardens and her plants on a daily basis than she found herself to be at present. All of the adventures she had gotten up to with Beryl since her friend's arrival the previous autumn had thoroughly distracted her from her ordinary routines. As she glanced about the beauty surrounding her at Maitland Park, she wondered how she might manage to make a little more time for her own beloved gardens.

Simpkins might find the property inspiring, too. She made a mental note to find the right time to ask Constance if she might invite him to join her for a tour of the grounds during her stay. To her knowledge, neither the house nor the gardens had ever been open to the public for tours, and he would surely be delighted by the opportunity. He would certainly find it educational.

They stepped into the edge of the wood and Edwina felt grateful for the leafy canopy above them providing a bit of shade from the warm afternoon sun. The sharp scent of pine needles filled the air as the trio crushed them beneath their feet as they strode along a winding path worn through the wood by decades upon decades of use.

Constance seemed to know just where she was headed and hurried on with a degree of vigor that Edwina admired. Constance was, at a guess, perhaps ten years older than Edwina, but she moved with the limberness and speed of a woman still in the prime of youth. After a few minutes of walking at a brisk pace, their hostess stopped abruptly and called out to someone.

"Cressida, I'd like to introduce you to our latest guests," Constance said. "You remember me mentioning them earlier, don't you?"

"She doesn't look crazy, does she?" Beryl whispered startlingly in Edwina's ear.

Walking in the woods with Beryl was always a disconcerting experience. She made so little sound when she walked that one almost forgot she was present. Edwina attributed this to her friend's many years spent gallivanting about the globe in search of adventure. Many's the time the pair of them had whiled away a quiet evening with Beryl regaling her homebody friend with tales of her adventures on safari or traipsing through dense jungle in search of exotic fauna. Edwina supposed it would not be possible to track down elusive creatures if one went thrashing about through the wood with no thought to the sounds one made.

Edwina had to agree with Beryl's initial impression. Although she could not have said exactly what she would have expected Cressida would look like, Edwina was sure it would have been at odds with the woman who popped out from behind a large clump of shrubbery to stand before them. With her light brown hair, average height, and cheerful countenance, Cressida appeared to be an entirely ordinary sort of a woman. Edwina would not have entertained any notion that she had struggled with delusions or any manner of mental anguish based on the first impression she made. As she stepped forward to greet the newcomers, Cressida adjusted the neckerchief of her Girl Guides uniform and graced them with a wide smile.

"You must be Beryl Helliwell and Edwina Davenport. Constance has told me so much about you," Cressida said. Dropping her voice slightly lower, she continued. "I understand we are to say that you are assisting me with the Girl Guides, Miss Helliwell, and that you, Miss Davenport, are here as an artist's model."

Cressida went on to give them an extravagant wink. As if to reinforce her point, in case they had not picked up on her meaning, she tapped the side of her nose with a bony forefinger. Perhaps she was not quite as stable as she appeared at first glance, Edwina thought. Beryl apparently felt the same, as she poked Edwina sharply in the back. Edwina hoped Cressida would prove to be far more subtle when they were with other members of the household. If she behaved in such a way in front of Ursula or worse, Hubert Maitland, it would prove very awkward indeed.

"May I assume we are quite alone at present?" Beryl asked, glancing about conspiratorially.

"Voices tend to carry a bit in the wood, so you might want to lower yours," Constance said. "But there is no one in the immediate vicinity."

"You are quite right about our cover stories," Beryl said. "But, as I am sure Constance has informed you, we are here to make a thorough investigation of your allegations concerning Ursula and one of the artists here at the colony. Louis is his name, I believe."

Constance nodded but gave no sign there was anything insincere going on. Her demeanor betrayed no sign that she was involved in an elaborate ruse. While Edwina was well aware that there was a need for those in the upper classes to comport themselves with even more self-possession than those in lower echelons of society, Edwina was impressed by Constance's easy manner in the face of a lie. Edwina wondered if their hostess's ability to disguise her true purpose had been formed through breeding or through years of experience.

It begged the question of whether Cressida had required delicate handling for many years, or if she had recently become far more unstable. It was a sad fact that the war years, and the economic downturn that followed, had left many of her fellow countrymen and women with emotional scars. As Edwina stood wondering whether Constance had used her flexibility with the truth when she had engaged their services, she regretted not asking a few more pointed questions about Cressida and what they might expect before they accepted the job.

"I am so relieved that you are able to take on this case. I am absolutely certain poor Hubert is being made to look an absolute fool by that little gold digger," Cressida said, two bright spots of color appearing on her otherwise flawless complexion. "I've tried my best to warn him, but he is simply too smitten by her obvious charms to listen to his family. Isn't that right, Constance?" She turned to her cousin and tugged at her sleeve as if she were a small child looking for attention from a distracted governess.

If such outbursts occurred routinely, Edwina could easily understand why Constance had hired them to help quell Cressida's concerns. She certainly did not mince words about the new lady of the house. Edwina would have been mortified if she were Constance, especially if such things often took place in front of visitors. Most families preferred not to air their secrets in front of outsiders, and old, prominent families seemed to like it even less. In this case, it would appear that Cressida not only made a point of sharing secrets, she herself was one of them. She glanced over at Constance and then at Beryl before stepping in to offer what she hoped would be helpful words.

"Please be assured that we will make every effort to get to the bottom of your concerns. However, you must remember that in order to do so we will need to rely on your complete cooperation concerning our supposed reasons for being here at Maitland Park. If you were to give any hint to Ursula that we were investigating her behavior, I am certain she is sensible enough to take steps to curtail her activities, and thus it would be much more difficult to prove any inappropriate goings-on," Edwina said.

Constance gave the barest nod of approval. Cressida bobbed her head up and down enthusiastically. She yanked up and down on Constance's sleeve once more. With her own Girl Guides uniform, she put Edwina in mind of an overgrown child.

"You can rely on me to safeguard your true purpose here. I've always been quite good at amateur theatrics. This will be rather fun, don't you think, Constance?" Cressida asked, turning to her cousin.

"I believe we should regard this as an entirely serious matter, Cressida. After all, one does not take infidelity lightly. I would not have engaged these two professionals if this matter were not very serious," Constance said.

"Of course. I didn't mean to sound as though it were a light-hearted matter. I only meant to show my unreserved support for this course of action. Do tell me how I may be of assistance," Cressida said.

"I think the most helpful thing would be for us to be introduced to as many of the people staying here just as soon as is possible," Beryl said. "Ursula mentioned that Louis Langdon Beck was likely to be found somewhere here in the wood sketching. Do you know if that is the case?"

"I know right where he is. Of course, I'm not surprised Ursula does, too," Cressida said. "If you'll just follow me, I will introduce you to him. The glade where he has set himself up every day is on my way to collect a group of the Girl Guides, so it's no trouble at all."

"Since that's settled, I will leave you in Cressida's competent hands. I have other matters to attend to back at the house before dinner," Constance said. "I'll see you both then."

Edwina felt a ripple of unease as Constance left them on their own with Cressida. They held back slightly as she led them farther and farther along a path through the wood in order to observe her without being seen to do so. Surely Constance would not have left them alone with her in a far-off part of the property if she posed any sort of danger, would she?

Cressida moved along swiftly as though the uneven path littered with pine needles and pebbles was as familiar to her as one of the plushly carpeted hallways in the main house. To watch her gave no indication that there was anything unstable about her in the least. In fact, she gave off a confident, wholesome, and capable air. After a few moments, she stopped behind a large rhododendron and beckoned for them to join her.

"This is where he'll be," Cressida whispered, lowering a

leafy branch and pointing towards a sheltered glade opening out in the woods just beyond them. Through the small gap, Edwina could just make out the back of a man's golden-blond head atop a billowy white smock and a hand grasping a long-handled paintbrush. Even out in the open, the scent of mineral spirits hung heavily in the air. Edwina wrinkled her nose.

Fortunately, Charles preferred to paint with watercolors, she thought, as she considered her cover story of being his model. Beryl touched her on the arm and pointed towards the ground at their feet. The earth around the back side of the rhododendron had been well beaten down, as though someone had spent a great deal of time hiding in that very spot.

Before she had time to consider what that might mean, Cressida let out a startled gasp and darted around the bush and into the glade. Beryl hurried off in pursuit, and Edwina followed immediately behind her. As much as she was loath to involve herself in awkward situations, she could not very well leave Beryl on her own to endure it. Before she reached her friend's side, however, the sound of Cressida's shrill shouts filled her ears.

At first, she saw nothing to provoke such a commotion. Cressida stood next to the artist, waving her arms wildly and shouting.

"What in the world do you think you are you doing?"

"I should think that what I am doing is quite obvious, but I cannot imagine how it is of any business of yours. Or is that the trouble? Are you beset by envy? If you want to model for me, all you need to do is to ask."

The man adjusted his stance slightly and noticed Beryl and Edwina's presence. He smiled broadly at them before turning back to his easel.

"This is absolutely outrageous, even for someone like you," Cressida said.

She reached out, and Edwina felt her breath catch in her

throat as the man grabbed Cressida's arm and prevented her from snatching the canvas from his easel. She yanked her arm away from his grasp, then turned and addressed someone beyond Edwina's view.

"Janet, what on earth would your mother think if she found out you were involved in a thing like this?" She stepped forward and pulled a girl of about fifteen years to her feet.

"You won't need to tell her, will you?" Janet asked. It looked as though the girl were about to burst into tears. Her lower lip wobbled, and her face had flushed bright scarlet.

Edwina took a step forward. She did not at all like the look on Cressida's face. Perhaps a well-placed word would defuse the situation. But the sight in front of her as she peered around Cressida's back drove all words from her lips. There, in the center of the glade, reclining on one elbow, lay a slim woman with hair of such paleness it was almost white. It hung over one shoulder, almost entirely obscuring the right side of her face.

Her skin was, for the most part, equally fair. Edwina could say that without reservation as so very much of it was on display. With the exception of a long string of bright blue beads, the woman stretched out on a blanket in the center of the grass was entirely nude.

Edwina averted her eyes, took a step back, and the only thought she could put together was to flee. It was one thing to be confronted with a completed painting hanging in a museum or featured in a book that depicted an unclothed human body. It was an entirely different matter to stumble upon such a figure in the flesh. Try as she might, Edwina could not think what one ought to do under the circumstances. She had no notion of what to say or even where to look. Gratefully, she felt Beryl place a steadying hand on her back.

"We will discuss this later. Now, you go on back to the Girl Guides campsite and don't let me catch you lurking around here again or there will be serious consequences," Cressida said.

"I cannot see what all the fuss is about," Louis said. "What could possibly be wrong with appreciating the beauty of the human form? Don't you agree, Tuva?"

"It is not my place to agree or to disagree. I am merely the model," the model called out from her place on the blanket.

"There is nothing in the least mere about you, my sweet," the man said. "Although I will say I am quite taken with the idea of trying my hand at capturing the essence of Cressida, too, now that the notion has occurred to me. Can I not persuade you to throw off the trappings of convention in order to pose for me for a few hours? I would have to insist that you remove most of that childish ensemble you are wearing, but I would permit you to leave your kerchief wound round your neck if it would put you at your ease." He playfully pointed a palette knife at Cressida.

"I know you enjoy flaunting convention, but some of us believe in common decency and all that entails," Cressida said. "If I hear the slightest whisper of you having anything further to do with Janet, I will report you to the police for attempting to corrupt a minor." With that, she turned on her heel and headed off through the woods in the same direction as the girl.

The pale woman stood and slowly crossed the grass to a tree, from a branch of which a dressing gown hung fluttering in the light breeze. Without the slightest appearance of self-consciousness, she slipped her arms into the robe and without haste buttoned the garment up. Edwina was struck by the impression that she was some sort of forest nymph rather than a mortal woman. That said, a rather angry nymph at that. Edwina noticed how the young woman's gaze followed Cressida's retreating back with undisguised hostility.

"Well, that is rather disappointing. I think Janet added a certain something the painting was lacking. Wouldn't you agree?" he asked, turning to fully face Beryl and Edwina.

Edwina steeled herself and glanced over at the painting propped on the easel before him. She wondered how he could say anything of the sort. The canvas was covered with irregular blotches of paint in earthy tones, none of which looked the least bit like people. In fact, the more she looked at it the more it looked like a rag someone had wiped a dirty brush on than a work of deliberate creation. Once again, she found herself robbed of the power of speech. Beryl gave her a reassuring pat on the back and launched into the breach.

"Perhaps someone else could be convinced to stand in for her," Beryl said. "After all, I am sure there are plenty of people who would be happy to be captured on canvas by an artist with as much acclaim as you have earned, Mr. Beck."

"What a charming creature you are. But you have me at a disadvantage as you seem to know my name, but I do not know yours," he said.

"I am surprised at you, Louis," the woman said. "Do you not recognize the famous Beryl Helliwell?"

She took a step towards them and swept her hair away from her face, perhaps for a better look. Edwina was shocked once again by the woman's appearance. The entire right side of her face was covered in a fine tracery of scars. As Edwina looked down, she noticed red scars covering the model's bare feet as well.

"I beg your pardon. Of course, I should have recognized you without being prompted to do so. I can only justify the oversight by saying I would never have expected to encounter an adventuress like yourself in such a quiet little backwater as Walmsley Parva. What brings you here?" Louis asked.

Edwina had not been predisposed to like a man suspected of cavorting with another man's wife. She did not approve of ogling naked women, even for artistic purposes. She especially did not hold with exposing young girls to the sort of moral decay that most likely ate away at his soul. But she simply could not abide the sort of person who dismissed her beloved village as nothing more than a backwater. She was about to school him concerning his unwarranted prejudice, when Beryl spoke again.

"And unless I miss my guess you are the famous dancer Tuva Dahlberg, are you not?" she said.

"I am surprised to be recognized in my altered state, but you are correct." Tuva gestured to her face. "Not that I am a dancer any longer."

"Allow me to introduce my friend and business associate, Edwina Davenport," Beryl said.

"Pleased to meet you both. Are you in the art business or the tobacco business?" Louis asked.

"Neither. We own a private enquiry agency right here in this little backwater," Edwina said, finally finding her voice.

"Astonishing. Are you here on a case?" Louis asked.

"I've been asked to give a few talks on topics of interest to the Girl Guides, and Edwina has offered to serve as an artist's model herself for Charles Jarvis," Cressida said.

"Good for Charles," Louis said. "I hadn't any idea he was the sort of fellow to be open to using a model. I do hope you will not let Cressida's prudish attitude keep you from enjoying yourself at it."

He winked at Edwina in a way that made her feel lightheaded. Was he implying that she might pose in a state of undress? Worse yet, would Charles expect her to do so? The glade in front of her began to flit in and out of focus, and the back of her neck felt as though it had burst into flame. Beryl seemed to sense her discomfort and tucked her arm through Edwina's own, holding her upright as she felt her knees begin to wobble.

"Speaking of Charles, you don't know where we might find

him, do you? We were hoping to speak with him before dinner," Beryl said.

"Ever since he arrived, I believe he has been painting in the Japanese garden," Tuva said.

"It is a predictable sort of space but one I am sure will be livened up immeasurably by the inclusion of a model," Louis said with another wink before turning back to his canvas. "Tuva, let's get back to work before we lose the light for the day."

Beryl propelled her away as Tuva's dressing gown slipped from her shoulders.

Chapter 6

Beryl continued to lend a sturdy arm to Edwina as they beat a hasty retreat from the artist and his model. While Beryl had long been accustomed to the sorts of experiences one might encounter when mixing with those who claimed the title of artist, she very much doubted Edwina had ever witnessed such a scene in all her life. She had considered mentioning that there might be some unexpected behavior from the participants at the colony, but she had selfishly been so eager to leave the Beeches and Beddoes's relentless cleaning that she did not wish to give Edwina any reason to refuse the case. From the way Edwina sagged against her, she felt overwhelmed with regret at not better preparing her friend.

Beryl found herself in the unusual position of having absolutely no notion of what to say or to do. As they moved farther from the glade and its startling occupants, an uncomfortable silence hung between them. Beryl was accustomed to being the one to offer up a shocking comment or to suggest taking a bold action.

In this case, she was merely a witness to the comments and

actions of others. She had grown familiar over the course of the past few months with how far to push Edwina as concerned new ideas and experiences. She thought nude models might have been a great many steps too far.

As they came to the end of the path at the edge of the wood, Edwina stopped abruptly and took a step back from Beryl. She closed her eyes, drew in a deep breath, and then shook her head slowly as she exhaled. When she opened her eyes once more, she trained her gimlet gaze on Beryl's face with the same expression she used when questioning suspects who were telling half-truths and outright lies.

"Why didn't you tell me there might be such goings-on at an artists' colony?" Edwina asked.

Beryl was of two minds as to how to answer. She was sorely tempted to claim that the haste with which they departed the Beeches had left little time for such discussions. But Edwina had many gifts and the detection of lies, even those offered in her best interest, was one of them. Beryl did not want her friend to feel she could not trust her.

After all, the business they were building together depended on uncovering secrets and unmasking untruths. She couldn't very well hope they would be a success if she sowed such seeds of deceit between them. Perhaps she could simply parry the questions.

"While I was aware such informality between an artist and his or her model likely could exist, surely you don't believe that I could have anticipated that proof of it would be thrust upon us so unexpectedly," Beryl said.

Edwina narrowed her eyes and pursed her lips.

"I suppose you could not have expected that. I am sure even you could not have imagined that such a debauched scene would take place out in the open air where anyone might unwittingly stumble across it," Edwina said.

Beryl knew that Edwina had not been all that interested in art classes when the two of them had attended Miss Dupont's Finishing School for Young Ladies, but she had not realized how little familiarity her friend must have had to the works of great artists throughout time if she had the impression that nude figures appeared only in interior scenes. While she did not wish to leave Edwina even more ill at ease, she did wonder if she ought to mention the enthusiasm so many artists had for painting in plein air or the way abundant natural light was so highly prized by them.

All in all, she decided that if Edwina had survived one such shock, she would be capable of enduring another. They could not very well pretend to be investigating the case if one-half of their duo could not bring herself to leave her room for the remainder of their stay for fear she might encounter another scantily clad model.

"Perhaps they will be more considerate of the feelings of others from now on," Beryl said. "I expect they noticed your surprise at coming upon them like that."

"I should hope so. I don't know how I shall be able to face either of them again should the situation present itself. How does one make polite dinner conversation with someone as morally bankrupt as those two?" Edwina asked.

Beryl could not agree with Edwina's assessment. Her own life had provided her with a great many unorthodox experiences, and she would not have traded them for anything. That said, she did not feel that Edwina needed to hear a lecture on open-mindedness just then.

And Beryl could see Edwina's point, too. Every society needed rules, and Edwina's adherence to the expectations of the citizens of Walmsley Parva had made her a respected and even powerful member of the community. Beryl knew she could take as many lessons from her straitlaced friend as Edwina could from her.

"Perhaps it won't be necessary. Constance did say the artists' colony attendees tend to be very irregular in their attendance at meals," Beryl said.

"If we are lucky, we won't be here long enough to face many meals where they might appear," Edwina said.

"I wouldn't count on that," Beryl said. There was no way she was going to encourage Edwina to entertain the idea of returning to the Beeches before Beddoes had finished wearing herself out with the cleaning.

"Surely after witnessing the scene this afternoon, Cressida must realize that if Louis is conducting an affair with anyone, it is Tuva," Edwina said.

"Why would you believe that had any bearing on her suspicions?" Beryl asked. "As far as I could tell, Cressida wasn't surprised by Tuva's state of undress. She was only upset by one of the Girl Guides being a part of the painting, too."

"So, you don't think there is something going on between Louis and his model?" Edwina said, her eyes wide.

"Artists and their models often have a close relationship, but it does not guarantee a romantic entanglement. I don't expect your offer to serve as a model for Charles was meant to encourage him to attempt to woo you. Speaking of which, isn't that Charles up ahead?" She pointed to a pair of figures approaching from the direction of the main house.

As they stepped out of the wood onto the sprawling green lawn, Beryl wondered if she had gone too far in her teasing of Edwina. Her friend seemed almost as tongue-tied as they came to a halt beside Charles and a slightly younger man as she had on their retreat from the glade. She had not meant to make Edwina uncomfortable, but she did think it rather insensitive of Edwina not to take notice of Charles's feelings for her. Beryl could not understand why Edwina had no interest in reciprocating his affections. Beryl thought they were quite a good match, and that a little romance livened up almost everyone's life.

Come to think of it, she thought, it had been rather too long since she'd had any affairs of the heart herself. In fact, since her unexpected meeting with her old friend Archie Harrison some weeks earlier, she had not met any gentlemen who caused her heart to beat a little faster in her chest. Not that she hadn't had offers, mind. Rarely was there a visit to the pub that did not involve rebuffing the enthusiastic advances of one resident of Walmsley Parva or another.

It was a pity, Beryl thought as she allowed her gaze to linger on the shabbily dressed man standing at Charles's side, that so far no one of interest had yet presented himself at Maitland Park. She would very much like to encounter someone she was not in the least inclined to rebuff. Charles's companion was definitely not that man.

"Hello, Charles. Edwina and I were just talking about you," Beryl said. Charles quickened his pace, and Beryl observed the way his face softened as his glance turned towards Edwina.

"You must allow me to introduce you to my favorite pair of ladies," Charles said to his companion. "Spencer Spaulding, allow me to present my dear friends Miss Edwina Davenport and Miss Beryl Helliwell. Spencer is the artist I was telling you about, Edwina. The one who wangled the invitation for me here at the artists' colony."

Spencer Spaulding waved off the compliment with a paint-stained hand clutched around a pipe. "Charles is being far too modest. He would have been here on his own merits if only Ursula had already been aware of his interest in painting. He has real talent and is a whole lot more enjoyable company than some of the other participants here at the artists' colony," Spencer said.

"I thought that a retreat such as this one would bring out a sense of camaraderie between fellow artists," Beryl said.

"I'm sorry to say there are artists who believe they have no fellows. Some seem to think they inhabit a plain far above the rest of us poor mortals. Isn't that right, Charles?" Spencer said.

Charles cleared his throat slightly. "I'm sure I couldn't say as I admire everyone's work that is in attendance."

"See what I mean about him being such agreeable company? But being his friends, you must know that already," Spencer said. He cocked his head and looked Edwina over carefully as though she were an apple in a barrel in front of the green-grocer's shop he was considering for purchase. He took a step towards her and snapped his stubby fingers. "Am I imagining things, or is this the woman you have portrayed in several of the watercolors you have shown me?"

"I am delighted my efforts to depict her have proven recognizable. Edwina has very kindly offered to model for me during my time here at the artists' colony. She knew I would want to take full advantage of the unprecedented opportunity this time affords me, and that it would be most advantageous to work with a familiar subject, albeit in a new setting," Charles said.

"I can see why you have painted her again and again," Spencer said. He lowered his pipe and knocked it against the sole of his scuffed shoe, scattering the ash on the pristine lawn. He reached out and laid a stained finger against Edwina's cheek and gently tilted her head to the side. Edwina stiffened, and her eyes grew almost as wide as they had when she had spotted Tuva in the glade. "You could be a professional model if you so choose. Should you ever grow tired of sitting for Charles, please do seek me out. I am looking for a new source of inspiration and you might just be it."

"I have no experience at modeling so I am sure I would prove a grave disappointment," Edwina said stiffly.

"Nonsense. It takes very little effort on the part of the model. The work is all down to the artist. Besides, if you needed any help in learning what is expected, you could simply ask Tuva Dahlberg. She knows just what to do."

Chapter 7

When they reentered Maitland Park, the same well-trained young parlormaid greeted them and informed them that tea was being served in the drawing room. Edwina allowed the young woman to divest her of her hat and after checking her hair in a hallway mirror, followed the cheerful and chattering maid towards the soothing sound of teacups clattering against saucers.

As she felt the gravitational pull of the tea tray, she paused long enough to notice Beryl's decided lack of enthusiasm for the upcoming refreshments. She was becoming increasingly convinced that her friend would not ever truly warm to that most British of indulgences. Back home at the Beeches, by late afternoon or early evening, Beryl was much more interested in mixing up a batch of chilled American-style cocktails than in sipping a piping-hot cup of Darjeeling. She never seemed all that interested in the food, either.

All of Edwina's efforts to convert her to local ways had failed miserably. Try as she might, she could not seem to offer her friend any combination of teatime treats that elicited enthusiasm. As often as not, Beryl simply ate what was put before her without complaint but also without much sign of pleasure. The only times she seemed to relish a meal was when Simpkins tested one of his experiments on them.

After recently assuming responsibility for the Colonel Kimberly's Condiment Company, he had taken it upon himself to try to come up with some new recipes for the product line. And despite her efforts to train Beryl's palate to enjoy a rock cake or a tongue sandwich, she only applied herself with gusto to a plate filled with some sort of concoction Simpkins cobbled together from the depths of his imagination. The pair of them seemed to think a sensible British tea could be replaced by spicy curries served over rice washed down by dry martinis.

The sad fact was, if she were to admit the truth, she felt that Beryl had had more of an impact upon her own behavior than the other way round. Edwina had found herself rather more enamored of the rituals surrounding cocktails, not to mention the bracing quality they so often offered to her generally mild-mannered demeanor, than she would have cared to admit. She could not, however, imagine herself ever coming to prefer plates of foreign food teaming with onions and startling bits of fiery capsicum to a dependable pickle and cheese sandwich or a hot, fruit-studded scone.

The maid pushed open the door of the drawing room and held it open for them to pass into the enormous room. Long windows hung with velvet deep-rose-colored draperies flanked a wall paneled in ornately carved wood. Dotted about the room were more darkly moody oil paintings, this time depicting landscapes rather than dour Maitland ancestors. Piecrust tables clotted with bric-a-brac stood scattered about the room and despite the warmth earlier in the day, a fire cracked quietly in a vast fireplace situated at the far end of the room.

Even with its blaze the room felt chilly, and Edwina gratefully thought of the woolen shawl she had tucked into her valise before setting out from the Beeches. She suspected she might well be glad to have it wrapped round her shoulders when she climbed into bed that night. No matter what Beryl might say on the matter, it was best to prepare for every eventuality, especially when subjecting oneself to the twin unpredictabilities of country houses and what constituted English summer weather.

The maid gave a slight curtsey and withdrew. Edwina noticed they were not alone. A man in his early fifties sporting a full head of curly hair and a prominent nose sat on a damask sofa, his eyes trained on the door. Beryl gave a little gasp of surprise. Edwina took a closer look and felt far from favorably impressed by the man seated before her. Upon seeing the women, he rose to his feet and took a step towards them, his hand outstretched in greeting. She felt her lips pursing together ever so slightly. Without a doubt, he was the man who had almost run her down with the motorcycle the day before.

"Roger Hazeldine, as I live and breathe," Beryl said, not bothering to disguise the note of shock in her voice. "It seems forever since I last laid my eyes on you." Beryl turned towards her and began to explain her connection to the man before them. "Roger and I met before the war broke out."

"How well I remember those days spent painting you," Roger said, his voice pitched just slightly louder than Edwina would have deemed necessary in such a quiet room.

She felt Beryl stiffen as though she were a dog who suspected it had heard someone prowling the grounds outside its home. Edwina was not certain, but she had the impression that Roger Hazeldine had just changed the subject. But why would he have done such a thing? Who was this mysterious stranger who drove about recklessly on country lanes and yet seemed as though he wished to keep his connection to Beryl some sort of secret? More importantly, why was Beryl willing to go along with him?

In all her experience with her friend, Edwina had never known Beryl to be one who accepted direction from others, at least not without a great deal of fuss. It often took a large dose of finesse on Edwina's part to convince Beryl to do things in a way that made the most sense in a small country village. But here was a man Beryl had never mentioned spinning her about with less effort than the flick of a forefinger.

Ever a romantic, Edwina wondered if the two had once been in love before the war had thrown so much of life into turmoil. She allowed herself a moment to imagine a heroine in a novel who had been separated from her one true love by a cruel twist of fate in the form of the Kaiser. Beryl's voice brought her back to reality and with a pang of regret she focused her attention on the conversation taking place in front of her.

"I had absolutely no idea that you would be here. Are you taking part in the artists' colony?" Beryl asked.

"As a matter of fact, I am. I don't suppose I could convince you to sit for another set of cigarette cards, now could I?" Roger asked. "That first set proved to be some of my most inspired and impactful work."

"It's possible that that could be arranged. I'm here to provide some expert instruction to the Girl Guides who are spending time here this week. But I don't expect that will take all of my time and attention. I'd love to catch up with you and chat about old times," Beryl said.

Edwina again had the sense that there was a sort of subtext passing back and forth between the two other people in the room. She felt decidedly uncomfortable. Most often when Beryl was conducting conversations with more than one meaning, Edwina was in on the secret. It was very unpleasant to find herself on the outside looking in.

The only time she did not wish to join Beryl in her bouts of double entendre were when she was outrageously flirting with nearby men. But for some reason, Beryl seemed to be withholding her usual charms in her exchange with Roger. Whatever could be going on? Could it be that Beryl's feelings for Roger were so strong that she did not wish to cheapen them with her usual playful banter?

Edwina fervently hoped this would not prove to be the case. She had no intention of feigning approval of a man who so callously disregarded the rules of the road. Even before she had become the local magistrate, she had held very strong opinions concerning motorists and safe practices.

"I don't believe I've had the pleasure of meeting your friend. Won't you introduce us?" Roger asked.

He turned to Edwina, a broad smile spreading across his face. Edwina felt her blood begin to simmer. Not only did it feel as though he were driving a wedge between herself and her dearest friend, but he had no notion that she was the woman he had nearly run down.

"I'm surprised you don't recognize me as we very nearly met only yesterday," Edwina said.

Roger raised a shaggy eyebrow in surprise. "I'm sure I would have remembered a lovely lady such as yourself," Roger said. "Perhaps you are mistaken?"

"I fervently wish that I was, but I'm afraid the dramatic nature of our encounter made an unfortunately strong impression upon me," Edwina said. She could hear her voice taking on a slightly strident note but found that she did not care. It was a rare thing for Edwina to give vent to her spleen but once she did, she did a thorough job of it.

Her dander was well and truly up. Even if she had not been subjected to the encounter with Louis and Tuva and then the unsettling comments made by Spencer Spaulding, she would have found Roger's dismissal of her memory irksome. During the course of her life, Edwina had prided herself on being a noticing sort of person.

While Beryl's strengths lay in attempting daring deeds and

undertaking bold plans of action, Edwina's were more concerned with observing things closely and then mulling them over carefully. While she did make a habit of carrying a pocket notebook to record her thoughts or exact statements from persons of interest they encountered during their cases, the fact of the matter was that Edwina needed no such memory aid. She prided herself on paying attention in the moment and remembering what she heard and saw.

"Edwina is famous for her recall of faces," Beryl said. "Roger, if you have been in her path, she is sure to have remembered you." Slightly mollified, Edwina turned towards her friend and gave a slight nod of appreciation.

"It seems I must ask for your forgiveness. Please do me the favor of refreshing my memory as to our previous encounter," Roger said.

"I am the woman at the side of the road yesterday afternoon that you nearly ran down recklessly careening about on a motorcycle. Ursula Maitland was in the sidecar," Edwina said.

Edwina was pleased to see a deep flush creeping up Roger's neck. Perhaps he regretted the incident after all.

She crossed the room to a long sideboard practically groaning under the weight of an enormous silver tea tray and an assortment of tiny sandwiches and fruit-studded buns. There was even a selection of iced fairy cakes laid out temptingly on a tiered stand. With her back turned towards the others, she made a selection of refreshments and placed them carefully on a translucent bone china plate.

Turning back to face them, she looked about the room for a place to sit. Settling herself into a wingback chair next to a low table, she turned her attention to Beryl and Roger once more. Once again, she saw a look pass between them before Roger began to speak.

"I must beg your pardon. I'm afraid that I simply have no recollection of the incident of which you speak. I would beg you to pardon my driving, but I do have an ironclad excuse," he said with a smile.

"And what might that be?" Edwina asked as she neatly crossed her ankles one over the other.

"I regret to mention that Beryl is the one who taught me to drive," Roger said with a chuckle.

Chapter 8

Despite her relief at getting well away from Beddoes, Beryl was beginning to feel the case was an ill-fated one. Not only did Cressida appear to be less unstable than Constance had revealed when engaging their services, she found herself in the uncomfortable position of keeping a secret from her dearest friend. It felt particularly loathsome as the secret might prove important to their current case.

A strange sensation filled her stomach and Beryl struggled to put her finger on exactly what it might be. With a jolt of shock, she recognized that her conscience was pricking. While it was extremely rare, Beryl realized she was feeling an unnerving sense of guilt. The situation unfolding between Edwina and Roger did little to lessen her concerns.

Without a doubt, Roger was doing himself no favors in his attempt at mollifying Edwina. It was going to take quite a bit of effort on her part to smooth things over with her friend. His jocular attitude towards Edwina's discomfort appeared irresponsible and dismissive. While she would not have described Edwina as someone who was unduly sensitive, she did know that Edwina did not appreciate threats to her personal safety.

Edwina's recent appointment as the local magistrate had done nothing to make her less attuned to matters of security. If anything, it had caused her to be even more vigilant when traveling by motorcar. Beryl knew Roger well enough to understand that he meant no discourtesy, but she also knew that Edwina would likely not see it that way, especially in light of the shocks to her sensibilities she had already endured that day.

Edwina's posture had stiffened to an even more preposterously prim degree when Roger blamed his poor driving on her tutelage. What he didn't realize was that Beryl had spent considerable time instructing Edwina on that very same thing. And while it was true that Edwina had decided to complete her driving instruction with the Blackburns, a pair of siblings who ran the local garage and driving school, she had gotten her start behind the wheel at Beryl's insistence and encouragement.

While she would be the first to admit that she adored pushing her own vehicle to the limits of its speed, she would never agree that she did so in any way that endangered others. She was an expert driver, and she felt that anyone who had enjoyed her tutelage could say the same if they took her lessons to heart and applied them with verve. Fortunately for them all, a newcomer bustled into the drawing room before Edwina could formulate a response to Roger's clumsy effort to place the blame for his irresponsible driving on Beryl's shoulders.

Standing before them with a beaming smile was a tall man in his late fifties or early sixties running ever so slightly to fat. Corpulent was likely the word Edwina would use to describe him if asked to do so. The buttons on his tweed vest strained slightly as they valiantly struggled to span his waist in a way that signaled he was a man who tended, at least in the matter of his girth, to vanity.

No doubt it was a matter of pride, not of economic where-withal, that explained why he had neither had his clothing altered nor replaced when it no longer fit properly. Even from a bit of distance the quality of his clothing and of his highly polished brogues spoke of his social station. While his gleaming bald pate reflected the late-afternoon sunlight slanting through the windows, his luxuriant mustache, waxed and gracefully curved at the ends, more than made up for any lack of hair on his head. He gave off an air of authority, and Beryl suspected they were viewing their host.

"Miss Davenport, I am simply delighted to have the opportunity to host you in my home," he said with a gracious hint at a bow. "And, of course, I recognize you, Miss Helliwell, from your portraits on the series of cigarette cards we commissioned some years ago. Allow me to introduce myself. I am Hubert Maitland."

Beryl snuck a glance at Edwina and was relieved to see her friend's expression softening. No matter how offended she might have been by Roger's comments, Edwina would never cause awkwardness with their host over such petty concerns. She would consider such a thing to reflect not only an utter lack of breeding but also a moral failing.

While Beryl did not personally value pedigree, she had found Edwina's adherence to such things useful on occasion. This was clearly one of them. Taking advantage of the change of topic, she smiled at Hubert and extended her hand, which he quickly crossed the room to kiss.

"If I remember correctly it was for a set featuring lady adventurers, wasn't it?" Beryl asked.

"Right you are. I'll have you know it was one of our most popular series. Isn't that right, Roger?" he asked, turning to the other man in the room.

Beryl noticed that Roger seemed as relieved as she at the

change of topic. The red flush was receding down below his collar, and he had stopped jingling coins in his pocket.

"Those pieces were some of my finest work I would say, but the job was an easy one with such a beautiful subject to paint," Roger said.

"We feature many beautiful women on our cigarette cards, but I don't believe that adequately explains the popularity of that series. It is my firm belief that the world is rapidly changing, and people are eager to see women in new and exciting roles." Hubert looked around the room as if to check for other occupants. "I understand from my sister, Constance, that you two ladies have begun a private enquiry agency here in Walmsley Parva."

"That is correct. But I am happy to say that we are not here on investigatory business," Edwina said.

Beryl noticed that her friend did not look in her direction. She wondered if Edwina had picked up on the unsaid messages passing between herself and Roger. She hoped that Edwina had not taken offense. Once again, Beryl wondered if the case were off to a bad start.

"Well, that certainly is a relief. What brings you here if it isn't business?" he asked. "Are the pair of you artists as well as detectives?"

"Edwina is attending the colony as an artist's model, and I'm here to give the Girl Guides the benefit of some of my experience in the hinterlands," Beryl said.

"An artist's model, you say? Not quite what I would have expected from a lady such as yourself," Hubert said, stepping towards Edwina and looking over her a little too boldly. Now it was Edwina's turn for a creeping flush to suffuse her face.

"I'm only here as a favor to my good friend Charles Jarvis. He's taking part in the artists' colony and he expressed an eagerness to paint from a live model," Edwina said. "I cannot claim to be a professional. I save that for my role as an enquiry agent."

Hubert impudently ran his gaze over Edwina once more. "I suppose that would explain it," he said.

Beryl wondered if he had any inkling as to their true purpose in his home. Was Constance as protective of him as Cressida was? Surely, he could not be so obtuse as to have no notion of Cressida's feelings about his new bride. She decided to try to distract him. She turned one of her famous smiles on him and then sighed dramatically.

"You know, I feel quite envious of Edwina. I enjoyed my time spent posing for Roger enormously," she said, not entirely untruthfully. She would vastly have preferred to sit perfectly still while someone painted her rather than to be assigned the repellent task of demonstrating bush craft to a group of eager young girls.

"My dear lady, you've just given me the most marvelous idea," Hubert said, plopping into the seat next to Edwina's. "What would the two of you say to the possibility of a series of cards of the pair of you? I don't believe any cigarette company has ever featured lady detectives on their cards before. If lady adventurers caused a stir, I can only imagine how well packs of cigarettes with a series of cards featuring lady enquiry agents would move off the shelves."

Beryl wondered what in the world Edwina would say to such a suggestion. Her friend was known for her modesty and her persistent belief that it was not quite nice to push oneself forward into the public spotlight. Beryl had found it to be a bit of a damper on their company's ability to make great strides in their growth. Beryl often felt like she was dragging her friend into the spotlight whether in advertising, in talking about their business, or especially in the press.

She could hardly imagine Edwina consenting to her image

being splashed out over hundreds of thousands of packets of cigarettes. She decided for the good of the agency she would have to accept for them and then convince Edwina of the merits of the suggestion.

"We would be delighted to take part in such a scheme," Beryl said, plucking a fairy cake from the buffet and placing it on a delicate plate. Beryl nodded encouragingly at Edwina as she selected a minuscule sandwich and some sort of bun. "Of course, we shall have to discuss the details and find a way to fit any sittings in around our prior obligations."

"Splendid, absolutely splendid." Hubert rose to his feet and ambled towards the sideboard, where he poured himself a cup of tea and helped himself to a heaping plate of food. "Roger, I'm sure I can count on you to arrange this, can't I?"

Beryl thought that Roger looked anything but pleased to take on the commitment. She wondered if it had to do with Edwina's hostile attitude, their shared past, or something else entirely. Still, he seemed to know his place in the pecking order.

"I can think of nothing I would like more than to paint these two lovely ladies. I think the idea a marvelous one," Roger said. "But if I'm going to make time for that, I have some loose ends I need to tie up with other projects. If you'll all excuse me, I'll go sort out those details and check in with you ladies later on about when we could begin some sessions."

With that, he bobbed his head at Edwina and then at Beryl before hurrying out the door. Beryl wondered just what sort of business Roger might need to conclude. From the way Edwina turned her gaze on Beryl, she knew her friend would have something to say about Beryl's high-handed acceptance of Hubert's offer without consulting her.

But Edwina was far too well-mannered to voice such questions aloud, especially in front of the man who seemed to think he had done them a service by offering to make them famous. Beryl was certain that she would hear more on the matter as soon as the two of them had a moment to themselves.

Once again, she wondered why she had not been able to restrain herself from offering assistance to Beddoes. If only she had followed the rules of society for once, they would likely not have accepted the case from Constance. And the fact was that there was something irksomely underhanded about it all that left a bit of a bad taste in her mouth.

She had never felt inclined to judge how others conducted their marriages, and the notion of appearing to spy on someone concerning such things, even if it were just a pretense, was starting to feel grubby. When Constance had offered them a way to flee the Beeches for a few days, she had leapt at the opportunity. But now that she had had more time to consider it, she felt less sure that it had been a wise course of action.

The only positive in Edwina's opinion had been the possibility that Constance would recommend their services to others in her social set. Beryl was not so sure that any such recommendations could be relied upon. After all, not only could they not very well boast about conducting a sham investigation, surely Constance would not wish to admit to anyone else that she had hired them to pacify an unbalanced member of her household. Between the unsavoriness of the task, the dreaded Girl Guides, and the unexpected reappearance of Roger, she found herself wishing she could simply go home.

Beryl felt a startling lurch in her heart at the thought. She had, of course, lived in houses that belonged to her or to her parents or various husbands. She had even had an occasional flat of her own from time to time between sojourns off to the far reaches of the globe. But what she had never even given thought to was the notion of a home. With a bolt of clarity, she realized she thought of the Beeches as her home, and she was overwhelmed with the urge to throw her things in the motorcar and to rush back to it without delay.

Her throat tightened as she looked over at Edwina making polite conversation with Hubert. Maybe, just maybe, her boldness over the years had less to do with courage and more to do with having nothing in her life she was not prepared to lose.

Chapter 9

Edwina had been relieved when just as Constance had predicted, the artists, with the exception of Charles, had not appeared for dinner. Even Cressida had absented herself with the excuse that the Girl Guides required closer supervision than she had previously thought. Edwina had been profoundly grateful that no one inquired further as to why that might be.

The dining room was paneled in a similar wood to that of the drawing room and of a size that easily could have accommodated four times as many diners as were seated at the long, gleaming table. The flickering candles set in ornate silver holders threw the faces of the small, assembled company into wavering shadow. Once again, gilt-framed portraits painted in somber oils filled the walls. Edwina wondered if any of the men portrayed in them had served as inspiration for Hubert's mustache. Not one of the paintings depicted men who were clean shaven.

Above the fireplace hung a double portrait of Hubert and Ursula seated close together on a green settee, hands clasped and smiles upon their faces. Another, of Constance displaying a stern countenance, hung to the side. Edwina noted with interest she had yet to see a portrait of Cressida in amongst the others. What did Cressida herself make of the omission? How did she view herself in comparison with Hubert and Constance? Was part of her ire towards Ursula founded on a sense that an interloper was afforded a more important place in the family than was she?

How closely related was she to the Maitlands? If she were a distant relative, had she harbored some hidden feelings for Hubert? Could she be jealous of Ursula and if so, did that pose a danger to the younger woman? Perhaps Constance had hired them as much to prevent harm from coming to Ursula as she had to stave off any awkward social situations.

Not long after the excellent meal, the two sleuths begged to be excused when a rubber bridge was proposed. As there were four to play without them, it was no difficult thing to excuse themselves.

Upon reaching their adjoining rooms, Beryl opened the door connecting their two bedchambers and made herself at home on Edwina's bed, relaxing against a bank of plump pillows, her satin evening slippers discarded on the rug beside the bed. Edwina moved between the chest of drawers and the walnut wardrobe, looking over the manner in which the maids had unpacked her belongings.

"So, what do you think of our case?" Beryl asked.

Edwina was not entirely sure how best to respond. She did know she had no desire to dwell a moment longer on what they had seen in the glade. "I have to wonder if Cressida is as paranoid as Constance is making her out to be. After all, what was Ursula doing riding around the countryside in the side car of a motorcycle with Roger Hazeldine?" Edwina asked.

"Perhaps she was just out getting some air. Or maybe she likes to race about at high rates of speed. I happen to know that some women like that very much," Beryl said. "Although, in my case, I much prefer to be the one behind the wheel."

"I suppose that's possible, but I can't say that Mr. Hazeldine looked all that pleased when I mentioned I had seen them together," Edwina said. She wondered if that was perhaps a good way to broach the subject of Beryl's secretive behavior concerning Roger.

"I can imagine there might well be all sorts of reasons why he would not have wished to appear to be someone who is not beyond reproach. After all, Hubert Maitland is his employer in addition to being his host. If any suspicion were to attach to him in reference to his relationship with Hubert's wife, he stands to lose a great deal," Beryl said.

"I'm surprised that you did not mention your connection with Roger and even with Maitland Cigarettes when we were first approached to take on this case," Edwina said.

She turned to Beryl and surveyed her expression for any traces of disingenuousness. Her years of supervising her own domestic servants, as well as leading Sunday school classes, had taught her a great deal about ferreting out untruths from others. Beryl, however, provided a unique challenge. It was almost as though her friend had the ability to entirely disregard the difference between fact and the fictions she preferred. Maddeningly, that strategy often seemed to work in Beryl's favor.

"I knew the name Maitland was a familiar one, but I simply didn't put two and two together. After all, it had been several years since I had last encountered Roger. And to be honest, I didn't give the cigarette card project much thought. After all, I don't smoke and my involvement with the company ended after my modeling sessions were over," Beryl said.

She wriggled back farther into the pillows and leveled an innocent gaze at Edwina.

"Still, it seems as though you remembered them both quickly enough once you were reintroduced," Edwina said.

"The memory works that way sometimes, don't you think? And with all that had happened in the intervening years, with the war and all, there have been more important things on my mind than some silly marketing scheme," Beryl said.

"Speaking of marketing schemes, you don't really mean to make us go through with posing for Roger, do you? I feel very uncomfortable with the idea of our business being associated with a product I would not endorse," Edwina said. "Frankly, I am surprised you were willing to model for them yourself."

She watched as Beryl drew in a deep breath as if considering her answer. There was definitely something troubling her friend that she was struggling to keep to herself.

"I suppose I was in need of some ready money at the time. I was between husbands, if I remember correctly," Beryl said, keeping her eyes fixed on a spot on the wall somewhere over Edwina's shoulder. "If you don't wish to do it, I am sure we can think of an excuse and wriggle out of it. After all, it isn't as if we signed a contract to do so."

Edwina was not entirely satisfied by Beryl's answer, but she didn't feel that she could press any further without accusing her dear friend of something. And she wasn't inclined to make waves. Before Beryl had arrived unexpectedly at the Beeches the previous autumn, Edwina had been feeling unprecedentedly low. All of her accounts with local merchants were in arrears, her house was in need of some vital repairs, and her day-to-day existence was one of profound loneliness. Beryl's arrival had created an upswing in every facet of her life. She had no desire to drive any sort of wedge between them and return to her previous existence of solitary boredom.

If Beryl had things about her life that she wished to keep private, Edwina would hold her tongue no matter how it hurt her feelings to be excluded. Perhaps the best way to ignore it would be to create some secrets of her own. Sadly, her only real secret concerned her novel, and Beryl had already ferreted that one out. She consoled herself with the knowledge that others of her acquaintance, like Charles or Simpkins, knew nothing of her literary efforts. She decided not to dwell upon secrets between them and instead to focus on their reason for being at Maitland Park.

"What do you think of Cressida?" Edwina asked.

"I thought she seemed far less unstable than Constance made her out to be when she hired us," Beryl said. "She did get riled up about that Girl Guide being painted, though, didn't she?

"From what little I saw of the goings-on, I should say Cressida's reaction only strengthened my impression that she was more in charge of her senses than Constance implied," Edwina said. "In fact, in that situation, she seemed the most level-headed one there."

"Still, Cressida did make a great deal of fuss about it. If he hadn't stopped her, she definitely intended to strike Louis," Beryl said. "That is not the sort of thing one would expect from a lady of her station.

"Cressida may have behaved regrettably, but I can't say I disagree with her for trying to protect that young girl. If Janet were my daughter, I would not have felt at all comfortable with what was going on. I'm sure that Cressida feels her responsibility towards the Girl Guides acutely."

"Do you think she mentioned her concerns to Constance?" Beryl asked.

"I have no idea, but she certainly took action about it all herself, and decisively, too. She's not really what I would have expected, either, considering the way Constance described her when she engaged our services," Edwina said.

"No, she isn't, is she? I was expecting to encounter someone who was far less sensible than she appears to be. Or maybe sensible is the wrong word. Perhaps I was imagining someone who appeared more fragile and less capably involved with life here at Maitland Park," Beryl said.

"Perhaps we'll be lucky and discover that Louis is actually conducting a torrid affair with his model, and that will stop

Cressida from making her accusations about Ursula," Edwina said. "That would make quite a tidy resolution to the case, wouldn't it?"

"It certainly would be preferable to discovering that he was attempting to ensnare a girl as young as Janet," Beryl said. "And artists and their models are often romantically entangled."

Edwina felt the skin on the back of her neck grow hot. She fervently wished she had been brave enough to pose as a poet during their visit. A poet would not have had to worry about any state of undress or entanglements of any kind. She could have drifted about the estate with a notebook in her hand feigning fits of inspiration whilst actually making note of all that was going on at Maitland Park.

"Speaking of artists, Charles seems to be having a wonderful time, doesn't he?" Beryl said. "Have you scheduled a time to sit for him yet?"

Edwina's palms dampened in a most unladylike way. The conversation was taking an unpleasant turn. Beryl had a habit of dropping broad hints about Charles's interest in her, and Edwina never enjoyed them. Things were made even more uncomfortable by Beryl's mention of romance between artists and their models. Tuva lounging about in a state of undress had made her comments all the more unnerving.

"We have not yet had the opportunity to set any appointments to meet. I suppose I should make time tomorrow in order to keep up the pretense for our attendance," Edwina said.

"I am sure you will enjoy yourself. And rest assured that should you find yourself in danger of becoming entangled with the artist painting you, I shall not behave as Cressida did," Beryl said. "If I happen upon you behaving unconventionally, I shall simply avert my eyes and walk on past without comment."

Edwina's stomach lurched. The notion that Beryl could even

imagine that such goings-on might occur between herself and Charles made her feel slightly lightheaded. Her eyes were drawn to the bed at the center of the room and she wondered, not for the first time, what it must be like to be Beryl, to be so shockingly unconventional. Edwina preferred to leave the more fleshly exploits of the world in the shadowy recesses of her vivid imagination. Her notions of romance invariably stopped before anything turned the least bit carnal.

"Sleep well. Tomorrow will likely prove an exciting day," Beryl said. With that, she slipped off the bed, bent down to pick up her satin slippers, and strode through the connecting door.

Chapter 10

Beryl had spent her fair share of time as a guest at English country houses. She was accustomed to the informal atmosphere they generally provided as to breakfast. As a matter of fact, that was one of her favorite parts of stays at such establishments. Beryl was not one who was inclined to rise early but while she was disinclined to rearrange her preferred sleep schedule on anyone's account, she did not like to give undo trouble whenever she was a houseguest.

In fact, when she had first started living at the Beeches, it had taken some time for Beryl to convince Edwina that she should feel comfortable making breakfast just for herself and then to get on with the business of her day. Somehow Edwina had decided that a full English breakfast served at the dot of seven in the morning was what was expected of her as the lady of the house, and it had taken a great deal of reassurance that Beryl not only did not expect that sort of coddling, she actually did not like it.

Beryl vastly preferred wandering into the breakfast room whenever suited her best and helping herself to whichever of the breakfast offerings piqued her interest. Often when visiting the homes of others, she arose late enough to find herself completely alone in the breakfast room and able to enjoy her first meal of the day in solitude. Although she was a vivacious and gregarious sort of a person, Beryl enjoyed easing into her day over a strong cup of coffee, a piece of toast or two, and a leisurely perusal of several of the morning's newspapers. She lifted the lids on the various chafing dishes set out on the sideboard and wondered, not for the first time, how the English could bring themselves to face the day when confronted by such horrors as smoked kippers.

She eagerly poured herself a steaming cup of coffee and selected a boiled egg and a piece of toast. She had just settled herself comfortably in a seat near the head of the table and had turned her attention to a newspaper conveniently left discarded by a previous guest, when she noticed young Janet Brown waving her arms over her head and shouting. She was running across the lawn, hell-bent for leather, towards the French doors positioned all along the side of the breakfast room.

While never inclined to go out of her way to interact with children, Beryl promptly dropped the newspaper, rushed to the door, and popped it open. Even someone with as underdeveloped a maternal sense as Beryl had no doubt the child required attention from someone. As there were no other adults conveniently making their presence known, she stepped out onto the lawn and intercepted Janet.

The girl's eyes were opened wide and she was panting heavily as though she had run at great speed for some distance. Her uniform neckerchief was askew, and Beryl was surprised to see there were grass stains on her knees. She wondered if the girl had been chased by some sort of predator. She dismissed the notion that a four-footed creature had attempted to run Janet down and wondered if any of the two-footed variety had done so. She sincerely hoped that nothing so damaging had occurred.

"Are you injured in some way, Janet?" Beryl asked.

Janet began to answer but instead of explaining herself burst into a spate of blubbering. Tears streamed down her face, and her nose began to run. The girl was not much more than a child, and children were not Beryl's favorite sort of people. She was never quite sure what to do with them, especially when they started to cry.

She wished that Edwina were there. She would know what to do with a distraught young girl. Beryl looked around desperately, once more hoping for another adult to appear, preferably one with a clean pocket handkerchief. No such person loomed into view, and Beryl resigned herself to the role of comforter. She took the unprecedented step of patting the girl on the shoulder.

As if by magic, Janet's sobs quieted. She bent over and propped her hands on her knees, attempting to draw in great, ragged breaths. After a moment, she stood and patted her eyes dry with her uniform neckerchief and managed to recover her ability to speak.

"It's Louis Langdon Beck. I think he's dead," Janet said.

She grabbed Beryl by the arm and pulled her off in the direction from whence she had come. Beryl broke into a trot beside her young guide. She had not expected to need to wear sturdy hiking shoes so early in the morning and was sorry to see that her satin house shoes were not the best footwear for running along a wooded path. Not that footwear should be her main priority, she scolded herself. Not when a death might be at hand.

"Are you quite sure about that? It seems unlikely," Beryl said. "Perhaps he is only asleep."

"He didn't look asleep to me. I shook his arm and called his name over and over, but he didn't wake up," Janet said.

Beryl was slightly alarmed to see tears beginning to spill down Janet's face once again.

"Artists tend to be unorthodox in their habits, with an appalling tendency to the overuse of inebriating substances. I'd say that there's a very good possibility that he's simply sleeping off a night of excess," Beryl said as reassuringly as she could.

Janet shook her head back and forth furiously. "I'm not so young that I cannot tell the difference between dead drunk and simply dead. Besides, I've earned my first-aid badge, so I know a bit about injured people."

She hurried even faster along the path, pulling at Beryl's arm as she did so. Janet didn't speak another word until they reached the glade where Beryl and Edwina had met the young girl the day before. She remained rooted in place at the edge of the glade, hovering uncomfortably as if she might take flight back through the woods.

It was easy to see that Louis Langdon Beck was indeed there and positioned approximately the same place he had stood while painting Tuva and Janet. His French easel stood nearby in readiness, the painting he had been working on centered on its ledge. On a small folding table sat a few brushes and his palette covered with brilliant blobs of paint all squeezed out and glistening in the sun.

But unlike the day before, the artist himself lay sprawled out upon the grass, motionless. He lay on his back, and a shaft of sunlight reflected off his golden-blond hair spread out from his head, giving him the appearance of a sort of fallen angel. Beryl stepped towards Louis and knelt down beside him. She was never good at finding a pulse; she was simply too impatient. But with Janet making snuffling sobbing sounds behind her, she thought she ought to at least make an attempt to do so.

She lay her fingers along the side of his neck underneath his long curling hairline. With a start she realized how cold his skin felt to the touch. She loosened the first button on the collar of his billowy, paint-stained smock and then the second.

Chafed skin and a livid bruise clearly marked his pale throat. Beryl placed a forefinger on one of his eyelids and gently opened it. The whites of his eyes were crisscrossed with prominent red veins. There was no doubt in Beryl's mind what had happened. Louis Langdon Beck had been strangled.

Chapter 11

After witnessing the goings-on between Louis and Tuva the day before, Edwina had been dreading the very idea of taking up her modeling duties. She had no desire whatsoever to be associated with being an artist's model. But she had to wonder if she would have preferred it, despite any risks to her reputation or the ease of her relationship with Charles, to being questioned by an irate Constable Doris Gibbs.

She had found several vaguely plausible excuses to delay meeting Charles in the Japanese garden at the agreed-upon hour and as a result was still skulking about the main house when Beryl had tracked her down and made the surprising announcement that Louis Langdon Beck appeared to have been murdered. As they needed to keep the pretense that they were not investigating any crimes at Maitland Park, Edwina reluctantly persuaded Beryl that the best course of action, at least as far as their paying client was concerned, was to telephone for the police. Which is why she found herself standing in the glade being chastised by Doris well before luncheon.

"Why is it that every time someone turns up dead anywhere

in Walmsley Parva, the two of you are close on their heels?" Constable Gibbs asked. "We never had so many bodies in the village before you came to stay." She turned and gave Beryl a steady glare.

Edwina had thought that the three of them had come to an understanding after their last case, but perhaps she had been too optimistic as concerned the local constable. Constable Gibbs had attained her position during the Great War years when few men were available for any sort of work on the home front. That feat in itself had been remarkable. But what was even more astonishing was that she had managed to hang on to her position as the only law enforcement officer in the village after the war had ended.

Edwina did not find the constable's company particularly desirable, but she did admire the other woman's tenacity and ambition. She had wished they would continue to develop a mutually beneficial professional relationship, but everything about her behavior that morning seemed to discourage that hope. Edwina had not wanted to accept the case in the first place and finding the constable plunged into the middle of it made it even less appealing.

"I'm sure it has nothing to do with us. I should have thought you would be more pleased that we reported this to you straightaway," Beryl said.

"Are you implying that in the past you have not reported unexpected deaths to me immediately?" the constable said, crossing her beefy arms over her ample bust line.

The truth was that she and Beryl habitually had delayed including the constable in an investigation until they had had time to make their own assessment of the situation. Beryl had insisted that the police officer would exclude them as soon as she became involved and with the exception of their last case, this had proved true.

"I'm sure that's not what Beryl meant in the least," Edwina

said. "I think she meant that it's a good job you are able to be here as soon as the body was discovered in order to get on with your investigation. The sooner you get down to business the more likely it is to uncover whoever did this, isn't that the case?" Edwina turned towards Constable Gibbs and rearranged her face in what she hoped appeared to be a mask of innocent curiosity.

Constable Gibbs made a harrumphing sound down low in her throat that Edwina took to be a sign of begrudging agreement.

"What are the two of you doing here at Maitland Park, anyway? I was not aware that you were at such terms of intimacy with the Maitland family," Constable Gibbs said. "You're not involved with this artists' colony nonsense, are you?"

Beryl and Edwina exchanged a glance. As so often was the case when dealing with the constable, Edwina took the lead.

"I see we are going to have to beg for your discretion. As an officer of the law accustomed to investigating private matters and keeping your cards close to your vest, I am confident we can rely on you to keep what we tell you to yourself," Edwina said.

Edwina was startled to hear herself speak thusly. A phrase such as *close to the vest* was more akin to something the hero of her novel would say than would she. She told herself not to allow such things to occur too often or people would begin to ask questions, and she had no intention of sharing the secret of her work in progress with anyone besides Beryl. She certainly would not want to discuss it with Constable Gibbs.

"So long as whatever you have to tell me does not need to come out during the course of my investigation, I see no reason not to keep stumm about your business," Constable Gibbs said. "Mind you, what constitutes something relevant to the case will be entirely up to my discretion."

"Of course, we understand that you will do what you think

necessary," Edwina said, hoping she sounded conciliatory but not obsequious. Constable Gibbs would not respect such insincere flattery and might take it into her head to arrest them.

"We happen to be here on a case," Beryl said. "Although things are not exactly as they appear."

"Well, it appears there's a murder. Are you telling me that's not what your case is about?" Constable Gibbs asked.

"Certainly not. We were asked by Constance Maitland to appear to be investigating an illicit love affair between the victim and Ursula Maitland," Edwina said.

"She asked you to *appear* to be investigating?" Constable Gibbs said. "Why would anyone hire you to do something as useless as that?"

"Constance does not believe any such affair was going on. But her cousin, Cressida, has been making a nuisance of herself with accusations. Constance hired us to make a show of investigating it in order to appease Cressida and convince her to stop making the rest of the guests and household at Maitland Park uncomfortable with her accusations," Edwina said.

"It's really rather ingenious. Cressida believes that we are investigating, but that we are doing so under the cover of other reasons for being here at Maitland Park. I'm posing as an expert lecturer for the Girl Guides, and Edwina is serving as an artist's model for Charles Jarvis, who happens to be attending the artists' colony," Beryl said.

From the look on the police officer's face, Edwina could see that Constable Gibbs was having trouble taking it all in. To give the constable credit, it was an unusually convoluted set of circumstances.

"Regardless of the reasons that you are here, the fact remains that a man you are supposedly investigating for carrying on with the lady of the house has been killed," Constable Gibbs said. "Doesn't that make you wonder if he was up to no good?"

"It does rather put a new slant on things," Beryl said, giving

Edwina a significant look. "You will keep what we've told you to yourself, won't you?"

"I'm not sure I will be able to. That is, unless the two of you agree to fill me in on what it is that you know and then promise to keep out of my investigation," Constable Gibbs said.

Edwina noticed the triumphant look in Constable Gibbs's eye. It was not every day that the constable had sufficient leverage over Beryl and herself to get them to fully cooperate. She certainly had them at a disadvantage in this particular matter. Edwina nodded her consent without looking over at Beryl.

"We are more than happy to stay out of this. Our hands are completely full with our own investigation, or the pretense thereof, as well as the activities we've agreed to participate in here at Maitland Park. Ask us whatever you wish, and we will stay out of it from here on out," Edwina said.

Constable Gibbs squinted at her skeptically. "Did you uncover any evidence that this Mr. Beck and Ursula Maitland were romantically involved?"

"No, we did not. As a matter of fact, Edwina has far more suspicion that Ursula's attentions, if directed outside of her marriage, are pointed in rather a different direction," Beryl said.

"And to whom might that be?" Constable Gibbs asked.

"Edwina thinks she saw Ursula careening about on a motorcycle with another of the artists' colony participants a few days ago," Beryl said before Edwina could answer herself.

"And what is the name of this man?" Constable Gibbs asked.

"Roger Hazeldine. But I doubt very much there's anything to it," Beryl said.

"I'll be speaking to him soon. For all I know he and the victim were competing for Ursula's attentions and it ended in violence," Constable Gibbs said. "Thanks for the information. I will take it from here. I suggest that if the two of you want me to keep quiet about your business, take yourselves away from my crime scene immediately."

Although Beryl had every intention of honoring the promise Edwina had just made to Constable Gibbs, her eyes were drawn to some tracks through the grass at the edge of the glade. Surreptitiously, she motioned for Edwina to follow her. The sound of Constable Gibbs's voice faded as they followed the almost imperceptible trail into the woods. Beryl prided herself on her tracking ability. It had served her well on many an occasion whilst out on safari or when traipsing through the jungle in search of elusive creatures, especially those of the two-footed variety.

Beryl flung out an arm to hold Edwina back from trampling the subtle signs that someone had passed that way within the last few hours. She focused on small disturbances in the leaf litter, crushed pine spills, and freshly snapped twigs. As they proceeded cautiously, the trail ended right where Beryl had expected it might. The ground near the bushes where Cressida had stopped to covertly survey Louis Langdon Beck and his models the day before had most definitely been recently disturbed.

"Whatever are you looking for?" Edwina asked.

Although her friend was far more experienced at noticing the minutiae of the flora in their general vicinity than was she, Beryl had noticed her friend was not a particularly experienced tracker herself. Beryl might not know a hollyhock from a delphinium, but she did know when a plant had been recently jostled or crushed underfoot. She pointed to a patch of disturbed ground directly in front of them.

"There was a distinct trail leading from the crime scene to this very spot," Beryl said.

"I should think there would have been. We walked exactly this way ourselves just yesterday afternoon," Edwina said. "It would be more suspicious if there was no sign that someone had been this way recently."

Beryl shook her head slowly as she crouched down to take a closer look.

"The tracks are far too fresh to have been the same ones that we left yesterday afternoon. I would say they had been made within the last few hours. And it wouldn't surprise me if they had something to do with the murder," Beryl said.

"We just promised Constable Gibbs that we would keep our noses out of her investigation. You don't mean to tell me that you've broken our word already?" Edwina asked.

Her thin arms crept to a folded position across her chest. That never boded well. Edwina could be exceptionally stubborn when she set her mind to it. Her moral compass tended to be rather more fixed than was Beryl's own. This would take some convincing, there was no doubt about it.

"It's not breaking our word for me to have unconsciously exercised my well-honed tracking skills," Beryl said. "Perhaps this is the sort of thing that I will demonstrate to the Girl Guides while we're here. I can always say I wanted to be sure I wasn't rusty before a presentation for them," Beryl said.

"Are you trying to convince me that you're simply poking your nose in where Constable Gibbs does not want it in order to keep fighting fit for a demonstration for the Girl Guides?" Edwina said, squeezing her arms even closer to her chest.

"If it makes you feel any better, I am suggesting just that," Beryl said, leaning forward and peering more closely at the base of the bush in front of her. "Now, what do we have here?"

Despite herself, Edwina leaned forward as Beryl reached her hand under a tangle of branches and drew out a man-made object. She straightened, bringing the item towards her, then held it out so Edwina could view it, too.

"That doesn't seem like something that ought to be there, now does it?" Edwina said, peering at the length of rope in Beryl's hands.

"It looks too new to me to have been left lying under there for very long," Beryl said.

"It does look far fresher than any of the twine that I have used on my plants and left over the course of a season. It doesn't even look dirty," Edwina said. "And what a lot of knots it has tied along its length."

The length of rope was approximately three feet long and, as Edwina had observed, contained four different complicated-looking knots spaced at regular intervals along it. It certainly was not the sort of thing one would expect to find tucked under a bush in a wood.

"Have you ever seen anything like this before?" Beryl asked. Edwina nodded.

"I rather think it's something belonging to one of the Girl Guides. If my memory serves, knot tying is one of the skills for which they can earn a badge. This looks like a practice rope to me," Edwina said.

"It may be a Girl Guides practice rope, but I think there is a decent possibility that it may also be the murder weapon," Beryl said.

"Do you think so?" Edwina said.

"The victim was clearly strangled; a set of tracks led away from the murder scene, and now we find a rope of exactly the right length for doing the job hidden under a bush where the tracks end? What else can one think?" Beryl said.

"I suppose we shall have to give this to Constable Gibbs now that you've unearthed it," Edwina said. "Although I shudder to think of the fuss she will make about you finding it instead of her doing so."

"If you prefer, I could just tuck it back under the bush and hope for the best. It is possible that she might find it on her own," Beryl said.

"We can't do anything that would hinder her investigation," Edwina said. "There's no guarantee that she will find it if left to her own devices."

"But if we show her the rope, then we will admit to having involved ourselves in her investigation. I thought you didn't want us to do that," Beryl said.

"It's a question of the greater good. I'm afraid we're going to have to hand it over to her and live with the consequences," Edwina said.

"Perhaps it would be best if I tucked it barely back under the bush and we simply tell her we spotted that there was something poking out from there. She might arrest us for tampering with evidence if we were to remove it from its hiding place," Beryl said. Edwina nodded, and Beryl carefully replaced the rope in the exact spot from which she had retrieved it. "Will you tell her, or shall I?"

Chapter 12

It had been for the greater good, Edwina told herself as they took their leave of Constable Gibbs once more. As they had predicted, the constable had not been best pleased at their speedy discovery of a potential murder weapon. Still, since they did not keep the information to themselves, she agreed to maintain their pretense concerning their presence at Maitland Park.

Having delivered a stern warning not to involve themselves any further, the constable had turned her back upon them and, having retrieved the rope from its hiding place, had headed off in the direction of the murder scene. Edwina could only assume that the constable had every intention of comparing the rope to the marks on the victim's neck.

"That went better than it might have done," Beryl said, tucking her arm through Edwina's and urging her to beat a hasty retreat. "While she's still busy with the crime scene I think we should go and speak with Cressida."

"Are you absolutely determined to ignore the constable's warning?" Edwina said.

"I have no idea what you're talking about. I see no reason whatsoever that we should not speak with Cressida in the course of our own investigation. As the person most interested in getting to the bottom of a possible affair between Ursula and the unfortunate Louis, we owe it to Cressida to speak with her," Beryl said.

Edwina did not quite like the glint in Beryl's eye. She seemed to take a perverse pleasure in flaunting the rules. Still, her friend made a good point. Cressida was the reason they had been hired in the first place. They could hardly seem to be doing their job if they did not speak with her, and Constance for that matter, about the fact that Ursula's supposed lover had been found murdered on the property. Without giving it more thought, she hurried her pace and shortly found herself back at Maitland Park.

After making inquiries of the servants, they found Cressida in the morning room sitting at an ornate writing desk, apparently absorbed in her correspondence. A pile of unopened letters sat stacked near at hand, and several slit envelopes littered the remainder of the desk. She turned and offered them a friendly smile as they entered the room.

"Good morning, ladies. Is there something I can help you with?" Cressida asked. She lowered her voice slightly. "Do you need any help with the case?"

"As a matter of fact we have some news concerning that very thing," Beryl said, crossing the room to a comfortable-looking chair placed near to the writing desk. Edwina followed her to a matching seat and settled herself on the edge of it. Cressida capped her fountain pen and laid it on the desk before giving them her full attention. Edwina had to wonder if Cressida was arranging her thoughts before facing them.

"There have been some developments, then?" Cressida asked.

"I'm afraid you could say that," Edwina said. "Have you spoken with Janet Brown yet today?"

"No, not yet. Constance is busy with the Girl Guides this morning. I'm catching up on some long overdue correspondence and will join them after lunch. Has something happened with Janet?" Cressida asked.

Edwina thought the flicker of worry crossing Cressida's face seemed genuine. After the way that Cressida had behaved protectively towards the girl the day before it did not seem unreasonable that she would be concerned about anything that might involve her.

"Janet is perfectly fine, but I'm afraid she has had an eventful morning," Beryl said. "In fact, I'm afraid she was quite frightened by a distressing incident."

Cressida squinted and a deep furlough appeared between her eyebrows. "That horrid Mr. Beck did not make unwanted advances towards her, did he?" she asked.

"I cannot say whether he did or whether he didn't. Unfortunately, neither can he," Beryl said. She glanced over at Edwina, who gave a slight nod.

"I'm sorry to say that Janet found Louis Langdon Beck's body this morning in the glade where he had been painting the day before," Edwina said, keeping her gaze trained fully on Cressida's face.

While she justifiably prided herself on her ability to detect lies, having had a great deal of experience with errant house parlormaids and girls in the Women's Land Army during the war years, she could not say that she was as skilled with persons who were known to be mentally unbalanced. It was possible that anything Cressida revealed through her words or actions could be unreliable.

Cressida's hand flew to her throat and she placed it over her neck protectively. Her eyes widened and if Edwina had not been concerned about Cressida's reliability on account of her mental state, she would have believed the woman had no prior knowledge of the murder. It was, however, notable that Cressida covered her own throat upon hearing the news.

"The poor little lamb," Cressida said. "Is she quite recovered from the shock of it?"

Edwina couldn't help but note that Cressida's first concern was for the girl, not the murder victim. Clearly there was no love lost between Cressida and Louis Langdon Beck. Was that because she suspected him of predatory behavior towards Janet? Or was it on account of her suspicions concerning his interactions with Ursula and how that ignited Cressida's loyalty to Hubert? Or was it possible that she had another unknown reason to dislike him? Whatever her reason, her reaction seemed unusual.

"I believe she's being questioned by the constable at present," Beryl said. "If she needs any assistance, I'm sure she will think to ask for it. After all, she seems a sensible girl."

"For the most part that's true. Although I would say she has behaved very foolishly when it came to Mr. Beck," Cressida said, the furrow in her brow deepening. "How did he die?"

"It appears as though he was murdered. There was evidence of strangulation upon his body," Beryl said.

Edwina watched Cressida's face and noticed that her eyes widened. Had she seen a small flicker of approval cross Cressida's face before she arranged it to look as if she were shocked by what had happened to the victim?

"I suppose if you live the way that Mr. Beck did, a violent death would be a distinct possibility. The constable ought to stop wasting her time with Janet and begin questioning Ursula," Cressida said.

Beryl and Edwina exchanged a glance. Edwina retrieved her small notebook from her pocket and pulled out her tiny pencil. She made a great show of flipping it open and clearing her throat gently. Cressida turned her attention to her, a look of eagerness on her face.

"What makes you suggest that Ursula should be questioned?" Edwina asked. "You had given us to understand that she and the victim were enamored of each other."

"They certainly had been acting that way since he arrived at Maitland Park. At least until last night they did," Cressida said.

"What happened last night to change your opinion of how things stood between them?" Beryl asked.

"I saw them together yesterday evening. It was really quite late. Most of the household had gone to bed, but I happened to see them in front of the summerhouse," Cressida said.

"Was there something about the way they were behaving that led you to believe she might wish him harm?" Edwina asked.

"I could not quite overhear their actual conversation, but it was obvious to me that they were arguing," Cressida said.

"If you could not hear what they were saying, why do you believe that they were arguing?" Beryl asked.

"Some of the strident tone of their conversation reached me from where I stood on the edge of the lawn. But also, it was their gestures. Mr. Beck had a tendency to gesticulate wildly under the best of circumstances. But he appeared even more animated than usual during their conversation last night," Cressida said.

"Animated gestures do not necessarily indicate an argument. He could have simply been carried away with enthusiasm while delivering a discourse on a favorite topic," Edwina said.

"I don't think that that was the case unless Ursula was in some way offended by his enthusiasms. She attempted to slap him," Cressida said.

"Are you quite sure?" Edwina asked. "After all, wasn't it dark?"

"It was a clear night and my eyesight is very good. Not only did I see her raise her hand to strike him, but I also saw him seize hold of her arm to stop her before she did so. He must have squeezed her wrist quite tightly because she cried out when he grabbed it," Cressida said.

"And you think that might be enough for her to have killed him?" Beryl asked.

"She's clearly a woman of very poor character if she is running around behind her husband's back. I see no reason not to believe the very worst of her in all matters," Cressida said. "I know that I promised Constance that I would keep my suspicions concerning Ursula's infidelity to myself for the duration of the artists' colony, but if questioned by the police I shall be forced to do my duty and disclose my concerns to the constable."

"Of course, you must do as you see fit," Edwina said. She wrote down another note in her notebook, aware that Cressida was watching her very closely as she did so.

"Do you happen to know anything about lengths of rope with a series of knots tied along their length?" Beryl asked.

"You might be describing a demonstration rope for the Girl Guides. Or it could be a practice rope that one of the participants used to work on their skills. Constance did a presentation on knot tying just yesterday for the girls," Cressida said. "Why do you ask?"

"I happened to see a length of rope like that lying around and I was curious as to its purpose," Beryl said. "I can see that you are busy, so we won't take up any more of your time. Will I see you later this afternoon when I give my talk to the Girl Guides about building a fire under damp conditions?"

"I am sure you shall. I cannot imagine that we will need to make adjustments to the schedule just because of what happened to the likes of Louis Langdon Beck," Cressida said.

Chapter 13

It was not without trepidation that Beryl made her way towards the area of the property where the Girl Guides had made camp for the week. Edwina might have found the idea of camping to be off-putting, but that was not where Beryl's concerns lay. She was, of course, completely comfortable with all forms of outdoor living.

The fact of the matter was, she had very little experience with children and had no desire to change that. Unlike Edwina, she did not go out of her way to interact with the younger set. Given the opportunity, she actively avoided them whenever possible. If she were to be entirely honest with herself, children made her rather nervous. They were one of the only things that did.

Having been an only child, Beryl had never particularly enjoyed the company of other children even when she had been one. Her parents, when they noticed her at all, had treated her as a sort of small adult, and Beryl's youth had been an unorthodox one. The closest she came to feeling like an ordinary child had been the time she had spent at Miss DuPont's Finishing

School for Young Ladies, where she had first met Edwina. When her parents sent her off to boarding school she had felt like she was drowning until she spotted the reassuringly competent figure of a young Edwina in the midst of the chaos that was her assigned dormitory.

She could well remember how much better she felt about the entire experience once she and Edwina had become friends. Edwina had always been more capable of interacting with children than she, and she wished her friend had been with her for the Girl Guides presentations. While she prided herself in never having needed anyone else's encouragement to tackle most feats of bravery head-on, there was something about a nod from Edwina that made difficult things seem more doable.

The entire matter was altogether more irksome when she considered the fact that Constable Gibbs was spending that same time getting stuck right into an investigation Beryl felt would be better conducted by herself and Edwina. The idea that they had been relegated to the pretense of a farcical case to appease an unbalanced member of a privileged family rather than leading the hunt for a murderer stuck in her craw. Watching from the sidelines with a group of children simply made the sting more painful.

She heard the lilting sound of childish voices floating towards her with every step she took towards the campsite. Her palms felt just the slightest bit damp as she considered speaking in front of an eager group of them. She gave herself a stern talking to and squared her shoulders. If she could face down being stranded without sufficient supplies throughout an entire winter in a treacherous Andean mountain pass, surely she could teach a group of young girls how to build a fire on a pleasant day in the English countryside.

Before she reached the camp, she spotted Janet Brown heading in her direction. Perhaps she could distract herself from the coming ordeal by interviewing Janet concerning her possible involvement with Louis Langdon Beck's murder. While Cressida seemed to be concerned that Janet had been in danger from the victim, it occurred to Beryl that perhaps the opposite was more likely the case.

Girls on the cusp of womanhood were a tricky subset of the species and in her experience, limited though it may have been, rather volatile when it came to passions they developed towards another. How well she remembered her own early attachment to one of her father's business associates. While she had not been inclined to murder him for rejecting her interest, she had been thoroughly worked up about his engagement to a woman far closer to his own age.

Janet did not appear to be feeling particularly better than she had when Beryl had spotted her through the breakfast room window. Her eyes were bloodshot and puffy. Her posture oozed misery, and her Girl Guides uniform looked as though she had hastily thrown it on, taking little care with the tying of her neckerchief or the tucking in of her blouse. One of her socks drooped lower on her calf than the other, and her left shoelace flapped with abandon. Beryl could not claim to know Constance well but based on her limited experience with the other woman, she did not think that she would feel that Janet's appearance passed muster, even considering the harrowing morning the girl had had.

"Hello, Janet. I hope you've gotten over the shock of finding poor Mr. Beck, at least a little bit," Beryl said, closing the gap between the two of them. She did her best to try to sound maternal, going so far as to imagine what Edwina would do in the situation.

"I don't think I'll ever get over seeing Louis that way," Janet said. "I just keep seeing his face over and over again. It was simply horrid."

If Janet were lying about her reaction to discovering the body, she was doing a clever job of it. Beryl felt increasingly uneasy as she noticed tears welling up in Janet's eyes. Once again, she thought of Edwina and employed a brisker tone of voice.

"Speaking as someone who has encountered more than her fair share of corpses, I assure you that you will in time forget the initial shock. What you need is to take your mind off of things. I think it's very good that you have the Girl Guides activities to keep you busy," Beryl said. "I'm on my way there for the presentation myself. Are you headed that way, too?"

"Miss Maitland thought that my presence was distracting the other girls so she sent me off to see if I could find you and escort you to the camp. She thought I could use a little time on my own to gather my thoughts. She's very kind that way," Janet said with a sniff.

"That was very thoughtful of you both. It seems unlucky that you were the one to find the body. How did you happen to be in the glade in the woods at that time of day?" Beryl asked.

"I had set off early for the kitchen garden. I wanted to check on some of the soft fruits that were ripening there against one of the brick walls. I'm working on a jam-making badge, you see," Janet said. Beryl nodded for her to continue. "It's best to pick the fruit early in the morning, so I headed out first thing."

"The kitchen garden is quite a distance from the glade in the wood, isn't it?" Beryl asked.

She remembered Constance pointing in the general direction of a walled garden on their initial tour of the property and how she had mentioned that Maitland Park could produce most of the fruits and vegetables its residents consumed, even with the added numbers from the artists' colony and the Girl Guides troop. She had sounded proud of that fact, and Edwina had asked a few intelligent questions about specifics that Beryl had spent no time whatsoever paying attention to.

"That's right. They are on different ends of the property. You wouldn't want a kitchen garden to be too far from the house, now would you?" Janet asked. Beryl had never given such things any thought in the least, but she nodded as though she were an expert on household management.

"Then how did you end up finding the body?" Beryl asked.

A bit of color rose on Janet's cheeks and her voice sounded a little less confident. "No one saw me in the garden, but I overheard Louis having an argument with Mr. Maitland. There is a window built into the brickwork of the garden wall, and the sound of their voices passed easily through it. Louis sounded so cross about it that I decided to take him some raspberries to cheer him up," Janet said.

"Do you remember what they were arguing about?" Beryl said. "It might be important to the police investigation."

Janet shook her head, but Beryl did not feel convinced that she wasn't holding something back. If she could hear that there was an argument, why wouldn't she remember what it had been about? After all, it had only happened a few hours earlier.

"I've forgotten specifics. I just know that they sounded angry. Besides, with the shock of finding Louis dead, I don't seem to be remembering much else from the morning," Janet said.

"Did you find any fruit to pick?" Beryl asked.

"Yes, I got a large basketful. It amounted to several quarts. I do remember that I took most of them to the kitchen at Maitland Park. As much as we are doing most of our activities outdoors, jam making is best done in the kitchen, and we are processing the fruit there. That's when I decided to take a punnet of berries to Louis to cheer him up."

"Is that when you found his body?" Beryl said.

"Yes, it was," Janet said. "I knew he planned to paint in the glade again today because he mentioned it more than once. In fact, he had said that he planned to make that spot his base of operations for the rest of his time at Maitland Park. He liked the way the light filtered through the trees and cast interesting shadows on his subjects." Janet dashed some tears away from her eyes with the back of her hand.

"How long would you say it took between the argument you overheard between Louis and Mr. Maitland and when you arrived with the berries?" Beryl asked.

"I was probably in the garden picking fruit for about three quarters of an hour. Then I took the fruit to the kitchen, spoke with the cook briefly about where she wanted me to put it, and then walked to the glade, where I found him. All told I would say about an hour and a quarter or so. Do you think that is important?" Janet asked, peering up at Beryl.

"I think it might be very important. Did Constable Gibbs ask you about any of this?" Beryl asked.

"No, she seemed more interested in why you were in the glade than my reasons for being there," Janet said.

Beryl felt her frustration mount once more. It was just like the constable to be more concerned with any perceived meddling in those things she felt were her exclusive purview than she was in asking the questions pertinent to the case. Beryl felt more determined than ever to surreptitiously continue to investigate. Still, she was in no position to keep such an important lead all to herself no matter how much she might wish to do so.

"You need to share that information with Constable Gibbs," Beryl said.

"Do I have to? It doesn't seem very important to me and I already gave her my statement." Janet's eyes shone brightly once more, and Beryl again worried the girl might begin to cry.

Still, the information needed to be passed on to the constable, and it would not do her relationship with the police officer any good to relay it on Janet's behalf, no matter how she might wish to postpone her appointment with the Girl Guides.

"Your information has helped to narrow down the time frame in which the crime could have been committed. Constable Gibbs will want to know where anyone who might have been involved was at that time. I think you should skip the presentation I'm going to give on fire starting and repeat what you've just told me for the constable," Beryl said.

Janet looked hesitant and Beryl could not truly blame her. She had never found Constable Gibbs someone with whom she found it easy to interact, either. Still, it was the only thing to do.

"Are you sure it can't wait until later? I would hate to miss your presentation," Janet said.

Beryl thought the girl's hesitance had much more to do with a concern about being associated with a murder investigation rather than her own charisma. But why was Janet so hesitant? Was she simply displaying the usual sort of concern the public demonstrated when dealing with the police, or did she have something to hide? Regardless of her reasons, Constable Gibbs needed to hear Janet's version of events from her own lips.

"Isn't one of the tenets of the Girl Guides to be helpful and to tell the truth?" Beryl asked. Janet nodded slowly. "Then I'm afraid you know what you have to do. I can give you your own demonstration on the subject of fire starting later if that would help you."

"Will the Maitlands find out I was eavesdropping?" Janet asked, looking over her shoulder in the direction of the Girl Guides camp.

"I cannot imagine that Constable Gibbs would feel compelled to take any of the family into her confidence concerning the investigation, and I am even more certain none of them will think to ask questions about you. Now run along and look for the constable before it gets any later. She has set up a temporary headquarters somewhere in the main house."

With sagging shoulders and dragging feet, Janet headed back towards Maitland Park. As Beryl watched her go, she felt that she had done the constable a favor while appearing to stay out of the investigation. She also had to wonder which member of the Maitland family Janet was concerned about knowing she had been listening to a private conversation.

Chapter 14

Edwina did not know whether to be pleased or irritated with Beryl when she returned from her campfire demonstration. She had been concerned for Beryl when her friend had set off for her presentation. Although Edwina could not understand it in the least, Beryl was absolutely disinclined to engage with children. The only one who had ever managed to win her over was the local newsboy, Jack. All other young people appeared to leave Beryl cold.

If Edwina didn't know better, she would guess that to some extent they frightened her friend. So, she was relieved when Beryl had burst into her room with a triumphant look on her face. But when Beryl revealed that she was excited about a lead in the case rather than her time with the Girl Guides, Edwina felt her heart sink.

They did not need to have any trouble with Constable Gibbs. The Maitland family was in a position to do a lot of good or ill to their reputation as private enquiry agents. If they managed to conduct themselves in a way that Constance approved of, she would be likely to recommend them to others in her social set. Edwina did not think of herself as a snob, but she did understand that, fair or not, there were members of society whose opinions counted more than others. Hubert and Constance Maitland were just such people. Which was one of the reasons she was even more dismayed to hear what Beryl had to say.

"So, from what young Janet had to say, it's possible that Hubert Maitland's the one who strangled Louis," Beryl said as she plopped down onto Edwina's freshly made bed and stretched out her long legs. Edwina spun away from the typewriter and faced her friend.

"Are you quite sure that Janet was telling you the truth?" Edwina said.

"I think there is every possibility she wasn't telling me all of the truth. But I do think she wasn't making things up about an argument between Louis and Hubert. Why do you ask?"

"Hubert Maitland is our host and in a position to help us with our business. We don't want to offend him if we can help it," Edwina said.

"We can't help where the case may lead us. I'm sure you are not suggesting that we fail to follow up on a lead because the suspect is a powerful member of the community," Beryl said.

"I'm suggesting we don't follow up on any leads at all. Constable Gibbs was very clear about her desire for us to remain completely uninvolved in this investigation. Besides, we have a case of our own that we need to attend to," Edwina said.

"I would say that the two cases overlap entirely when it comes to any problems between Mr. Beck and Hubert. Maybe Cressida was correct in her assumption that Hubert was being cuckolded by Louis. That certainly would be grounds for murder," Beryl said.

"Yes, it would be. Although I would say it's not quite nice for you to use words like *cuckolded*," Edwina said with a shudder. If her mother could hear her using such language she would roll over in her grave. "I am certain that Constable Gibbs will be interviewing him herself and that we have no need to do so."

"I sent Janet to go and tell the constable what she had overheard. So, with what we had to tell her about our reasons for being here in the first place combined with that information, I am quite certain the constable will zero in on Hubert Maitland as her prime suspect. Which is why I suggest that we speak to him ourselves and fast," Beryl said.

"Now, why would we do that?" Edwina asked.

"Because the poor man is going to feel like he's been put through the ringer after the constable is done with him. What he will need is a sympathetic ear. A little bit of genteel handling. Between the two of us I'm sure he will feel supported rather than suspected," Beryl said.

"Well, since you put it that way, perhaps we would be doing him a service," Edwina said. "It's not that I think that Constable Gibbs is not good at her job, but she can be a bit heavy-handed sometimes." Edwina placed the cover over the typewriter and got to her feet.

Chapter 15

"Yes, the constable has already been here and put me through quite an interrogation, I can tell you that," Hubert said.

He looked none the worse for wear from the experience, however. Unlike Janet, he seemed almost invigorated by the brouhaha on his property. Edwina had to wonder if that had to do with the novelty of it or if he had private reasons for being glad that Louis was no longer amongst the living. As much as she thought it inadvisable to meddle in the case, she had to admit she was curious.

"I understood that you were heard arguing with the victim not long before he died," Beryl said.

"Now, how did you know a thing like that?" Hubert asked. "I didn't get the sense that the constable was too eager to share the investigatory spotlight with the two of you. In fact, she asked me if you had already questioned me when she began our interview."

"A person who prefers to remain anonymous told me she had overheard you and Louis arguing just beyond the kitchen garden," Beryl said. "Edwina and I thought that it might be wise to look at that conversation from a less suspicious angle."

"We understand that these things are not always what they appear on the surface," Edwina said soothingly. "A man with a reputation as sterling as yours surely has an innocent explanation for an altercation even if it's with someone who goes on to be murdered shortly thereafter."

Men like Hubert generally responded well to flattery, Edwina knew. She had overheard her father do much the same thing in his law practice over the years. Hubert spread his hands expansively as if to say such a thing was true, but they need not go into it further.

"What you have to understand about Louis was that he was the sort of person who loved to debate things. I can see how someone without an understanding of that unpleasant side to his character would misinterpret our discussion as an argument."

"And what was the topic of this particular debate?" Edwina asked.

"Why art, of course. Call me old-fashioned, but I don't see why there's anything wrong with plain old realism. I think a painting of a horse ought to look like a horse, not a series of swirls and cubes scattered about all higgity-piggity," Hubert said.

"And Louis did not agree with you?" Beryl asked.

"No, he did not. He went so far as to call me a Philistine. He said he did not know how I had managed to capture the interest of someone as sophisticated as Ursula with an attitude like mine. He was really very cutting about it all," Hubert said. "We had started off pleasantly enough and then, as was his habit, Louis began spouting nonsense and trying to get a rise out of me first thing in the morning. I'm sorry to say that was the last conversation I had with the man. But he was alive when I walked away from him. I'm sure that your eavesdropper can attest to that."

"Did you take offense at his comments?" Beryl asked.

Edwina would not have been quite so direct, but Hubert did not seem to think anything of her friend's frankness. Perhaps it was because she was an American. Everyone knew they were not skilled in the art of subtlety.

"Certainly not. If there's one thing I've learned in my business, it's that artists are not to be taken seriously. They do quite a fine job of doing that for themselves. Louis was an extreme example of the artistic type. It would be impossible to recriminate myself on account of anything he had to say," Hubert said. "Besides, artists are a volatile lot. Which is what I said to Constable Gibbs. I told her she'd be well served to turn her attention to the other members of the artists' colony rather than to me."

"Did you have any particular artist in mind?" Edwina asked.

"As a matter of fact, I did. As much as it pains me to say it as I rely on him for so much of the work that's done in our studio at Maitland Cigarettes, Roger Hazeldine has not been getting along with Louis ever since he arrived," Hubert said.

"What do you mean hasn't been getting along with him?" Beryl asked.

"There's been trouble brewing ever since Louis set foot on the property. Roger was here before him and was helping Ursula with some of the logistics for the artists' colony. The two of them have been friends for ages. I think you know that I met my wife while she was working at Maitland Cigarettes," Hubert said, pausing and glancing at each of the women in turn. They nodded and he continued. "Ursula and Roger worked together long before I paid any attention to the woman who would become my wife. She has depended on him completely as concerns the artists' colony. It is something the two of them share that I just do not."

"Did you have any sense of what the trouble was about?" Edwina asked.

"There is nothing specific, just ripples of tension flowing between the two of them this whole time. There was a sarcastic undercurrent in each of their conversations that I overheard. I think at the heart of it they viewed each other as competitors in the artistic world," Hubert said.

"And you don't think there was any other reason the two of them might not have been getting along? Nothing in their personal lives?" Beryl asked.

"Not that I'm aware of. But to be fair, I've made a point not to get particularly involved. Like I've said, the artists' colony is something that Ursula and Roger have been spearheading. I've allowed it to indulge my wife, but left to my own devices I would never have planned such an event and certainly would not have offered to host it at my own home," Hubert said.

"Has no one else said anything about noticing the problems between the two of them?" Edwina asked.

"Not that I can recall. I think the person the two of you ought to talk with about this is Roger. I have found in life, as well as in business, it's best to get straight to the point with those in the know. Now, if you ladies will excuse me, I need to make some telephone calls," Hubert said. He gave them a slight bow and left the room.

Edwina waited for the sound of his footfalls to fade before speaking her mind.

"You know, Cressida's concerns about Ursula's faithfulness may not be as baseless as Constance believes them to be," Edwina said.

"Did Hubert reveal something just now that led you to believe she really was conducting an affair with Louis?" Beryl asked.

"Not with Louis, no. It sounds as though Ursula and Roger have been close for far longer than I realized. She could be in love with him but made the shrewd decision to marry his employer instead," Edwina said.

She watched Beryl's face for a reaction. Beryl hesitated

slightly as if she might refute the notion, then shrugged as if Roger's exploits were of no concern of hers. Edwina was certain there was more to their interactions than a few innocent and forgettable sessions spent between artist and model some years in the past, but it seemed as though Beryl was determined not to share with her what they did entail. Edwina was enough of a romantic to wonder if maybe Roger Hazeldine was the one man who had managed to break Beryl's heart.

Chapter 16

After hearing from Beryl that there were fruits in the kitchen garden ready for picking, Edwina could not resist the urge to wander off to see them for herself. One of Edwina's chief delights in life was visiting well-tended, well-designed gardens. The grounds at Maitland Park were a feast for the senses. As she stepped through the arched entry in the south wall of the kitchen garden, her heart thumped a little faster. Once again, she resolved to ask Constance if she might invite Simpkins round to view what a well-maintained garden ought to look like. The one spread out before her was exactly the sort she most admired.

As she passed through the opening in the brickwork wall, her arm brushed against the leaves of a flourishing grapevine pinned expertly against the warm mellow brick on either side of the entry. The heady scent of basil wafted towards her from somewhere towards the center of the elaborate maze of raised garden beds.

Gravel scrunched beneath her feet as she gave in to the urge to wander about looking and smelling and touching the plants.

One long row of trellises was filled with plump black raspberries. As she bent over to pluck one and pop it into her mouth, enjoying the warm spray of juice, she caught a flicker of motion at the far northern end of the garden.

Spencer Spaulding stood in the shade of a dwarf pear tree. An easel holding a partially painted canvas stood in front of him as he rummaged through what appeared to be some sort of tackle box. Edwina heard a few choice utterances escape his lips before he noticed her approach. He straightened up and though he attempted to smile, she could see that he was out of sorts.

"Miss Davenport, please improve my day by telling me you have come here to announce that you have forsaken Charles and have resolved to model for me instead," he said as his gaze traveled her length with an ungentlemanly boldness.

Edwina's pleasure in her visit to the garden evaporated like morning dew from a stone path. His unwelcome glances brought the entire scene in the glade to mind once more. What was worse was the sense that he considered it possible that she and Tuva Dahlberg were two of a kind. He would need to be disabused of such notions if she were to endure encountering him throughout her stay at Maitland Park.

"I'm afraid you are doomed to be disappointed for I cannot assist you with that. There is nothing you could do to lure me from my obligation to Charles," Edwina said. "I must insist that you drop the matter entirely from your mind."

"How very vexing. Even so, your appearance here is most welcome," he said. "You didn't happen to see a sable brush as you traversed the pathway towards me, did you?"

Spencer looked back towards the tackle box, which Edwina could now see was filled with an assortment of neatly arranged art supplies. Brushes and palette knives and tubes of paint all seemed to be sorted into individual compartments in a manner that displayed a sort of care that Spencer's untidy appearance did not imply would be his habit. Everything about the man suggested an absent-minded, passionate artist.

While Louis Langdon Beck had been tempestuous and dramatic in his demeanor and attire, Spencer was more ethereal and reminded Edwina of a piano teacher she had once had in her youth. He seemed to be the sort of man who would look for a charcoal pencil that was tucked behind his own ear. He struck her as someone who would be so caught up in his work that he would forget to eat, bathe, or even to sleep. He gave no indication that he would be so particular with his art supplies.

He squinted over Edwina's shoulder.

"No, I'm afraid I saw nothing out of the ordinary, unless you count the astonishing degree of health in this garden," Edwina said. "Have you lost it?"

"It wasn't me. It was those damn Girl Guides. Completely without permission one of them has gone ahead and tidied up all of my art supplies," he said.

"They look very well sorted," Edwina said.

"Well, they're not. I had everything exactly the way I wanted it when I left off work this morning for a quick kip, then when I came back one of them was just leaving the garden with an enormous smile plastered across her goofy freckled face." He waved his arms wildly about his head, gesticulating in what Edwina supposed was the direction the girl had gone. "Now I can't find anything at all."

"Did she give any reason for having been so bold as to touch your things?" Edwina said.

"She said that the Girl Guides are encouraged to do good deeds wherever possible. She then gave me a lecture that she credited to that dreadful companion woman who herds them about. Her name sounds like some sort of a vegetable," Spencer said.

"You must mean Cressida," Edwina said, imagining the woman sandwiched between two slices of thin white bread and placed upon a dainty china plate.

Spencer snapped his paint-stained fingers together. "That's the one. Apparently, she's been encouraging the girls to do little helpful tasks around the property, including those involving the artists' colony. I've got a good mind to tell her what I think about her interfering. What's the world coming to when young women are taught to be so high-handed with the belongings of virtual strangers?" he asked.

Edwina was taken aback. The Girl Guides were generally considered to be a credit to their sex. The notion that the Girl Guides organization would be teaching young women to be interfering and unwelcome members of society was not one she had ever considered. Although, to be fair, an artist such as Spencer Spaulding did not represent the average man of his age in society. Or of any age, she thought. She could, however, commiserate with him concerning the rearrangement of one's possessions without having given permission for such a thing to have occurred.

While she was most appreciative of Simpkins's generosity in hiring and providing the wages for the impeccable Beddoes, it had startled her the first time that paragon of domestic service had made free with Edwina's cupboards and drawers. She had grown rather used to the sort of complete privacy and autonomy being without any household help had facilitated. She had not particularly enjoyed doing all of the household cleaning tasks completely on her own, but she had discovered how much she appreciated not feeling as though anyone were sitting in judgment of the way she arranged the stationery in her desk or the undeniably shabby condition of her underthings.

And hadn't she gone to great lengths to secure her manuscript and writing implements in a drawer to which she knew she had the only key? That urge had not been driven solely by a desire to keep secret her work upon a novel but also the realization that in order to create something from nothing but ideas, she needed to have her things be exactly as she expected them to be. Any barrier between her thoughts and the process of getting them down on paper might allow them to flit away, never to return. Her heart went out to the distressed painter, and she resolved to assist Spencer in any way she could in getting his toolbox sufficiently re-jumbled.

"I am sure that whichever of the Girl Guides it was, she meant well. But I agree with you that to do such a thing was very wrong of her. I know just what you mean about having things set out just the way you want them when you're going to use them and I, too, would have been distressed should such a thing have occurred," Edwina said.

Spencer took a deep breath and exhaled slowly. His gaze landed upon Edwina and she felt that he was looking at her clearly, perhaps for the first time. There was an intensity in his gaze that made her question whether or not he was as entirely off in his own world as he gave the impression of being. A slight shiver ran up her spine as she considered that he might not be just exactly what he purported to be. But as soon as she had the thought, his gaze shifted once more towards his box of tools and she chided herself for being notional. She had still not become used to the idea of being in the proximity of crime scenes, despite the reputation she and Beryl were attempting to build.

"You sound like someone who has endured such a thing personally. It's very nice to encounter a kindred spirit now and again," Spencer said. "I can see why my new friend Charles admires you as much as he does."

Edwina felt warmth in her face that had little to do with the sun beating down upon her head. Any mention that Charles esteemed her as more than simply a dear friend caused her extreme discomfort. She had grown rather weary of those around her making comments about her unmarried state. It was even worse when they suggested that the best way to correct such a deprivation in her life was to declare a romantic interest in Charles.

When she was a much younger woman, she had thought she

would like to be swept off her feet by a handsome stranger. She had not given much consideration to the idea that her life might not unfold along a similar path as her own mother's had done. It had simply been expected that she would marry a suitable man, preferably one who was known to the family, and would produce two or three children in rapid succession.

And it was true that she had felt the bitter pang of regret at her childlessness more often than she would have liked. But as the years had passed and no appealing romantic prospects crossed her path, Edwina had come to realize how much she valued being the mistress of her own affairs.

While her parents had been alive, it could not truly be said she had been able to direct her own life to the degree she desired. Once her father had passed away, her mother had come to rely upon her much as she had her husband before his demise. Edwina had taken over the household accounts and had made decisions about home repairs and even their investments. Her mother still made social plans without consulting her and ran a constant monologue concerning Edwina's duties, appearance, and social position.

While she missed her mother from time to time, it had not been an easy relationship and Edwina had found solace in her loneliness by wholeheartedly embracing the ability to direct her own affairs. The fact that so many eligible men had died during the war years and the influenza epidemic that followed so swiftly on its heels made surplus women a common thing. Once Edwina was reconciled to the notion that at her age she would be unlikely to find a husband, she enjoyed the fact that the world had started to recognize that a woman living on her own and making her own way in the world was far from rare and might even provide a certain value.

She found comments like Spencer's and, honestly, those of Beryl from time to time irksome. She was happy just as she was and had no interest whatsoever in changing her marital status.

Perhaps if she were more like Beryl she might consider a romantic entanglement without the institution of marriage being involved. But she was not like Beryl in that aspect. Not in the least.

"Charles is a very dear friend and it's always nice to hear that one is esteemed when one is not present. Could this be the brush that you were looking for?" Edwina asked, holding up a wooden-handled, sable-tipped affair with just the tiniest bit of blue paint clinging to the base of the bristles.

The blue was the exact shade of some blotches scattered about Spencer's canvas.

"How did you find it so quickly?" Spencer asked, reaching for it eagerly. "You are a marvel."

As he turned his attention towards his canvas once more, Edwina felt torn. While she had agreed to resist involving herself in the investigation into Louis's murder, she felt a certain professional obligation to provide whatever assistance she could without overstepping her authority. Surely, she could not be faulted for making conversation with a fellow visitor on the subject that would without a doubt be on everyone's mind. And, with his insider knowledge of the art world, Spencer might have some information concerning a possible relationship between Ursula and Roger. He might even have some notion which secret Beryl was so determinedly keeping from her.

"I'm surprised you can find the focus you must need to work on your paintings given what has happened with Louis," Edwina said as Spencer squeezed a blob of cerulean blue onto his wooden palette and mixed it with a bit of brown. His hand hovered over the palette for just a moment before he reached for his brush and dabbed it into the patch of color.

"I take as little notice of Louis Langdon Beck as possible. I would hardly allow any of his antics to distract me from my purpose here," he said, turning to the canvas and adding a streak of color to it.

Edwina had no idea what he was attempting to represent. There was nothing in her line of sight that looked remotely like the shapes he had blocked out on the canvas. She gave her head a slight shake and turned her attention back to the matter uppermost in her mind.

"I should hardly call getting oneself murdered an antic," she said.

Spencer whirled around without thinking to lift his brush, creating a long smear across his canvas. "Louis has been murdered? You may have disappointed me by refusing to model for me, but you have still managed to improve my mood." He turned back to his painting and, seeing the streak, began to curse.

"Surely you cannot be glad to hear that he is dead," Edwina said.

She thought nothing of the sort, of course. She might be new to the sordid side of private enquiries, but she had long been aware of the petty jealousies and brewing animosities one found in a typical village. Even her own beloved Walmsley Parva was not immune to such base emotions.

"I can and I am. Now, if you will excuse me, I feel unexpectedly inspired," he said.

Spencer turned his back on her, but not before she spotted a look of utter glee on his face.

Chapter 17

Beryl had wondered about the furrow that appeared between Edwina's brows when she had offered to question Roger Hazeldine by herself. If she had to guess, she would have said that Edwina looked as though her feelings had been hurt. Perhaps Beryl had not been subtle in hiding the fact that she and Roger shared a history with each other that he did not wish to announce to Edwina.

She regretted any pain she might have caused her friend, but she felt that in the hierarchy of choices, she needed to honor Roger's wishes. It would be easier to question him if she did not need to worry if she would slip up and reveal that she had disclosed something she ought not to have done.

After asking one of the staff for his likely whereabouts, Beryl discovered that Roger had staked a claim in one of the outbuildings on the property. As she approached it, she could not help but make a comparison to Simpkins's potting shed back at the Beeches. It was a small brick building with a great number of windows installed in the roof and along its walls.

Like the rest of the property, it was well cared for. The paint on the door and around the windows looked fresh. Lush planting beds surrounded the foundation, and the smell of something Edwina would undoubtedly be able to identify wafted pleasantly into Beryl's nose. She stepped up to the glossy black door and rapped firmly upon it. The sound of footsteps quickly approached, and Roger flung open the door.

He glanced over her shoulder and swept his gaze back and forth across the open field behind her. Some habits died hard. He motioned for her to join him and firmly pressed the door in place behind her.

"Still dragging trouble in your wake wherever you go, I see," Roger said. Beryl was not entirely sure that he was teasing. "I admit, a body appearing in less than twenty-four hours after your arrival is impressive, even for you."

"I shall take that as the compliment I am sure you intended it to be. But to be fair, for all we know the trouble has followed you rather than me," Beryl said. "I was asked to come here to investigate some trouble that had arrived before I did. Can you say the same?"

Roger's face broke into a wide grin.

"I see you're still happy to give as good as you get. I'm glad to see it. I wasn't sure how you would manage after the war was over. Some of our former acquaintances haven't adapted to peacetime all that well," Roger said.

Beryl knew just what he meant. The war years had asked much of so many and although there were horrors to be sure, there were events that made one feel alive in a way almost nothing else could hope to produce. Not everyone who survived was entirely glad that they had not gone down in a blaze of glory. Often those with the audacious nerve and a willingness to run headlong into the sort of danger some war efforts required were not well suited to quiet, law-abiding existences after the conflict had ended. Beryl thought that some of her ennui before arriving in Walmsley Parva had been born of such a difficulty in her own character. She once again thought of how fortunate she had been to have been welcomed into Edwina's world and to have begun the adventure of the private enquiry service.

"I've landed on my feet very nicely, thank you. It seems as though you have done the same," she said.

"I have been one of the lucky ones. Although you might be right about the trouble following me. After all, I'm far more embedded in this establishment than you are."

"It's my investigation into your association with the Maitland family that brought me down to speak with you. Do you have a moment, or are you caught up in a burst of creative productivity?" Beryl asked.

"You know I always have time for you," he said.

He gestured to a pair of chairs in the corner of the light-drenched room. As she sat in one, she glanced at a large sketch-book sitting beside Roger's own basket chair. A charcoal pencil and gum eraser lay atop a rendering of a circus elephant being ridden by a woman in a formfitting costume. She squinted at it closely and noticed the face of the woman closely resembled that of Tuva Dahlberg.

"I see that the murder has not interfered with your work ethic," Beryl said.

Roger shrugged. "Why should it? It's not as though I was particularly broken up about Louis's death. I can see no reason not to honor my obligations just because he's no longer preening about the place," he said.

"Was he that much of a nuisance?" Beryl asked.

"He was that and then some. I couldn't stand the man, and I see no reason not to admit it even though he's dead. I never did hold with the notion that one ought to lie about a person just because they had passed on."

"A lot of people would be tempted to shade the truth about that sort of thing if the dead man had been murdered," Beryl said.

"Are you accusing me of something?" Roger said. "I thought we knew each other better than that."

Roger picked up the pencil and the sketch pad and flipped to a new sheet. His gaze moved between Beryl's face and the paper in front of him. With a few deftly placed lines, he sketched out her profile. Beryl thought he had perhaps been a bit ruthless in his inclusion of a few wrinkles around her eyes and a slight softening below her chin. But, she had to admit, her likeness was instantly recognizable. Without a doubt, Roger was a very skilled artist who deserved his reputation. The fact that he had taken such a dislike to another artist of renown spoke volumes.

"It's not an accusation but rather just an observation. What reason did you have to dislike him so?" she asked.

"Louis had an enviable reputation. He promoted himself as an artistic genius and by and large the world bought it."

"But you didn't?" Beryl asked.

"I'm not saying the man did not have a great deal of talent, as well as ambition for that matter. But I think that his reputation had as much to do with his ability as a showman as it did with his art."

"He was rather a large personality, wasn't he?" Beryl said. "I only met him once before I saw his body sprawled out in the glade and that much was obvious even from such a short acquaintance."

"He did like to make a big first impression. I always felt that there was something too studied about his appearance. I couldn't stand his long hair and his floaty smocks and his overall air of affectation. But that wasn't what bothered me the most," he said, adding more details to his sketch.

Beryl watched as the wall of the building appeared on the paper along with a shaft of sunlight coming through the window and illuminating her hair in the portrait.

"If it wasn't all that, then what was it that did bother you so much about him?" Beryl asked.

"It was the way he made a point of running me down every time we were in each other's presence that made me loathe him," Roger said.

"What complaint could he possibly have had about you?" Beryl asked.

"Louis saw himself as in an entirely different echelon to grubby little commercial artists such as myself. He called me a hack at every possible opportunity," he said.

"Is that a common thing to have happen at an artists' colony such as this one? I thought that the reason such things existed was to be mutually inspiring and supportive."

"I think that Louis truly believed that nothing in the world existed except to be in support of him. It would have made no difference to him whether or not the art colony was designed for all of us. Louis saw himself as a star in a way that someone who earned a living from their art such as myself could never be," Roger said.

"But wasn't Louis well compensated for his own artwork?" Beryl asked. "I know I've read in the newspapers that his paintings often sold for outrageous sums of money."

Roger raised an eyebrow. "Louis did make sure to brag about the showings he was having at well-respected galleries and indirectly dropped hints about the sums of money gleefully forked over for his latest masterpieces. Which is why it gave me a great deal of pleasure when I suspected that he was having financial difficulties."

"What made you think that?" Beryl asked.

"Why else would he have agreed to license his work to Maitland Cigarettes?" Roger said. "I had a good chuckle about it, I can tell you. That's what we were arguing about the last time I saw him." He erased a bit of shadow from his sketch and carefully blended it with his forefinger.

"I had heard that you were going at it with him hammer and tongs," Beryl said. "What did you say to him?"

"I told him he needed to come down off of his high horse since we were both in the same boat when it came to being a hack. He was not best pleased to find out his new commercial venture was a matter of public knowledge," Roger said, smiling once again. "The look on his face when I mentioned that Hubert told me about his project with the company absolutely made my summer."

"Is sounds to me like you really hated him," Beryl said.

"I did hate him, but I certainly wouldn't have killed him," Roger said as he held up the sketch for Beryl to see.

"Besides our shared history, why should I believe you?" Beryl asked.

"Because, my dear, if I had killed him, I would not have had the opportunity to torment him about his commercial artwork, and I absolutely assure you that I would have done nothing that would have gotten in the way of me being able to enjoy that," Roger said.

Chapter 18

Edwina was enormously relieved to part ways with Spencer Spaulding. There was something a little worrisome about his reaction to Louis's murder. She had perhaps been foolish to bring it up with him when no one else was around to witness the conversation. Ever since the war, there were many more people functioning under considerable mental strain than was usual. Maybe he had simply developed a callousness from some horrific experiences that explained his cavalier attitude to the death of an acquaintance.

She was glad, too, to take her leave of him for a reason beyond concerns for her safety. His constant stream of unpleasant chatter had dramatically reduced the pleasure of visiting the otherwise delightful garden. She resolved to return later and explore it in greater depth when no one else was about it. Or, perhaps, she told herself, she could arrange to visit at a time when the gardener was present.

She was startled to catch herself wishing that Simpkins could have been the one to be there with her. As much as he was not always the most energetic worker when it came to doing the actual tending, she found he understood the inherent value and loveliness of both individual plants and good design as much as she did. She resolved to ask Constance as soon as she encountered her for permission to invite him to stop by for an inspirational tour of the grounds.

As she made her way back towards the house, she heard someone calling her name. She stopped and turned to see Ursula waving from the summerhouse, a notebook held in her hand.

"Just the woman I've been looking for," Ursula said, beckoning Edwina to join her. She diverted from her course for the main house and entered the cool shade of the summerhouse instead.

"I am at your service. May I help you with something?" Edwina asked.

"I certainly hope so. I am just about at my wits' end," Ursula said. She tapped loudly against the hard cover of her notebook with the end of her capped fountain pen.

Edwina wondered if she were being called upon for some sort of investigative counsel or a rather more mundane household concern. Edwina knew that her reputation as someone who could be relied upon to help organize events and domestic difficulties was well known in Walmsley Parva. While she was loath to refuse a request from her hostess, she rather hoped that Ursula wanted to speak with her in a professional capacity.

Edwina found she was less and less likely to be inclined to be pressured into assisting with church fetes and the like ever since she and Beryl had opened their private enquiry agency. But perhaps Ursula wished to confide something concerning Louis's death to her. Constable Gibbs could not consider it meddling if one engaged in polite conversation with one's hostess.

"That sounds most unpleasant. With what do you need my help?" Edwina asked as she settled into a basket chair in the dappled shade of a thriving wisteria vine.

"I'm in dire need of inspiration. I'm a poet, you see," Ursula said. She tapped on her notebook once again. "And despite all the fervor of creativity wafting off the artists at the colony, I'm afraid that I'm suffering from a beastly bout of writer's block."

"I'm not sure how I could possibly help you with a thing like that," Edwina said. A niggling bit of suspicion darkened the corners of her mind. Had one of the domestic servants heard her tapping away at the typewriter and made mention of it to the lady of the house?

"I thought I might pick your brain for some tips, being a fellow writer and all," Ursula said.

"Whoever gave you that impression?" Edwina asked.

"Why your friend Beryl, of course. She was telling me all about the fact that not only are you a professional private enquiry agent, but that somehow you managed to find time to be a dedicated novelist as well. How do you do it all?" Ursula asked, holding her hands palms upward.

She leaned forward eagerly and Edwina felt flustered. Ursula's unexpected comment drove all thought of the investigation from her mind. It was one thing to have become used to the idea that her closest friend in all the world knew she was working on a novel. It was quite another thing for such news to be broadcast about to virtual strangers. But, surprisingly, the experience was not entirely unpleasant. She was quite shocked to see a look of attentive wonder on Ursula's face.

Edwina felt that she was still so new to the notion and practice of writing that she had no wisdom to offer. However, Ursula did not seem to be remotely aware of that fact. It was all a great deal to take in without warning. She found herself wondering what Beryl would do in just such a circumstance. Edwina doubted very much that Beryl would reveal her inner turmoil and lack of confidence.

No, Edwina decided, Beryl would push on ahead as though she were an expert in the matter. And it did sound as though her friend had enough confidence in her abilities for the two of them. Perhaps it would not be so very wrong to borrow just a little bit of it in this case. What could it hurt? Besides, she had rather longed for someone else to discuss writing with ever since Beryl had mentioned she knew what Edwina was up to with the Remington typewriter.

"I suppose I just make a point of making a priority of those things that are most important to me in any given day," Edwina said. "After all, what is life for if not to pursue one's enthusiasms?"

There, she thought, that sounded rather like Beryl even to her own ears. Although, now that she came to think of it, it was a sentiment with which she entirely agreed. While she valued duty and community service, the more confident she became in directing her own life and deviating from societal expectations, the less inclined she was to let the priorities of others crowd out her own plans for herself.

If she were not going to be pursuing a traditional life of domesticity making herself available at the beck and call of a husband, why should she not indulge herself in the pursuit of those things she most held dear? Edwina had not given the topic a great deal of thought until that very moment when she heard herself announce it with such boldness. A flicker of delight passed over Ursula's pretty features.

"I think you've put your finger right on the heart of it. I've been so busy making sure that everything was running properly for the artists attending the colony that I have not been making time for my own work," Ursula said. "I suppose you would have to be rather wise to be a private enquiry agent, wouldn't you?"

Edwina had not given any thought to that, either. But, she supposed, it did take an understanding of human nature to be able to imagine motivations and spot connections that rippled under the surface of polite society. Whether or not that could be considered true wisdom seemed debatable, but she was flattered nonetheless.

"I think it may be more a matter of being the sort of person who notices things. I know what you mean, though, about small household inconveniences causing difficulties with one's creative work," Edwina said.

She thought of the many, many times that an intrusion by Beryl or Simpkins or even Beddoes had caused her to lose track of an important thought or just the right phrase as she attempted to work on her novel. She had sometimes wished that the hero of her story could come by with his lasso and hogtie one of the offending household members before they landed a knock on the morning room door while she was working.

"It happens to me rather more often than I would prefer as well. That must be the appeal of something like an artists' colony. To be able to be removed from one's usual routine creates a sort of creative bubble in which to thrive. I'm sorry the same cannot be said for you as the hostess."

"A murder occurring in the middle of the creative bubble hasn't helped much, either, I can tell you," Ursula said.

"I'm sure as a hostess you must feel his death keenly. Were the two of you friends of long-standing?" Edwina asked.

"I would not have said we were friends of any particular standing. We tended to find ourselves at the same exhibits and openings, and we discovered we shared some mutual interests. He always made a fuss of the women in his orbit and I unwittingly encouraged Louis to take rather more interest in me than I would have preferred. I am afraid it caused some unpleasant speculation about what might be the connection between us," Ursula said.

Since Edwina still had not been told by Constance that Ursula had been apprised of her real reason for visiting Maitland Park, she did not feel it prudent to give any indication that she was aware of such rumors.

"I cannot imagine you comporting yourself in any way that was improper," she said.

"It wasn't anything I did to encourage him. It was that he was particularly taken with the fact that I consider myself to be a poet and that I mentioned that I was interested in the Dada movement," Ursula said.

"I've never heard of the Dada movement," Edwina said. "Is it a type of art?"

"It is more about thinking that anything can be art and therefore nothing is. It is a recent movement that includes painting, sculpture, poetry, and even dance. It's very popular on the continent," Ursula said.

"That sounds controversial," Edwina said. "I cannot imagine that his fellow artists would have taken kindly to him dismissing their efforts as nothing if he proposed that art did not exist."

"He did have a knack for alienating other artists," Ursula said. "I suppose it is no wonder really that he ended up being murdered. He managed to outrage the art world over and over again. I suppose it is one of the reasons his own work became so well known."

Edwina wondered if that outrage had extended to the art colony participants. Spencer had been happy to see him dead. Could Roger and Tuva feel the same? And what about Ursula? Did she have a reason to wish him harm?

"I only met him briefly, but the experience was one I shall never forget. I can imagine he left others similarly impressed," Edwina said.

"Louis was a very passionate man. He could expound for hours on his favorite topics, and I think that even when others agreed with some of his views, they found him tedious. I almost think that his insistence on discussing my work leached the lifeblood out of it. Do you not find that's the case for your own writing? Don't you find that keeping it to yourself, and working away on it in complete privacy, allows it to flourish, whereas letting it out in the light too soon just scorches it all away like the mist on a hot summer morning?" Ursula asked.

Edwina thought that regardless of whether or not she felt uninspired, Ursula brought poetic imagery to her ordinary conversation. And she knew just exactly what Ursula meant. She instinctually had sheltered her work from the prying eyes and knowledge of others until Beryl announced that she already knew what Edwina was up to. If it had not been for that announcement, Edwina would still be working away under the shroud of secrecy.

Still, she was finding it rather nourishing to be able to discuss such concepts with another writer, and so perhaps the time for working in solitude needed to be balanced with the vulnerability that came from exposing one's work to others. It was something she would have to give some thought to as she added more pages to her manuscript.

"I know just what you mean. I think the trick might be to decide ahead of time whether or not you wish to discuss your work with another. It's a small and fragile sort of thing that in the beginning requires shelter and coddling. As much as it is a tragedy, perhaps Louis's death may free you to return to your work with renewed enthusiasm," Edwina said.

Ursula seemed to be a woman with a level head upon her shoulders, but Edwina well understood how passionately she had felt about her own writing project. Was it possible that Ursula could have been driven to the point of murdering Louis just to get him to stop pestering her and creating difficulties with her poetry? Before she had begun working on her own novel, Edwina would have dismissed such a thing as an outrageous suggestion completely outside of the realm of possibility. But as her stack of manuscript pages had grown, she had become more and more passionate about her project.

"I suppose there is a silver lining to every dark cloud, now that you mention it. Cressida was saying just such a thing only an hour or so ago," Ursula said.

"Was she referring to Louis's death?" Edwina asked.

"Yes, she was. For some reason, Cressida has taken rather a peculiar dislike to Louis. I can't see why as she had never met him before he arrived for the artists' colony. Although, I'm afraid she does get rather notional from time to time," Ursula said.

"Constance had mentioned that Cressida could be a bit extreme in her feelings towards others," Edwina said.

"Well, that's certainly the case. She dislikes me intensely, although I can't imagine why," Ursula said. "Ever since I arrived at Maitland Park I've tried my very best to not rock the boat as far as the already established female members of the household are concerned."

"I noticed that Constance appears to have continued to run the household as though she were still the lady of the manor," Edwina said.

"I had no desire whatsoever to dethrone Constance. She and I get along very well indeed. She has always done such an extraordinary job functioning as the head of the household that I couldn't imagine trying to take over for her. I have no interest in doing so, and I'm quite certain I would not be able to hold a candle to her abilities," Ursula said.

"I'm sure that Constance appreciates your good sense about the arrangements," Edwina said.

"If only Cressida felt the same way. She is fiercely loyal, and I am given to understand from comments she has dropped ever since my arrival that she believes I only married Hubert for his money."

Cressida was in good company with her opinion. Most of the village of Walmsley Parva had come to the very same conclusion with much less evidence than Cressida had at her disposal. Still, such allegations were often the case when an older wealthy man married a younger beautiful woman. Ursula could not have had any expectation that such things would not be said in her case.

"You seem to be taking it all in stride," Edwina said.

"There's really nothing else to do about it. Besides, Cressida is one of those people for whom one simply feels quite sorry. She's a poor relation and a distant one at that. And she has had trouble throughout her life with being somewhat unstable. If I were the constable, I would be taking a long, hard look at Cressida and her vehement dislike for Louis."

"Are you saying that you suspect Cressida of being the one who murdered him?" Edwina asked.

"I'm not saying I suspect her. But I am saying that if it turns out that she's the one who did it, I would not be in the least surprised."

Chapter 19

Beryl did not know whether to be flattered or annoyed when Janet approached her at the end of her presentation and tagged along as Beryl attempted to make a hasty retreat. She had been hoping to complete her obligation with the children as quickly as possible and to get back to investigating the case. Janet, it seemed, had no intention of letting her get away so easily.

Furthermore, it appeared that she found Beryl's company rather more desirable than she would have preferred. Perhaps channeling Edwina's patient attitude and openheartedness towards the younger set had not been the right strategy after all. Clearly, when it came to Janet, it had worked far too well.

"I went to Constable Gibbs just like you said that I ought to and told her what I had overheard," Janet said as soon as they were out of earshot of the rest of the Girl Guides and Constance.

At least, Beryl thought, Janet wished to discuss something connected to the case rather than badges handed out for attempts at climbing trees or building shelters from evergreen brush. While Beryl absolutely applauded the organization's efforts to develop a sense of self-reliance in young women, as well as an enthusiasm for outdoor life, she could not whole-heartedly embrace their emphasis on things like doing good deeds and telling the truth.

Beryl had always found that a flexible sense of morality had served her enormously well. Despite the organization's efforts to support modern attitudes towards the place of women in the world, she couldn't help but sense an underlying patriarchy lurking in the shadows.

"What did she have to say about what you told her?" Beryl asked.

"To be honest, I thought she would be far more interested in what I had to say than she appeared to be." Janet dropped her voice and looked over her shoulder. "I think it may have had something to do with the fact that what I had to say cast a dark cloud over the Lord of the Manor."

Beryl looked at Janet with new respect. Perhaps the girl was not quite so young as she first seemed to be. In her experience, many of the inhabitants of greater Walmsley Parva tended to accept their social positions without question. Beryl had always found the practice entirely baffling, and it irked her to no end when those, by accident of fortunate birth, were given a pass on things like police scrutiny.

In her experience with Constable Gibbs, she had found that the police officer was no more immune to such prejudices than the average British subject. And here was this slip of a young thing looking straight into the face of injustice and calling it by name. Perhaps there was hope for the next generation after all, Beryl thought.

"Did she say as much?" Beryl asked. She did not want to in-fluence Janet's answer or to disparage the constable in front of the girl. There would be no faster way to get on Constable Gibbs's bad side than to cast aspersions upon her professional behavior. Beryl had always found that in situations involving those people one did not know exceedingly well and trust implicitly, keeping one's cards close to the vest was by far the best route to take.

"She said very little; that was what led me to believe she did not want to hear much about it. When I took the information about Mr. Maitland to her, she asked almost no questions. As soon as she heard that Louis had been arguing with Mr. Maitland, she snapped her notebook shut and stuffed it back into her uniform pocket. It almost seemed like she didn't want to know that Mr. Maitland had been arguing with Louis," Janet said.

Even for Constable Gibbs that sounded egregious. Beryl wondered if the constable had another suspect in mind and had been hoping that Janet would simply be confirming that line of enquiry. It would be worth checking later, if she could manage to dislodge her young fan from her side at some point in the course of the afternoon.

"Perhaps the constable has another line of enquiry she is following," Beryl said. "Was she speaking to anybody else about the case when you arrived to report your suspicions?"

"She had been taking a statement from Tuva Dahlberg when I arrived to speak with her. But she was just finishing up. I think that Tuva was waiting to speak with me because she was still there when I finished, not that it took very long until after I had made my own statement to Constable Gibbs," Janet said.

"What made you think she was waiting around for you? Do you know her well?" Beryl asked.

"I wouldn't say that I know her at all well; the Girl Guides are too busy to have much time left over to mingle with the artists, but the day that I first met you and Miss Davenport I'd spent quite a bit of time with both Tuva and Louis. Tuva and I spent the afternoon chatting while he painted us," Janet said. "Well, at least I did until Cressida found me there and made such an embarrassing scene."

"Cressida did make her feelings very clear to Louis and Tuva after she sent you off. I expect you heard an earful yourself when she caught up with you," Beryl said.

"She was very worked up about it. I can't see what all the fuss was about. Louis said blindly going along with society was what got so many people killed during the war and that we should reject its rules, especially when it came to self-expression," Janet said.

Beryl couldn't disagree with the sentiment. She had seen too many people blindly following inept orders that had led to misery during the war years to believe that traditional thinking on any subject should be accepted without question. That being said, she thought Cressida's concerns about Louis and his ultimate intentions towards Janet might be well founded. What better way to appeal to a girl of Janet's age than to speak to her as if she were an adult capable of discussing radical ideas?

Beryl would not have considered Janet to be a classic beauty, but there was something undeniably fresh and appealing about her youthful, open-faced appearance. Depending on Louis's inclinations, and taste, Cressida might well have had reason to fear for her young charge and even for the reputation of the Maitland family. If Louis had lived long enough, he and Janet might have embroiled the Maitlands in a scandalous situation. After all, they had scheduled the artists' colony and the Girl Guides' week at their estate at the same time. Some people might argue that they should have known that the girls could be in danger.

"Did you tell Cressida about Louis's ideas?" Beryl asked.

"I knew better than to say anything about all that. Cressida already thought that both Louis and Tuva were corrupting influences, and it would have only made her more worked up if I had given her any more reasons to dislike them. Besides, I thought he was probably right, but I thought if I gave away that I thought so she might have decided to send me home," Janet said. "I wouldn't have liked that at all."

Beryl felt her heart lurch in her chest. She knew exactly what it was like to be willing to do just about anything to avoid returning to her parents' home whenever the situation seemed to call for it. It was one of the reasons she had been so grateful for Edwina's friendship when they were about Janet's age. Edwina had gone about finagling repeated invitations for Beryl to stay with her during school holidays through increasingly outrageous stories about Beryl's parents.

Although not a liar by nature, Edwina had always possessed the soul of a storyteller. By the time they had finally left Miss Dupont's Finishing School for Young Ladies, Edwina had invented sufficient bouts of scarlet fever, influenza epidemics, and highly contagious skin lesions supposedly contracted by Beryl's parents to fill an entire hospital wing. As Edwina's mother was a confirmed hypochondriac, it was an easy matter to convince her to insist that Beryl not risk the health of her fellow students by returning home and exposing herself to such pestilence. Apparently, the Girl Guides functioned in a similar way for Janet.

An unexpected and unsettling thought flitted through Beryl's head. As she looked at Janet, she wondered if she found children to be so unnerving because being in their presence brought back so many unpleasant memories of her own childhood. She gave herself a mental shake. Surely not. It was much more likely she found them to be poor conversationalists and inclined to need regular feeding. Still, she was impressed at Janet's insight into how best not to further provoke Cressida.

"I never liked being at home, either. I suppose that is why I have made travel my life's work," Beryl said. "How did you manage to defuse the situation?"

"When Cressida got round to asking what sorts of foolish notions they had filled my head with, I just told her that they gossiped about the other artists," Janet said. She shrugged as if to say it had been easy.

"Did they really gossip about anyone, or did you tell her a fib?" Beryl asked. A faint blush rose on Janet's cheeks. But apparently she was sufficiently enthralled by Beryl and her charismatic demeanor that she did not feel inclined to hold back. Or perhaps her forthrightness could be attributed to the Girl Guides' value of such things.

"Tuva had a few things to say about the other artists and also about Ursula. I don't think she likes our hostess very much at all."

Beryl wondered if that could be on account of the same sort of jealousy she might have about a relationship between Louis and Ursula. Could Tuva have been in love with him? The more she got to know about the household, the more she wondered if Cressida was as paranoid as Constance had led them to believe. Over and over things pointed to the possibility that the affair between Louis and Ursula was not simply an imagining of Cressida's.

"I wonder why that might be?" Beryl said.

"I don't know that it was anything personal. I'm not even sure that Tuva liked Louis all that much really," Janet said. She stooped and pulled up one of her uniform socks, which had crept down into a bunch around her ankle.

"Why would you say that?" Beryl asked.

"Because she took me aside later that day when she found me running an errand for Cressida and told me that I ought to be careful when dealing with Louis," Janet said.

Beryl noticed a knowing glint in the young girl's eye. It seemed at odds with her otherwise youthful appearance.

"Careful in what way?" Beryl asked.

"She said that he had a fearsome reputation with women, and that I did not want to become one of the many girls he had left in bad situations," Janet said.

"Perhaps that didn't mean that she didn't like Louis but rather that she was concerned about you," Beryl said.

"It wasn't just what she said but rather the way that she said it. She called him a womanizer and told me that if I knew what was good for me I would keep my distance from him because he simply could not be trusted," Janet said with a shrug.

Beryl wished she could have heard the conversation for herself. There was nothing about it that indicated to her that Tuva was not trying to dissuade Janet from her attention to Louis for her own purposes. She left the conversation with a great deal to think about. Where did Tuva really stand in relationship to Louis? And was Janet really as naïve as she first appeared?

Chapter 20

An unsettling notion had occurred to Edwina. Now that Cressida could no longer suspect an illicit affair between Ursula and Louis could be turning Ursula's head away from her own marital state, would Constance wish to continue to retain their services? Could their presence at Maitland Park be of value to her any longer? And more importantly, would she be satisfied with the service they had rendered with such an unexpected ending to the case?

Not the least of her worries was the concern that should Constance no longer wish for them to remain at Maitland Park, they would naturally return to the Beeches, likely before Beddoes had had the opportunity to complete her frenzy of cleaning. If Beryl was no more willing to desist with her interference in such matters than she had been before they left, Edwina shuddered to think of the consequences.

After having the pleasure of being tended to by such a professional and accommodating staff at Maitland Park, Edwina did not like to consider any possible change to her own pleasing domestic arrangements. Still, needs must, and she determined that the right thing to do was to simply approach Constance about the status of their case. Even if the news from Constance proved disheartening, knowing for certain was preferable to worrying. Edwina had had enough of that during the war years and those just prior to Beryl's arrival in Walmsley Parva some months before.

Edwina sought Constance out and found her in the scullery speaking with Mrs. Morton, the cook. Edwina stood some distance away, providing the semblance of privacy the lady of the house needed when soothing agitated servants. Servants abhorred being associated with a house in which anything untoward had taken place. The involvement of the police made matters even more disgraceful and in a social climate such as theirs, the stakes ran very high.

Edwina had found it difficult enough in most ways to run a household the size of the Beeches without any assistance outside of an occasional charwoman to help with the heaviest of cleaning or the young girl from the village to help hand round sandwiches and glasses of punch at an open garden day fundraiser. She could not imagine the chaos that would ensue if a household the size of the one ensconced at Maitland Park was forced to run without the assistance of full-time staff.

"I assure you, Mrs. Morton, this unpleasantness in no way reflects upon any member of the household here at Maitland Park. I am certain that this will turn out to be an unfortunate incident wholly unconnected with any of us," Constance said.

Edwina inwardly applauded her hostess for doing a remarkably fine job at keeping panic from her voice. The look on Mrs. Morton's face did little to encourage Edwina to believe that the excellent dinners gracing the tables of Maitland Park were destined to continue in force for long.

"That well may be, Miss Maitland, but I don't hold with scandal. I am afraid that a stain will attach itself to anyone associated with Maitland Park on account of this tomfoolery," Mrs. Morton said, propping up a plump fist on each of her hips.

How much had changed in the few short years since the war had broken out. Edwina could well remember a time when no domestic servant would have dared to speak to an employer in such a manner. Not only would a servant not dare to speak to his or her own employer thusly, someone of the serving classes would not deign to act so brazenly towards their betters regardless of any economic connection to them. Constance opened her mouth as if to give a reassuring reply when she caught sight of Edwina hovering nearby. Constance beckoned her to join them with a hopeful gleam in her eye.

"Mrs. Morton, I shouldn't like for you to feel that we were not doing our very best to return things to normal here at Maitland Park, which is why I will include you in a private matter and trust that you will respect my confidence," Constance said.

Mrs. Morton removed her hands from her hips and crossed her arms over her chest instead. Despite the activity in the kitchen, Edwina noticed that the cook's starched white pinafore remained spotless. Not only was the table she provided of consistently high caliber, Mrs. Morton knew how to appear reassuringly neat and tidy as well. Edwina found that, despite the circumstances, she rather envied Constance as she allowed her thoughts to harken back to the disheveled appearance of her own Beddoes upon their last interaction.

"I'd be glad of a reassurance as to why I should remain in your employ," Mrs. Morton said, eyeing Edwina up and down as though she were a goose on offer at Sidney Poole's butcher shop. It gave Edwina rather a nasty turn and she wondered if Constable Gibbs had made any enquiries into motives of the domestic staff in Louis's murder.

"While she is here as a model for one of our artists' colony participants, Miss Davenport also happens to be a private enquiry agent. I have asked her, along with her business partner, Beryl Helliwell, to conduct their own investigation into this dreadful matter," Constance said, giving Edwina a steady gaze she interpreted to mean that Edwina was to agree with her story.

"Is that right?" Mrs. Morton said. "A private enquiry agent? Someone had said something like that was going on in Walmsley Parva, but I didn't connect you with any of that. I thought you were just one of those useless women who lounged about all day being painted."

"I shall take that as a compliment," Edwina said.

"So, you see, Mrs. Morton, it is vitally important to Mr. Maitland and myself to get to the bottom of the travesty that has occurred on our property. We are willing to enlist professionals outside the scope of the local police in order to get to the bottom of it. I hope that that will reassure you of my confidence in the members of our household and their lack of involvement in any wrongdoing," Constance said.

"I suppose it does put a new light on things. I can't see you or the master laying out for the expense of such a thing if you weren't convinced that you'd be happy with the results," Mrs. Morton said. "I can't promise that I won't hand in my notice if you're wrong about where you've placed your faith, though."

With that, Mrs. Morton turned her back on her employer and bustled off in the direction of a younger woman scraping potatoes at a worktable at the far end of the scullery.

"Things just aren't what they used to be, are they?" Constance said, as she observed her cook scolding her underling. "I never thought I would see the day when I had to go groveling to one of my own servants."

"I know just what you mean. I am inordinately grateful to have some help at the Beeches and because of that fact find myself walking a delicate balance between overfamiliarity and giving offense that would cause her to leave my employ," Edwina said.

"Just so. Now that I've said it, I would be most obliged if you and Miss Helliwell would turn your investigatory prowess from your previous endeavors to the investigation of Louis's death," Constance said.

"I had wondered if you would still find need of us considering the fact that Ursula could no longer be suspected of conducting an affair with the victim. In fact, that was why I came to find you. I wanted to ask for further instructions on this matter," Edwina said.

"I'm sure that Constable Gibbs is exceptionally good at her job. After all, if she were not extremely capable, I'm sure she would have been replaced when the men returned from the front," Constance said. "That having been said, I am sure that she would not begrudge someone such as myself the privilege of a speedier resolution to this nasty business."

"I'm not entirely certain that Constable Gibbs would see things that way. She might feel that we were treading on her toes if Beryl and I were to become involved with this case," Edwina said.

"Then she must be prepared for her feet to feel sore. My family is not without a certain degree of influence in the district, and I will impress upon her the fact that her cooperation and solicitousness to my wishes would be in her best interest," Constance said. "The fact that she has managed to keep her job as long as she has does not guarantee that she will continue to do so in future if she manages to put the backs up of the wrong sort of people."

Edwina glanced over at Mrs. Morton once more and wondered if Constance was not taking her frustration with her household staff out on Constable Gibbs. A woman such as herself who had spent her entire adult life having her every whim indulged by her social inferiors could not possibly find the new way of things terribly agreeable.

While it was true that the power of the domestic servant had irreparably shifted, the same could not be said for employees in other spheres. The unemployment rate in the United Kingdom remained at alarming levels. Edwina was not at all sure what Constable Gibbs would find to do with herself if she had the misfortune to be removed from her post.

While Edwina did not always see eye to eye with the constable, she did not wish for anything truly unfortunate to happen to her. And in a way, Constable Gibbs's position as a female law enforcement officer helped to pave the way for the community to accept a woman in a role such as hers and Beryl's. It would be very much in everyone's best interest for Constable Gibbs to continue on as the face of law enforcement in Walmsley Parva.

"Perhaps you would permit me to speak with Constable Gibbs before you approach her yourself. We have worked together in the past on cases, and I believe that she would be open to the idea of a collaboration in this instance. She is a very reasonable woman, and such overt pressure is likely unnecessary. I'm sure you have more than enough to do without adding a conversation with the local constable to your list of duties," Edwina said soothingly.

"You really are running a full-service enquiry agency, aren't you?" Constance said. "I would appreciate your assistance in this matter. But please do impress upon her that if Constable Gibbs refuses your offer of assistance, I will make my displeasure felt."

Chapter 21

Edwina considered her options. She could scurry about the estate in search of Beryl in order to apprise her of their new circumstances as regarded Constance's wishes. Or, she could head directly to the makeshift office Hubert had assigned to Constable Gibbs as a temporary headquarters. Its location reflected his lack of pleasure in a police presence at Maitland Park, Edwina thought as she made her decision. Beryl would surely applaud her for taking decisive action, especially if it meant continuing their stay at Maitland Park and avoiding a return to the scowling oversight of the formidable Beddoes.

And, not least of which, Edwina was quite certain she would make far better progress with Constable Gibbs in a one-on-one scenario. There was something about Beryl's attitude towards the social niceties in Britain that made such delicate negotiations oftentimes more difficult. And, she had to admit, if she were Constable Gibbs, her ability to set aside her own pride would be greater if she had an audience of one rather than two. Especially if the two were a team.

Thinking of things that way, Edwina had to give Constable

Gibbs credit for all of the work she did completely on her own. Policing the village of tiny Walmsley Parva would likely not present the same quantity of challenges as a similarly sized district in say, London or even Manchester. But then, police officers in those locales surely would not have been asked to do so single-handedly.

Constable Gibbs had much to be commended for even though she often seemed to go out of her way to be abrasive and unpleasant, especially towards Edwina and Beryl ever since they opened their private enquiry agency. Edwina really had thought they were improving their relationship with the constable some weeks earlier when a matter involving the national census had cropped up. She had felt a bit offended when the constable so firmly shut the door to the investigation into Louis Langdon Beck's murder in her face.

Perhaps Beryl was not the only one who would derive some satisfaction from being in a position to insist upon their inclusion in tracking down the murderer. As the buttery was a short distance along the corridor from the kitchen, Edwina had little time to plan her approach with the constable. She paused outside the buttery door and knocked on it firmly, but not too firmly. She wished to be heard, but not to be seen as demanding.

When she heard the constable's voice from within beckoning her to enter, she turned the knob and stepped inside. The sight that greeted her was pitiable. Doris Gibbs looked as though she had not had a moment's rest since Louis Langdon Beck's body had been discovered. Never in the time Edwina had known her had Constable Gibbs ever appeared to be anything but well turned out and somewhat intimidating.

The woman before her could only be described as frazzled. Edwina's heart gave a squeeze as she noticed a dollop of something that looked suspiciously like mud clinging tenaciously to the lapel of Constable Gibbs's uniform jacket. Her coarse and slightly wavy hair made so bold as to escape her hairpins. Gray smudges stood out below Constable Gibbs's brown eyes.

"I hope you're not here to report the discovery of another body," the constable said, scowling at Edwina. Edwina closed the door behind her and approached the table the constable was using as a makeshift desk. While the constable's words sounded cross, it was plain to see that Edwina's appearance was not the source of her distress.

"Mercifully, I am not." Edwina took a seat opposite the constable and made herself at home.

"You haven't been running about investigating things you shouldn't, have you?" the constable asked.

"I have refrained from poking my nose in where you've asked it not to be, as agreed," Edwina said.

She refrained from mentioning any investigations that Beryl had been conducting or information simply offered up to her as a sympathetic ear. She had not poked her nose in; she had simply been observant and competent. Certainly, the constable could not fault her for that. Technically, it didn't even seem to be an untruth if one sliced it finely enough. "But I would have to be a very poor investigator not to notice that something is troubling you, Doris."

The constable's mouth popped open in surprise. Edwina rarely addressed her by her Christian name. Edwina felt that the constable deserved her title to be used and as their relationship did not tend to be a social one, she could see no reason not to do so whenever the two met. But something about the other woman's demeanor made it feel as though this were a personal interaction rather than a professional one.

"Is it that obvious?" the constable asked.

"You do not appear to be your usual self." Edwina pointed to the spot on the constable's lapel. "When was the last time you had a hot meal?"

"I suppose it was at teatime the evening before the call came in about the victim," Constable Gibbs said. "I was out on another call all last evening and I've been running on cups of tea and the odd biscuit for good measure ever since."

It was times like these that Edwina appreciated her upbringing. The constable had been raised in a family that, while well respected and not impoverished, was not the sort familiar with the ins and outs of a large country estate. She also had chosen to enter a profession that was not widely respected by those members of society who owned stately homes.

Edwina could well imagine that it would not have occurred to the constable to have assumed she might simply order a tray of food to be brought to her wherever she wished. At the very least, Edwina could assist with a small thing like that. She stood and left the room without a backwards glance. In less than five minutes' time she had approached Mrs. Morton and requested that a tray filled with a variety of sustaining comestibles be prepared directly. Edwina stated that Mrs. Morton should expect to send a similar tray to the buttery at dinnertime that evening. She returned to the makeshift office holding the tray aloft.

Constable Gibbs's eyes widened at the sight of the food. Edwina placed the tray on the table in front of her and took her seat once more.

"You must be absolutely famished. Go on and have something to eat. I've asked that the cook send some supper around to you this evening as well," Edwina said.

From the look on the constable's face, Edwina thought she might just burst into tears. Edwina certainly hoped that it would not come to that. She was not sure that either of them would recover from such an intimacy. Still, she would have to risk it. She was certain there was something else that was distressing the constable.

"I'm sure that a few missed meals and hard work cannot completely explain your demeanor. Won't you tell me what is wrong?" Edwina asked.

Constable Gibbs looked her in the eye for a moment as if weighing a decision. She exhaled deeply and seemed to have made up her mind.

"I regret that my personal life has intruded on my professional duties to the point that a civilian would notice something was troubling me," Constable Gibbs said. "I'll have you know this is the first time such a thing has happened in the course of my long tenure as the face of law enforcement in Walmsley Parva."

"I would concur without reservation. You always present a stoic and professional appearance to all members of the village. I do hope you will feel you can unburden yourself to me as one professional woman to another. There are not so very many of us in the community, and it seems to me we ought to stick together."

The constable nodded slowly. "You know that I'm a woman who takes my obligations seriously, don't you?" Constable Gibbs said.

"It's one of the things I respect most about you, Doris," Edwina said. "I don't think that anyone would ever accuse you of doing otherwise."

"I would never put my outside interests before my duties," Constable Gibbs said.

"I can't imagine who would. What's all this?" Edwina said.

"You may not be aware of it as I do not broadcast the details of my personal life, but I happen to be a member of a brass band," Constable Gibbs said.

"No, you have kept that information quite to yourself," Edwina said. "Which instrument do you play?"

"I play several, including the French horn and the tuba," Constable Gibbs said. "I happen to be rather good at them both."

"I'm sure that if you approach your musical endeavors with the same verve that you bring to your police duties you are an outstanding success," Edwina said. "But how does that explain you falling down on your duties in some way?"

Constable Gibbs took another deep breath and exhaled

slowly once more. "The band with which I play has earned a position at an upcoming competition. We are supposed to compete at the weekend, but if I do not wrap up this investigation before then there is no way I will be able to participate."

"I see the difficulty. Of course, you could not leave the case unsolved while you hie off to make music, no matter how pleasantly you do so. Who is it that does not understand where your loyalties need lie?" Edwina asked.

"Thanks to the local gossip mill, I've just received word from our bandleader that he has made it quite clear that if I do not manage to appear on Saturday morning as expected he will replace me with another. Artemis Jennings has just been itching for the opportunity to take my place. She's been pestering about it for years," Constable Gibbs said.

"You know that Beryl and I would be happy to assist you in any way possible in this investigation, don't you?" Edwina said. "I think it unlikely that most police departments would be expected to take on a murder investigation with only one officer working the case."

"Would you really be willing to help me? After all, I have not been all that welcoming towards your participation in the past," Doris said, looking down forlornly at her half-eaten sandwich.

"I completely understand why you would not wish to compromise your reputation in the village by enlisting the assistance of civilians. If I were in your position, I likely would have behaved precisely as you have done. That said, I do not think that you should be punished in your personal life for your commitment in your professional one. I, for one, would not like to see you dethroned from your spot in the band by a woman named Artemis," Edwina said.

Constable Gibbs looked up from her plate and gave Edwina a hint of a smile.

"I really don't know what to do. On the one hand, I'm feeling rather prideful about my position as the constable, and on the other, I couldn't agree with you more about the name Artemis. What were her parents thinking?" the constable said, before taking another bite of her sandwich and chewing it slowly.

"What if you were able to say that you were forced to accept our assistance because of outside pressure beyond your control?" Edwina said.

Constable Gibbs swallowed. "What sort of pressure did you have in mind?"

"What if, should anyone question you for bringing us on board, you were to say that Constance and Hubert Maitland had insisted on hiring us as an independent investigative duo because as wealthy landowners they felt themselves too important to simply rely upon the normal police procedures?" Edwina asked. "That would provide you with a reason for allowing us to assist you that did not reflect on you in any way."

"I should think it might bring the average citizen of Walmsley Parva over to my side of things. As much as the Maitlands are respected in these parts, I'm not sure that most residents of Walmsley Parva would appreciate them throwing their weight around like that," Constable Gibbs said. "But what if that tale gets carried back to the Maitlands? Won't they be angry about it?"

"I should think they would be flattered to have a rumor spread about claiming that they exerted so much influence in the community. Besides, people like the Maitlands rarely pay attention to the tittle-tattle of the rest of the villagers. Should anything unpleasant come of it, I will take full responsibility."

"You would really do that for me?" Constable Gibbs said.

"I most certainly would. If there's one thing I've learned in this business, it's that professional women should stick together. Now, where should we begin?"

"That is one of the things about this case that has been worrying me the most," Constable Gibbs said. "You know I wouldn't let a murderer go unpunished just because he or she is a powerful person, don't you?"

"You have always applied the law without regard to station as far as I recall," Edwina said. And it was true. The constable might have her faults, but playing favorites was not one of them.

"It seems to me, considering why Constance hired you, that the folks who appear at a glance most likely to benefit from the victim's death are the members of the Maitland family," Constable Gibbs said.

The constable was right, of course. Unless they unearthed some more compelling reasons why anyone would want Louis Langdon Beck out of the way, the Maitlands were the ones who stood the most to gain. Hubert could have wished to eliminate a romantic rival. Ursula could have wished to preserve her marriage. Cressida had two strikes against her. Not only did she have a fierce loyalty to Hubert, she had a deep-seated dislike of Ursula. Her mental instability could have pushed her to lash out with violence.

"As much as it puts both Beryl and me in an awkward position considering Constance is both our client and our host, I would have to agree," Edwina said. "One of the Maitland family seems to be the most likely suspect. And, unfortunately, considering the way Cressida reacted to Louis when she found him using one of the Girl Guides as a model, she tops my list of suspects."

Constable Gibbs raised her eyebrows in surprise. "Did she behave violently?"

"While I would say that Cressida truly was provoked, the fact remains that she did attempt to strike him. I understood from Constance when she asked us to take the case that Cressida has a history of paranoia that has produced some violent behavior. As much as I realize it may make your job more difficult, I think you should start by looking into her movements when the murder took place."

"Even with your help, I am not sure I am going to get out of this case with my job still in place. Families like the Maitlands take offense when someone pokes into their business, and they are especially tetchy when any secrets they have been keeping tucked deep in their wardrobes get hauled out into the light of day," Constable Gibbs said.

"I know it will prove difficult, but you haven't remained constable for all this time by only doing your job when it was easy," Edwina said. "If you were such a person, I would never have respected you enough to have offered to help."

Two spots of color appeared on the constable's cheeks. She swallowed twice in quick succession, and Edwina wondered if the police officer had been moved almost to the point of tears. Then she spoke again.

"This doesn't mean you should expect to simply stick your nose into any future cases," Constable Gibbs said. "As far as I am concerned, you are still a civilian."

"I would expect nothing else," Edwina said with a smile.

Chapter 22

It had been clear to Beryl from the first time she had met Charles that he esteemed Edwina above all other women of his acquaintance. When she had arrived in Walmsley Parva the previous autumn, she had recognized that fact. It was not often that when Beryl was in a room she was not the greatest source of the gentlemen's interest. As much as she was flattered by their attention, as often as not, it could be exhausting. But Charles, as polite as he was, and to be completely fair in her assessment of the situation, slightly starstruck by her celebrity, he truly only had eyes for Edwina.

For her part, Edwina seemed determined to take absolutely no notice of his feelings for her. Every time Beryl raised the subject, her friend became flustered and hurried to change the subject. Beryl was not of the opinion that women were without value unless they married. However, she saw no reason why her friend could not enjoy the excitement of a little dose of romance in her life, and so she often found herself thinking of little ways to put the two of them in close proximity. Serving as an artist's model for Charles might just be the thing that pushed them from long-term loyal friends into something a bit more.

She quietly approached the area of the property where she knew Charles intended to paint Edwina that day. One might even say, if observing her, that she snuck up on the site as though she were hunting for an elusive quarry that she did not wish to startle away. In actual fact, Beryl had hoped she might spot them in a scene of tenderness and demonstrated fondness that she had no desire to interrupt.

Instead, as she approached the carefully contrived Japanese garden where Charles had staked his claim, he appeared to be entirely alone. Beryl could see over his shoulder and onto his easel. She could make out an upright stone standing in a bed of carefully raked gravel and a weeping maple tree sketched upon a large sheet of paper. Of Edwina there was no sign, either in person or on paper. She abandoned her stealthy demeanor and strode briskly to his side.

"Didn't you have a sitting with Edwina scheduled for today?" she asked.

"We were supposed to meet over an hour ago, but she still has not turned up. I feared she might not prove to be the most enthusiastic artist's model, but it's not like her to leave me wondering what's become of her," Charles said. "Still, I think I've made good use of the light." He stepped back away from his easel and chewed at the end of his paintbrush.

Beryl did not know a great deal about art. She had spent considerable time with artists, as she enjoyed their iconoclastic ways and unconventional lifestyles. She did not particularly care, however, to pay particular attention to all that they had to say about philosophies and techniques. That being said, it was clear to her that something had shifted fundamentally in the way that Charles had gone about painting the work on the easel in front of them.

If she had to describe it, she would say that there was a boldness to it that had been lacking in his previous paintings. A sort of a verve and a confidence in the strokes of paint, as well as a deeper saturation of the colors than was typically his style, were on display before them. Beryl wondered what could account for this sudden deviance from Charles's more timid previous attempts.

"I think you've made a good job of it. Have you changed the paints that you're using?" Beryl asked.

"I've been picking up some tips from the other attendees here this week and I thought that I would try some of them out. It's the same paint that I've always used, it's just that I'm laying it down a bit differently," Charles said, squinting at the painting. "I've been focusing more on the mood of the painting than on accurately portraying the details. Strangely enough, I think the paintings end up looking more representative of reality by approaching them this way than they have when worrying so much about realism."

"This new approach seems to suit you. I think you'll find that this time at the artists' colony will prove to be a good investment for you," Beryl said.

"I think so, too. I still can't believe that I managed to be invited. I feel as though it's a chance of a lifetime," Charles said.

Beryl thought it just might be that. Not only did Charles's painting seem to be more full of life than his previous efforts, but the man himself seemed somehow changed. His posture was more erect, and he moved his hands about animatedly as he spoke. Beryl wondered if he would transport these changes with him when he went back to his regular life as a country solicitor. She hoped he would find a way to integrate some of his newfound confidence into his day-to-day life in Walmsley Parva. Perhaps if he did so Edwina might be more interested in paying attention to his shy advances.

"You said that Spencer Spaulding was the one who asked you to attend, didn't you?" Beryl asked.

"Yes, it was Spencer who asked me," Charles said.

"Do you know him well?" Beryl asked.

Charles turned from his painting and gave her his complete attention; Beryl noticed he seemed a little reserved. Not that he wasn't often quite reserved. The best solicitors made a habit of keeping much of what they knew to themselves. Still, there was a subtle shift in the atmosphere between them.

"No, I would not say I know him well in the least, which is partly why I feel so lucky to have been invited. It's not as though he had any obligation to me as an old friend or even an acquaintance of long-standing," Charles said. "Why do you ask?"

"I wondered if you might happen to have any idea if Spencer had a reason why he might be a good suspect in Louis's murder?" Beryl said.

Charles dropped his gaze from her face and made a point of looking at something in the middle of the Japanese garden. He was so slow to answer, she wondered if he was going to refuse to do so.

"I've been waiting to be asked a thing like that. The answer is that my new friend Spencer had very good reason to have hated Louis Langdon Beck."

"Anything you'd care to share with me?" Beryl said.

"To be honest, I would really rather not mention what I know. Spencer told it to me in confidence, and considering how much I feel that I owe him on account of the invitation to Maitland Park, I would feel like a complete cad if I betrayed his trust," Charles said.

"You know that these questions are going to come up from someone. Wouldn't you rather discuss it with me than with Constable Gibbs?" Beryl asked. "I expect I would be a whole lot more likely to look kindly on whatever unorthodox things an artist gets up to than Constable Gibbs will be inclined to do."

"When you put it that way, I suppose talking with you about it would be the lesser of two evils. Especially since I don't think that Spencer seems like the sort of person who would harm another," Charles said. "You will keep this in confidence if you don't need to use it, won't you? After all, Spencer shared this with me with the understanding I would keep it to myself."

"You know that I can be discreet if necessary, Charles,"

Beryl said. "I will only mention to the constable any of those things that seem to be relevant to the case. Now, out with it."

Charles reached over and placed his paintbrush into a cup of water and began swishing it about.

"Louis Langdon Beck was not just any artist. His paintings were well regarded and sold for amounts that most other painters could only dream of. But he also had considerable influence with art critics," Charles said.

"Let me guess, he was not a fan of Spencer Spaulding's work?" Beryl asked.

"Exactly. And not only was he highly critical of Spencer's work himself, he made a point to encourage all of his contacts in the art world to feel the same disdain that he did."

"Did he have a reason for that?" Beryl asked.

"Spencer didn't tell me there was a particular reason. He just said that Louis hated him and took every opportunity to destroy his reputation. In the end, it sounds as though he managed to do a remarkably thorough job of it," Charles said.

"How did he accomplish that?" Beryl asked.

"Spencer had a high-profile exhibition at a well-respected gallery to unveil a new school of artistic thought. It deviated from Louis's own philosophy in ways that were most likely quite irrelevant to those not intimately involved in the art community. From what Spencer said, Louis wanted to be seen as an authority, and the fastest way to become one was to push someone else down. Louis wrote to at least half a dozen art critics of his acquaintance, providing them with his take on what Spencer was trying to accomplish through his work. He ridiculed it soundly and encouraged them to do the same," Charles said.

"And did they?" Beryl asked.

Charles nodded. "The coverage of the exhibition was scathing. It closed two weeks earlier than it had been scheduled to do, and Spencer has not been able to persuade another gallery to consider hosting his work since. His reputation is in complete tatters."

"I know that you like Spencer and feel grateful to him for including you in this opportunity, but I have to say, that sounds like an extraordinarily poisonous relationship between him and the victim. If I were Spencer, I think I would have been willing to consider doing away with Louis should the opportunity arise," Beryl said.

Charles's shoulders slumped and without meaning to, Beryl realized she had helped to return him to his habitual posture. Still, it could not be denied that it sounded as though Spencer had a strong motive.

"I'm afraid you just might be right," Charles said.

Chapter 23

Edwina left Constable Gibbs to finish her plate of sandwiches and pot of tea in peace. She was most eager to tell Beryl about the understanding she had reached with the law enforcement officer. As she hurried away from the buttery, she imagined Doris Gibbs firmly clutching a French horn beneath one of her muscular arms and puffing away furiously. Somehow the image seemed to form easily in her mind's eye.

Edwina felt pleased to discover that the constable had something in her life about which she cared a great deal other than enforcing rules and regulations throughout the village. Having developed some new pleasing interests and pursuits of her own, she was delighted when she recognized others enjoying leisure pastimes, too.

Edwina made her way past a warren of small rooms in the utilitarian section of Maitland Park and entered a long corridor that led towards the drawing room. As she began to pass by an open doorway, she heard someone calling her name. She turned towards the sound and spotted Tuva Dahlberg curled up on a chaise longue placed in front of an enormous, carved marble fireplace. The younger woman raised a slim, scarred hand at Edwina, as if to beckon her inside.

Although there was no other visitor to Maitland Park she would less like to encounter than Tuva, Edwina could see no polite way to ignore her invitation. As she stepped into the room, she consoled herself with two facts. The first was that she now knew where to locate the library. The second was that Tuva was fully clothed.

The library was an enormous room with built-in bookcases stretching from floor to ceiling, filling the better part of all four walls. Wooden ladders hung from polished brass rails, making even the shelves located high above Edwina's head easily accessible. As her gaze wandered across the spines of the leather-bound books, her palms itched to pull down something to read rather than to make polite conversation with Tuva. After all, what did one say to someone one had seen in a state of nature? Nothing in her sheltered spinster's life had prepared her for such a thing.

Tuva seemed to have no qualms about renewing their previous acquaintance. Perhaps, Edwina thought, that was the most baffling thing of all. Tuva had shown no sign of awkwardness when she and Beryl had come across her in the woods, and she seemed equally nonplussed to encounter Edwina in the more formal setting of the library. Or perhaps she was simply showing signs of shock after the news of Louis's death reached her.

As she looked at the young woman, she felt her attitude towards her soften. If the relationship between artists and their models was as close as Beryl had led her to believe, surely Tuva was suffering a bereavement, and that fact alone warranted an attitude of compassion. After all, Edwina knew what it was like to have lost many of those closest to her and had appreciated small acts of kindness offered by her neighbors and acquaintances.

Edwina crossed the room and took a seat in an overstuffed

wingback chair beside Tuva. It reminded her of her own favorite chair in the parlor at the Beeches, and she felt a sudden
longing to have her dear little dog, Crumpet, at her feet and a
knitting project in her hands. Still, the sooner she helped Constable Gibbs get to the bottom of Louis's murder, the sooner
she could return to her own home. And who better to provide
some information about the victim than his own model?

"Please allow me to extend my condolences about Louis. I
expect his death came as a terrible shock to you," Edwina said.

"That is very kind of you to say. It does not seem real to me
that he will no longer be striding around waving his brushes in
the air and commanding me to move in this way or that," Tuva
said. "I was so distressed by the news that I came in here to collect my thoughts. To my mind there is no place as comforting
in times of trouble as a library."

Edwina was surprised to share such a deeply held conviction
with Tuva. After what she had been so unfortunate to have witnessed in the glade the day prior, she would not have thought
the two of them would have anything in common, let alone a
love of libraries.

"I could not agree more. And this room is such a beautiful
example of a library that I can imagine that it would be very
soothing," Edwina said.

"I have found it so throughout my stay here at Maitland
Park. Ursula mentioned to me that you are here as a model for
Charles Jarvis and that it is your first time posing for anyone.
How are you enjoying the job?" Tuva asked.

Edwina felt a gasp escape her lips. She had completely forgotten about her appointment with Charles. She hoped that he
had found something else besides herself to paint, as she was
well over an hour beyond their agreed-upon time. She would
have to apologize profusely and offer to make up for it somehow. But knowing Charles, he would be very gracious about
the whole thing, especially considering he knew that she was

working on a case and he kindly encouraged her in all such endeavors.

"I haven't actually sat for him yet. Louis's death seems to have rather thrown things off schedule. I was supposed to sit for him an hour ago, but Constable Gibbs needed to speak with me and I was delayed," Edwina said.

"I wish you luck with it when you have the time. It's actually much more difficult than people assume," Tuva said.

Edwina wondered if Tuva was speaking of difficulty in sitting in a single position, or if she referred to cultivating an attitude of nonchalance as concerned nudity. As she could not imagine discussing states of undress with anyone, she decided to assume the former.

"I imagine it must be tiring to remain motionless for as long as a painting would take to create," Edwina said.

Tuva smiled and nodded vigorously. "That's exactly what I find. People do not appreciate how taxing it is to sit perfectly still for long stretches of time. I tried to tell that to that young girl who kept following Louis around like a puppy pestering him to paint her. I told her how much work it was, but she didn't believe me. I'm glad to see that somebody understands," she said.

"I'm sure someone as experienced at modeling as you would find it much easier than will I," Edwina said.

"I am not as experienced as a model as you might think," Tuva said, tapping the book in front of her. "Not all that long ago, I was a dancer." She lifted the cover on the oversize volume and pointed to a newspaper clipping pasted to one of its pages.

"Is that you?" Edwina asked. She leaned towards the photograph at the center of the newspaper article.

"Yes, I was a dancer for longer than I have been a model. But things change, don't they? Sometimes in the blink of an eye." She absentmindedly ran a slim finger over a thick scar running along her cheek. Edwina had become more and more used to seeing disfigurement on young men, but she was less hardened to the sight of the same degree of injuries appearing on women.

Although she did not wish to seem like she was prying, Edwina was extremely curious about Tuva's scars. The young woman made no attempt to hide them and it was easy to see how they ran all along the side of her face, down her neck, and disappeared below her collar line. More scars covered her arm and hand.

"How long did you model for Louis?" Edwina asked.

"For about two years now I have been his primary model. I suppose you could say his best one," Tuva said. "He told me I was the one who inspired him the most in his whole career."

"Is your scrapbook all about your dancing, or does it include your appearances in the art world as well?" Edwina asked.

"This book is entirely filled with my dance career. I was one of the premier dancers in all of Sweden," Tuva said. "Before my accident, that is."

Edwina wondered if the accident she referred to explained how she ended up with her scars or if it was a separate matter altogether. She was not quite sure how to broach such a sensitive subject.

"I've met many people whose lives were changed by unexpected injuries, but certainly you must know such people yourself. The war did so much to knock lives off course, didn't it?" Edwina asked.

"Indeed, it did, but this was nothing to do with the war years," Tuva said. "I was badly injured in a tragedy and my legs never recovered."

"That must have been terribly distressing," Edwina said.

She wondered if Tuva had been involved in a road accident. She had many times imagined being in a tremendous automobile wreck. In fact, it happened almost every time she found herself in the motorcar with Beryl behind the wheel. An involuntary shudder ran down her spine as she recalled the near miss she had had with Roger Hazeldine and the motorcycle.

"It was. Perhaps you heard about my accident?" Tuva asked.

"I don't believe so. There have been so many dreadful events over the last few years that I have made a point not to listen to those that did not touch my life directly," Edwina said.

"I was injured by a bomb blast in a café. I spent months in the hospital recovering from the severe burns. But I was one of the few lucky ones. I only lost my career. Several others in the restaurant that day lost their lives," Tuva said.

"I am so very sorry to hear that. Did it happen in Sweden?" Edwina asked.

"No, I was in London at a Swedish café visiting with friends and enjoying some of my favorite pastries from my homeland when suddenly something exploded and the entire place went up in flames," Tuva said.

Edwina watched the color drain from the younger woman's face as she spoke. Her heart went out to the former dancer. "I cannot imagine how much you have suffered. I had no idea that you had endured such a frightening experience."

"It was absolutely the worst way for my career to end. Still, I've managed to find other ways to occupy myself, as you can clearly see," Tuva said.

"It seems you've certainly remained in the public spotlight as an artist's model," Edwina said. "After all, Louis's paintings are internationally well known."

"That was one of the reasons that I agreed to model for him. That and the fact that he found my disfigurement to be beautiful in its own way, as opposed to something that would best be politely ignored or covered up."

"I can imagine that that would hold a great deal of appeal," Edwina said. "But clearly not everyone thought so highly of him. If they did, he would not have been killed."

"He was kind to me and very generous, but he was not always an easy man to get along with. He was a perfectionist. He was arrogant, and he could be extremely outspoken about his opinions regardless of who was hurt by them," Tuva said. "But let us not speak ill of the dead. Would you like to take a look at my scrapbook?" Tuva tapped the page beneath her finger.

"I would love to see some of your clippings. I've always admired those people who are good dancers. It's not one of my own gifts," Edwina said.

Tuva readily agreed and chatted away animatedly as she pointed to various photographs, programs from performances, and newspaper clippings mentioning her appearances. It was an exhaustive quantity of information and memorabilia, and it was easy to see how much that time period in her life meant to Tuva.

Edwina wondered briefly if Tuva felt sidelined by her position as an artist's model. Certainly, her face was still famous as one who appeared on Louis's canvases. But there must have been something rather different about being the one praised for one's own performance versus simply being a supporting role in someone else's fame.

"Thank you so much for showing this to me. I do love a scrapbook. You know, I keep one very similar to this of my friend Beryl and all of her exploits," Edwina said, as Tuva gently closed the book and placed it on a low table beside her.

"I have heard of your friend, the grand adventuress," Tuva said. "I'm sure she appreciates the scrapbook and must enjoy looking at it from time to time."

"To be honest, I've never shown it to her," Edwina said, feeling rather shy. "It was a way for me to keep tabs on her adventures from afar for the many years when we were not in direct contact very often."

"She's lucky to have such a good friend as you. I'm afraid

that there is no one I know who has made any scrapbooks of my career other than me," Tuva said.

"Surely you have friends and family who are delighted with all that you have accomplished," Edwina said.

"I wish that were the case, but I'm afraid it is not," Tuva said sadly. Without another word the former dancer got to her feet, picked up her scrapbook, and walked out of the room.

Chapter 24

The day had turned out to be another picture-perfect one and as she had attempted to find a place out-of-doors to sit and to gather her thoughts, Beryl had encountered artists, Girl Guides, and members of the staff all staking claims on desirable spots about the property. It had taken some doing, but she had spotted a bench placed at the far side of the enormous man-made pond she had noticed when they first arrived at Maitland Park. As she sat down and leaned back against the wooden slats of the bench, she thought it the perfect place to mull over the case.

It seemed to her as though the past days had been a blur. She felt a bit of a pang as she noticed a flash of orange beneath the surface of the pond. The sleek carp moving through the water reminded her of those in Edwina's goldfish pond at the Beeches. She was surprised to realize she missed the intimate charms of the house and gardens at the Beeches, as well as the occupants left behind like Crumpet and Simpkins. She even spared a fond thought for Beddoes.

She suddenly had an overwhelming urge to wrap up the case

and to head back to all those familiar comforts. The thought occurred to her that perhaps now that Louis was no longer at Maitland Park to agitate Cressida, it was possible that Constance would no longer require their services. She was surprised at how cheered she felt by the notion.

Unexpectedly encountering Roger and feeling obliged to keep secrets from Edwina had diminished the enthusiasm she usually felt about pursuing a new case. She had spent an unaccustomed amount of time tossing and turning in her bed the night before thinking about the past and how much she preferred the present. A poor night's sleep of unsettling dreams had left her drained and eager for her own bed back at the Beeches. Matters had not been helped by Louis turning up dead before she had even finished her first cup of coffee.

The heat of the sun and the droning of the bees in the nearby flower beds worked their magic and before she knew it, Beryl had nodded off. She woke with a jolt sometime later to the sound of someone calling her name. Beryl opened her eyes to see Edwina steaming towards her with uncharacteristic speed.

Her diminutive friend was always inclined to stride along as though she knew exactly where she was going no matter whether she was on her way to track down a suspect or simply to take her terrier, Crumpet, for a leisurely ramble along a country lane. But no matter how swift was her usual gait, she always gave off an air of ladylike self-control.

But in this particular instance, Edwina looked more like a schoolgirl who was desperately trying to catch a train. Beryl could only surmise that Edwina was most eager to share a development in the case with her. She raised a hand in greeting and moved over to make room for her on the garden bench.

She must have been asleep for more than a few moments. The sun had moved in the sky, and a shadow from a nearby tree had spread over the bench. Edwina dropped down next to her and fanned herself with her hand as she struggled to catch her breath. She put Beryl in mind of Janet that morning when she appeared outside the breakfast room with news of Louis's demise.

"You look as though you've had a break in the case," Beryl said. "Or have you come to tell me that we have been dismissed from our position now that Louis is dead?"

"Not only have we not been dismissed, we have been asked by Constance to conduct an independent investigation on behalf of the Maitland family," Edwina said.

"Why should she want that if Constable Gibbs is already here and doing her job?" Beryl asked.

"She wanted to reassure her cook that she was taking stern measures to see the situation resolved before scandal could attach itself to Maitland Park and its residents," Edwina said.

"I can't imagine our involvement will help very much as far as keeping a scandal at bay goes. Unless I miss my guess, the rumors about a sudden death on the estate will have started circulating just as soon as Constable Gibbs left the police station," Beryl said.

"I am not sure that it will do any good in the long run, but it did seem to pacify Mrs. Morton, the cook," Edwina said. "After the meal we had last night I can easily see why Constance would do whatever was necessary to keep her on staff."

"Maybe that is the solution to the case. Perhaps Louis did not show sufficient appreciation for Mrs. Morton's culinary prowess," Beryl said.

Edwina cocked her head to one side as if actually considering her suggestion as a possible motive. Once again Beryl thought of the near miss they had experienced with Beddoes. Perhaps she ought not to be so very eager to return to the Beeches so soon after all.

"As intriguing as that theory might be, I would have to stick with what I said to Constable Gibbs about suspecting Cressida," Edwina said.

"You've spoken to the constable?" Beryl asked.

"I felt it my duty. Constance threatened to tell her that if she was unwilling to accept our help with the case, she would see to it that Constable Gibbs was ousted from her position. I offered to deliver the news myself," Edwina said.

"I can just imagine how delighted the constable would have been for you to give her that message. I'm surprised she didn't arrest you on the spot for interfering in an ongoing investigation. Or perhaps even assaulting a police officer," Beryl said.

Edwina's lips spread into a wide grin. "Believe it or not, Constable Gibbs is eager to have our assistance for a change."

"You are pulling my leg. The way she insisted that we refrain from becoming involved when we were giving our statements back in the glade makes it seem unlikely she would have had a change of heart," Beryl said.

She thought of the constable as bullheaded and unreasonable and not given to easy changes of heart. In fact, it was a total shock to have found how well she had worked with herself and Edwina during the course of the last case they had investigated. But that change in attitude had required the intervention by an official placed high up in the bureaucratic machinations of the British government. Unless something similar had occurred whilst she dozed on the bench, she could not credit the constable's willingness to accept their help. It was simply not in her nature.

"I promise you she wants our help. And you will never guess why." Edwina paused for effect. "Doris Gibbs plays the French horn in a brass band and if she cannot wrap up the case by Saturday, the group's leader has threatened to replace her at a competitive event with a woman named Artemis. She is beside herself at the very thought of it."

"I should think so. What sort of a name is Artemis?" Beryl asked. "I am surprised at the French horn, though. I should have thought that any musical inclinations the constable might have would show up in a love of a more brash sort of an instrument, like the cymbals."

"Apparently her passion is for the horn. I promised her we would do our very best to help her to be available to puff away to her heart's content on Saturday. She agreed with me that Cressida is both the most likely suspect as well as one of the most inconvenient, at least as far as keeping scandal away from the Maitland family," Edwina said.

"I can imagine that they would not be too eager to have one of their own accused of murder," Beryl said. "I doubt they would be too happy for the public to know about Cressida's history of instability, either."

"Exactly. I suggested that Constable Gibbs look into Cressida and that we focus on the other possible suspects and also on the victim. After I left her, I stopped to speak to Tuva. I thought that if anyone might know why someone would harm Louis it would be her."

"Did she have anything useful to say about him?" Beryl asked.

"Not really. I found out that she had not been his model for all that long. She said Louis hired her in part because of her unusual appearance."

"I would have thought it was because they were fellow Swedes," Beryl said.

"That wasn't what she said. Did you know that her career as a dancer was ended in a bombing in a Swedish café in London?" Edwina asked.

"What a pity. I remember the incident now that you come to mention it. I believe the papers reported some sort of English anti-immigrant group was to blame," Beryl said. "So, she didn't give you much to go on as far as enemies he might have made?"

"She only told me things we had seen for ourselves upon briefly meeting him. She said he was arrogant and that he didn't keep his opinions to himself even if they were offensive," Edwina said. "I am not convinced being unpleasant is enough to drive someone to murder a person."

"I heard something a bit more concrete that I think is worth looking into. Charles told me that Louis ruined Spencer's reputation in the art community," Beryl said.

"How did he do that?"

"Charles told me that Spencer confided that Louis had gone out of his way to influence critics to write scathing reviews of Spencer's work a couple of years ago. They seemed to have agreed, and the result was that Spencer couldn't even get any galleries to agree to allow him to have showings at their establishments."

"That sounds almost vindictive. Did Charles say why Louis would want to destroy Spencer's reputation?" Edwina asked.

"Spencer thought it was because Louis wanted to be seen as the voice of authority, and a shortcut to being considered one was to focus on nitpicking minor differences between his own artistic philosophy and Spencer's. According to Charles, the two were remarkably similar and the whole situation seemed unnecessary."

"So if Spencer arrived to discover his greatest professional enemy was here at the artists' colony, he might have killed him out of revenge," Edwina said.

"I think it is a possibility. But it is too early in the investigation to close our minds off to the possibilities. I think what would be best is for us to take a step back and gain a little perspective," Beryl said.

"I think that a good idea. What do you say to the idea of running back to the Beeches just for an hour or so to let Crumpet know we have not abandoned him altogether?"

Beryl felt her spirits rise. She could think of nothing she would like more than to spend a few quiet moments at home.

Chapter 25

The day was a beautiful one and as they made their way along the long gravel drive from the house out towards the road, Beryl slowed the motorcar and paused to enjoy the view around them. As they turned out onto the open road, Beryl reminded herself to proceed at a sedate pace. Or rather at a more sedate pace than she would be inclined if she were alone in the motorcar.

She would not say that she and Edwina were on the outs per se, but she could not help but feel that there was still a lingering residue of tension from her reticence concerning her history with Roger, as well as the way she could not refrain from encouraging a bit of romance with Charles. Beryl was eager to do nothing that would exacerbate any existing unease between them.

While Beryl thought of herself as someone who enjoyed the company of others, she had not lived a life that had developed many true intimacies. Certainly, she had people upon whom she relied and who, in turn, relied upon her during the war years. She also went out on expeditions where lives were at stake and trust had to be developed between group members. But in the everyday, humdrum world, she had functioned far more on her own. By and large she valued her independence and had been unaware of any downsides to the life she chose to lead.

But after having tossed up at the Beeches some months earlier, she had discovered how lovely it was to have someone with whom she could share the small incidents and excitements of the day-to-day and to feel as though those things were valued and understood by another. The idea that Edwina might feel there was some cause for estrangement between them produced in Beryl a sharp pang of unease and even trepidation. The least she could do to restore a harmonious balance was to not indulge her driving preferences when such things gave Edwina palpitations.

She felt Edwina stealing glances at her from the passenger seat. As they crawled along at a pace Edwina could easily outdo upon her bicycle, her friend felt she could contain herself no longer.

"Have you done something I ought to be worried about?" Edwina asked. She turned in her seat and looked squarely at Beryl.

"What would make you say a thing like that?" Beryl said, hoping that her nonchalance would move the topic along.

"Are you ill? Have you been diagnosed with something dreadful? Am I ill and simply do not know it?" Edwina asked.

"I cannot imagine what you're talking about. What could be wrong on such a fine summer's day?" Beryl asked, waving her arm out through the open window at the landscape slipping along beside them.

"You have never driven this slowly in my presence before. Is there some reason that you are not eager to get back to the Beeches?" Edwina asked.

Beryl clutched at the offered straw. "That's it exactly. I feel that Beddoes has been far better off in my absence, and I wish to do nothing to provoke her. When we left, it had crossed my mind that she might be considering giving her notice," Beryl said.

Edwina leaned back and faced forward once more, a flicker of relief passing over her face. "I'm afraid Beddoes was, quite rightly, offended by your offers of assistance with her house-keeping, but I'm sure that she has managed to put things to rights for the most part while we've been gone. As long as you keep your nose out of her business, I'm sure she will refrain from leaving us, at least for now," Edwina said. "But if you really are concerned about it, perhaps we ought to take her a peace offering of sorts."

"What do you have in mind?" Beryl asked.

"As much as I'm sure she would not admit it, Beddoes has a rather wicked sweet tooth," Edwina said. "Why don't we stop at Prudence's shop and pick her up some candy? We can tell her that it's just a little something to show our appreciation for her expertise."

Beryl nodded and depressed the accelerator with a little more gusto. The motorcar shot forward and they took the turn into Walmsley Parva with zest. By the time Beryl had stopped at the curb in front of Prudence's stationer-cum-post office-cum-sweetshop, Edwina had resorted to once more clinging to the dashboard as was her habit.

Prudence Rathbone stood behind the gleaming glass counter looking much as she ever did. Beryl always thought that her expression could be described best as a portrait of someone who had simply smelled something unidentifiable and unpleasant and was trying to track down the source of the scent. Edwina had always said Prudence had a nose for gossip. Apparently, as much as she was attracted to it, the smell did not agree with the shopkeeper.

She bustled out from behind the counter with a surprising degree of enthusiasm. One never knew how one would be received at the shop. If Prudence had something she wished to unearth or if she had some juicy news to impart to others, she could be quite welcoming.

Should she feel that a customer offered neither of those opportunities, she often made people feel as though they were disrupting her more important work of polishing the glass cases above the chocolates or refilling the racks of picture postcards and pads of notepaper. Clearly today they were to be bestowed with her enthusiasm.

"I'm surprised to see you here in the village. I had heard that you were transported to a far more artistic environment than we have on offer in conventional Walmsley Parva," Prudence said. Beryl could practically see Prudence's ears waggling as she waited to hear something about the artists' colony.

"I see news of our invitation to Maitland Park has reached you," Edwina said. "How did you happen to hear about it?"

"One of the Girl Guides was in here purchasing some sweets and she happened to mention it. That Janet Brown, it was," Prudence said. Beryl was quite sure that Janet Brown had happened to mention absolutely nothing. Prudence would have pressed the young girl for information ruthlessly from the moment she stepped through the door.

"That's just what we're here for," Beryl said, hoping to distract Prudence from the topic of their presence at Maitland Park. Even if it made no difference to their case or to the privacy each and every one of their clients was entitled to, it was a matter of principle with Beryl not to allow Prudence to satisfy her curiosity so easily. It was one of the things upon which she and Edwina invariably agreed.

"Do you happen to have any Turkish delight?" Edwina asked. "I'd like to buy a pound of it to take back to the Beeches."

"Leaving Maitland Park so suddenly? I should have thought with a murderer on the premises you would have been right in the thick of things with no desire whatsoever to leave."

Prudence made her way around the counter once more and withdrew a paper box from a drawer before placing it on the gleaming glass counter. Beryl noticed she made no move to remove the tray of Turkish delight from its place in the glass case. Prudence would not be hurried.

"Is that something else that Janet just happened to mention to you?" Beryl asked.

"No, as a matter of fact, I heard it from the doctor. He does happen to know about any bodies that turn up in the general area, as I'm sure you know," Prudence said. "Janet had a lot more to say about the goings-on of the living at the artists' colony rather than the dead."

"I think I will have a pound and a half of the Turkish delight now that I come to think on it," Edwina said, tapping just above the candy on the glass case.

Prudence bent and pulled out the tray and placed it on the counter. With agonizing slowness, she plucked one piece at a time from the tray and placed them gently into the box with maddening precision.

"That is, she was nattering on all about it until one of the other residents of Maitland Park came in and gave her an earful," Prudence said. "I felt rather sorry for the poor girl even though I don't think someone as young as Janet ought to go round with her face made up like some sort of music hall tart."

"I can't say that I've ever seen Janet wearing any cosmetics," Edwina said. "She always seems like such a fresh-faced young woman to me."

"Well, she strode in here bold as brass with her face plastered with powder. She had painted her lips in a screaming scarlet and had ringed her eyes with some sort of dark muck. I don't hold with that sort of thing myself, but Cressida made a right fuss about it all," Prudence said.

"I'm sure Cressida would have been far too well bred to cause a scene here in your shop," Beryl said.

If there was one way to provoke Prudence into sharing what she knew, it was to imply that she knew rather less than she claimed. It invariably managed to pluck any bits of gossip she held clutched jealously to her heart and toss them out into the open to be evaluated by those with more generous turns of mind.

"You would think so, wouldn't you, with her being related to the family at Maitland Park." Prudence added a few more pieces of Turkish delight to the box. "But I assure you she did not behave like a well-bred lady of the manor. As soon as she spotted Janet in here, she made a beeline for her as though she had been searching for her. She gave me a nasty shock when she grabbed Janet by the arm and shook her like she was a madwoman. I thought I might have to call Constable Gibbs in to intervene."

"She must have been outraged about something to behave in that way," Edwina said.

"It was the cosmetics. She told Janet that it was not the sort of thing that any Girl Guide should go about wearing if she wished to continue to be holding a leadership role. She said something about the danger of trying to look older than she was. She went so far as to pull a hanky from her own pocket and wipe the lipstick off Janet's lips before dragging her out of the shop. I had to call after them to come back in order to be paid for Janet's purchase." Prudence slapped the lid on top of the box of candy, a look of triumph across her face.

Beryl reached into her handbag and fished out payment for their purchase. Given Prudence's inclination towards gossip, they did not want it said that they did not pay their own bills. She looked over at Edwina as Prudence was placing the payment in the till. From the look on her friend's face, she knew she wasn't the only one thinking that maybe Cressida really was as unstable as Constance had implied. So far, she was the only person involved with the case who was known to behave violently when angered. The question was, had Louis angered her enough to resort to strangling him?

Chapter 26

Crumpet had been exceedingly glad to see them when they arrived at the Beeches. He capered around Edwina's feet like a soul possessed and refused to leave her side for the entirety of their stay. She realized with a jolt that it was the longest length of time she had spent away from him. Edwina was determined to make a fuss of him and headed straight to the kitchen to unearth something tasty for him from the icebox by way of an apology for her absence.

While she stood mincing a bit of ham for him, she spotted Simpkins emerging from the garden shed looking a bit rough around the edges, too. She wondered if he had missed them as much as Crumpet had. He looked through the window and when he noticed her his craggy face split into a wide grin. She felt a strange warmth spreading across her chest as she considered that he was delighted to see her returned home.

She still had not become entirely used to the notion that her jobbing gardener had become a permanent resident at the Beeches. Nor, for the matter, had she completely reconciled herself to the idea that he had invested a considerable sum in both the property and the private enquiry agency, albeit secretly. She lifted a hand to wave at him and before long, she, Beryl, and Simpkins were all seated round the kitchen table with Crumpet sprawled happily beneath it.

As soon as she realized they had returned, Beddoes had insisted on halting her cleaning duties in order to prepare a pot of tea for them. Despite how busy she must have been during their absence she had found the time to bake a sponge cake and placed it in front of them before leaving them to chat amongst themselves. Edwina was pleased to see that Beryl refrained from inviting her to join them. She simply handed Beddoes the box of Turkish delight with no fanfare or explanation. Perhaps Constance's fears concerning her own staff had driven home the point of how best to show servants respect.

Whatever the cause, Edwina thoroughly enjoyed her brief trip home. She mentioned to Simpkins that she hoped he would take the time to visit Maitland Park to see the grounds and he readily agreed. Since he had moved into the Beeches, he had let his own cottage and surrounding small farm to the Prentice family, and he was eager to bring the father, Frank, to Maitland Park in order to see the kitchen garden and the fruiting trees and shrubs.

The time passed too quickly, and it was with regret that Edwina gave Crumpet a last scratch behind the ears before waving good-bye with the assurance they would be back just as soon as they could. Simpkins stood on the doorstep, holding Crumpet in his arms to keep the little dog from running down the drive after them.

As they pulled away from home and once again headed towards Maitland Park, Beryl must have sensed her heavy heart. She remarked that if all went well, they would be back in no time and turned their conversation to the confrontation between Cressida and young Janet.

"I have to wonder if what Prudence had to say makes it seem like we ought to consider Cressida as a very strong suspect for Louis's murder," Beryl asked. "After all, her temperamental behavior is the reason we were asked here in the first place."

"If that's the sort of stunt she would pull in public, I can only imagine how unpredictably she might have behaved in the privacy of her own property," Edwina said.

"It does make one wonder if she has the capacity for murderous violence if provoked sufficiently," Beryl said.

"Before we jump to any conclusions, I think we had better speak with Janet about what happened," Edwina said. "Perhaps Prudence exaggerated for the sake of a good story to bandy about to her customers."

"Why don't you go ahead and talk to her about it. You have such a way with girls of that age," Beryl said.

Edwina understood just exactly what Beryl meant, but it had very little to do with any skills on her own part. Beryl had absolutely no enthusiasm for young people, even those who were at the tail end of childhood. Edwina, on the other hand, had always found children to be a delight, even those at the awkward age, which Janet currently occupied. She readily agreed and parted ways with Beryl as soon as they reached the main house.

As she was dressed for town, Edwina went to her room and changed into something more suitable for a walk through the woods. The Girl Guides were scheduled to be involved with outdoor activities every afternoon, rain or shine, and Edwina was quite certain she would find Janet out-of-doors.

Sure enough, she located Janet in the Girl Guides campsite only a little while later. Here and there girls in uniforms stood about in small groups tying knots, attempting to start campfires in rings of rock, and scurrying about busying themselves with the construction of unstable-looking shelters. By and large they all appeared to be having tremendous fun.

Janet stood a little way away from the group, looking off at nothing as far as Edwina could tell. Cressida was nowhere to be seen, nor was Constance. Perhaps in her role as a young leader of the Girl Guides Janet had been left in charge. The girl looked up and gave Edwina a half-hearted smile as she approached.

"Good afternoon, Janet. May I speak with you for a moment?" Edwina asked.

"I'm supposed to be supervising the younger Girl Guides with their projects towards some of their badges. I can't leave the area or I'll be in trouble with Cressida and Constance."

"We can stay right here and talk if that won't prove to be too disruptive," Edwina said. "It shouldn't take long."

Janet nodded and gestured for Edwina to accompany her to a large, flat rock nearby and invited her to sit. "What is it you wanted to talk to me about?" Janet said.

In such matters as these, Edwina often found it to be best to get straight to the point. There were those people who opened up fastest if one employed a bit of jollying along before one got to the point, but with the way that Janet's eyes kept wandering back to the younger Girl Guides, Edwina thought it best to hurry things along.

"I was at the post office today and happened to hear that you had a terrible confrontation with Cressida over some cosmetics that you were seen wearing."

Janet's eyes widened and her cheeks grew rosy. "I suppose gossipy old Prudence Rathbone told you about that," she said.

"Yes, she did, and I am not asking because I am equally interested in idle tittle-tattle. Perhaps you know that Beryl and I are employed as private enquiry agents when we are not busy with other things."

"Is that why you're both here at Maitland Park?" Janet asked.

"That's not why we came here in the first place, but we have been asked by Constance to help Constable Gibbs with her enquiries. It simply is a courtesy to them both that we are involving ourselves in this matter. Anything unusual that has happened either here at Maitland Park or between those people who were here at the time of the murder is of interest to the investigation," Edwina said.

"And you think that my argument with Cressida might have had something to do with Louis's murder?" Janet said.

"That remains to be seen. But I do need to know why Cressida was so upset with you that day. It seems out of character for her to comport herself like a fishmonger's wife rather than a member of the Maitland family and moreover in front of someone as inclined to gossip as Prudence Rathbone," Edwina said.

Janet nodded her head. "Miss Rathbone delights in making things sound more dramatic than they really are. At least that's what I've noticed. Cressida was upset to see me wearing cosmetics, especially in public. She came in and demanded that I behave in a more ladylike manner. She said to do otherwise was to betray Constance's faith in me and the values the Girl Guides uphold," Janet said.

"I heard she practically dragged you out of the shop after wiping the lipstick from your face," Edwina said. "Prudence said she was tempted to call for the constable. That sounds like it was quite a dramatic confrontation to me."

"I know it might have seemed unreasonable, but Cressida was very concerned about me interacting with Louis. She seemed to think that he might have some sort of nefarious designs concerning me, and she said that the only reason I was wearing cosmetics was to appear more appealing to him. It really put her back up."

"It's only natural for someone your age to wish to appear more sophisticated and mature," Edwina said. "Do you think that Cressida was simply looking out for you? You sound as though you are willing to make light of what she did."

Janet nodded. "Cressida always has the best interests of all the Girl Guides at heart. And really it was not as much of a brouhaha as Prudence made it seem. I had practically forgotten it already. If you want to know about fireworks, you should talk to Roger Hazeldine about his argument with Louis. That was where the real scene was that day in Walmsley Parva."

"You saw an argument between the two of them on that same day?" Edwina asked.

"You bet I did. Roger had both of his hands on Louis's shoulders and was shaking him. Louis pulled away and then he threw a punch that knocked Roger to the ground," Janet said.

"Where did you see them arguing?" Edwina asked.

"They were in the village green near the duck pond. I couldn't believe that they were behaving like that right out in the open where anyone might see them. Perhaps if Cressida had seen what they were up to she would've left me well enough alone," Janet said.

"Do you remember exactly which day this was?" Edwina asked. "Prudence wasn't clear about that detail."

"I do. It was actually the same day that you and Beryl arrived at Maitland Park. It took place late in the morning. I had forgotten all about it, with what happened with Louis that next morning and all," Janet said. "Do you have any more questions for me? I need to get back to supervising the girls."

Janet pointed at two much younger children who were inexpertly attempting to chop some green saplings into smaller lengths with an ax.

"No, I'll let you get back to your responsibilities. Thanks for being willing to give me some of your time. And, Janet, I think you look just lovely without any cosmetics at all," Edwina said.

The girl gave her a warm smile before hurrying over to the

shelter builders. Edwina watched her retreating back and wondered if everyone at Maitland Park had more of a temper than it first appeared. Roger Hazeldine had been careless about life and limbs while careening about on his motorcycle. Would he have been as cavalier about murder?

Chapter 27

"I think that we should speak to Hubert. I'm sure he must have known that his longtime employee Roger and Louis did not get on all that well," Edwina said. "One of the things that was so important in a house party guest list is compatibility amongst the people invited. After all, one never knows if the weather will be uncooperative and the entire party will be cooped up for days on end together."

"I know just what you mean. I had the misfortune of attending a house party during the rainy season in India many years ago. There were three divorces under way by the end of it, including one of my own," Beryl said. "When do you think we ought to approach him?"

"Well, as he is our employer's brother, as well as our host, we do not wish to give offense. I think we ought to be sure to catch him in a good mood," Edwina said.

"I know just the thing. A man like Hubert seems unlikely to turn down an American-style cocktail and it's getting to be just about a socially acceptable time for such things," Beryl said.

"I could do with a bit of a pick-me-up myself," Edwina said.

Beryl was surprised to hear her say that. Generally speaking, Beryl was the one who was more interested in imbibing them than was Edwina. Unless coaxed to do so, her diminutive friend generally stuck to drinks of a more ladylike nature, such as lemon squash or the ubiquitous cup of tea. Beryl wondered what had caused this change of heart and thought fleetingly once more of the strain she had felt rearing its ugly head between them.

"That's rather unlike you to say such a thing. What's gotten into you?" Beryl asked.

"I don't know. Perhaps it's the artistic attitude in the air. Or maybe it's that it seems like the sort of thing a successful novelist might say," Edwina said, gazing off at a spot somewhere near the ceiling.

Beryl felt cheered at the notion that Edwina was willing to discuss her literary pursuits with such ease. It was only a few weeks earlier when she had been willing to admit at all that she was involved with the writing of a novel. Now here she was saying so out loud where anyone might hear her. Not only did Beryl think that Edwina deserved a pick-me-up, she thought she deserved something worthy of celebration. She wondered if the Maitland cellar ran to bottles of decent champagne.

"What has brought about this change in your attitude towards discussing your novel?" Beryl asked.

"I had an interesting chat with Ursula. She said that you had mentioned that I was working on a novel and she spoke to me about her own writing. Apparently, she thought I could offer her some advice," Edwina said.

"Should I not have mentioned it to her?" Beryl asked, hoping she had not added petrol to the fire of discord between them.

"I will admit that I was a bit surprised, but in the end I felt surprisingly elated by having a conversation with someone else on the ins and outs of creating such work. I went away feeling valued and I must admit, I rather liked it," Edwina said.

"That calls for a celebration." Beryl tucked her hand through Edwina's arm. "Unless I miss my guess, we'll find Hubert Maitland in the drawing room seated conveniently near to the drinks tray."

Beryl had a sixth sense for such things. Hubert looked the soul of prosperity as he sat stretched out in a high wingback chair, his legs extended in front of him, grasping the cocktail Beryl had easily convinced him to accept. In truth, it was not the first nor the second but rather the third that he had clutched in his hand at the moment. Beryl noted his ability to imbibe without becoming an embarrassment to himself.

While his words remained unslurred and his voice grew no louder, a rather merrier demeanor suffused his slightly flushed face. Edwina displayed the good sense of not removing her notebook from her pocket as she sat in a nearby chair sipping at a saucer of inferior champagne. Beryl did not know if that was all the Maitland cellar contained or if Hubert had been unwilling to pull out the good stuff for the two of them. Perhaps he was simply ignorant on such matters, she thought to herself, glad that she had decided to stick to cocktails rather than champagne.

"I'm sure that by now your sister has mentioned to you she's asked us to look into Louis Langdon Beck's death," Beryl said, introducing the subject on her mind before Hubert got too squiffy to formulate a coherent answer.

"Constance has always been quite a treasure at managing the household no matter how unexpected the things that crop up might be. Although I must say, a murder was the most unexpected thing ever to happen here," Hubert said. He took another sip of his cocktail and leaned his head back against his chair.

"I really don't know how she's done it all with the Girl Guides, the artists' colony, and now the murder. I'm not sure I've ever seen the like of her capability at managing a household," Edwina said. "Although I suppose that might explain any hiccups in the guest list."

Beryl wondered if Edwina had perhaps overstepped the boundaries of politeness by her remark, but Hubert seemed to take no offense.

"A hiccup you say?" Hubert smothered a small hiccup of his own with a tightly clenched fist.

"Well, it does seem rather an oversight on someone's part to have invited Spencer Spaulding, Roger Hazeldine, and Louis Langdon Beck to the same week here at Maitland Park," Edwina said. "But perhaps Constance did not know that the three men disliked each other so intensely when she wrote up the guest list."

"What makes you say that they hated each other?" Hubert said.

"Because we asked both Spencer and Roger and each of them told us that they couldn't stand the man," Beryl said. "When there's been a murder done it's important to find out who might have wished harm to the victim, as I'm sure you will agree."

"I'm sure that Connie had no idea that they felt that way about each other. I had no idea about it myself, so I can't imagine how she would. But I don't get involved in any of that sort of thing. I leave the running of a household completely in Connie's capable hands," Hubert said.

"How long had Louis worked for you?" Beryl asked.

"Technically I don't suppose that he did. Roger works for me as a studio artist, but Louis simply agreed to license his work for us to use on the cigarette cards. I'm sure he would never have considered himself as someone who works for anyone," Hubert said. "He was rather superior about that sort of thing."

"You don't sound as though you particularly liked him, either," Edwina said.

"It wasn't really a question of liking or disliking him. It was just business. Besides, he was a foreigner, and you know what that means," Hubert said.

He glanced over at Edwina as if to include her in such a sweeping statement. Even though English was a common language for Americans and the British, oftentimes Beryl felt at least as much of a foreigner in England as she did when much farther from her roots. She especially felt that way at times when it was clear she was not quite one of the natives.

"I'm not sure I know what that means, being a foreigner myself," Beryl said, attempting to keep up a bantering sort of tone.

"Oh, yes, I seem to have forgotten that I was in mixed company. Please forgive me," Hubert said. "It was just that he wasn't entirely simpatico with the types of things the average British man would value."

"What sort of things?" Edwina asked.

"He was a bit of a braggart, not to put too fine a point on it. And he made sure that everyone knew how valuable he thought that he was," Hubert said. "I wouldn't be surprised if that was one of the reasons that Roger did not esteem him. I expect that was quite off-putting."

"So, Louis thought rather a lot of himself, then?" Edwina asked.

Hubert nodded, causing a bit of the liquid in his glass to slosh about.

"I'll say he did. He made sure to tell me he was repulsed by the notion of something so crass as mass reproduction of his art," Hubert said.

"If he found the idea of licensing his work to you offensive, why did he do it?" Beryl asked.

"I assumed he needed money, like so many people do in today's economic situation. I didn't think it my place to pry into his affairs," Hubert said, taking another sip of his drink. "I suppose in a way it's a good thing for Maitland Cigarettes that he will not be making any more paintings."

"Why would you say a thing like that?" Edwina asked.

"Well, for one thing, it will drive up the value of his work overall if he's not going to be creating any more of it. Not to mention that the sensational nature of his death will certainly bring a great deal of attention to him posthumously," Hubert said.

"You don't seem at all perturbed by the prospect. In fact, that's a bit mercenary, isn't it?" Beryl asked.

"Like I said before, it was a business relationship, not in any way a personal one. I'm just looking out for my company's best interests."

"Is there a possibility that the contract will fall through now that he has died?" Edwina asked. "Is there any way that his estate could revoke the license, especially in light of the fact that his work may be more valuable than it was prior to his death?"

Hubert sat up straighter and took another sip of his drink. "You've got a businesslike mind of your own, don't you? I asked Charles Jarvis that as soon as I heard that Louis was dead. Charles did me the favor of looking over the contract and he said it was his opinion that it should hold up no matter what any heirs to Louis's estate might have to say about things," Hubert said.

"Do you have any idea who those heirs might be?" Beryl asked.

"No, I haven't the foggiest notion. I believe Louis wasn't married, at least not at the time of his death, and as far as I know he had no children. I suppose some relative or other will appear and make a nuisance of themselves before long. But as far as I'm concerned it makes no difference to me. We plan to roll out the cigarette cards on a timeline that corresponds with whatever publicity happens to come as a result of Louis's death. Maybe if we are lucky there will be a sensational murder trial and we can time it to release with that," Hubert said.

Beryl looked over at Edwina, who had proved unable to stifle a small gasp. Fortunately, their host seemed to have imbibed sufficiently to pay no attention to such things. Beryl wondered how ironclad the contract with Louis had been. She looked at Hubert with new eyes. Was it possible that Hubert could have engineered the murder in order to bolster sales of his cigarettes? It seemed unlikely, but one never knew.

Chapter 28

Edwina was not sure if her head felt swimmy from too much champagne, or if she was becoming affected by the overall atmosphere of the artists' colony. But one thing was for sure—as she wended her way towards the appointment she had suggested for a sitting with Charles, she did not feel like her usual self, not in the least. Edwina reflected on her recent past and even the overall pattern of her life and found herself marveling at the changes that had occurred in such a short period.

The death of each of her parents had grieved her, as had the death of her brother, but she found that her life was so filled with interesting and alternate outlets for her energy and enthusiasm that those old wounds had faded to a familiar ache rather than an acute stabbing pain. Fading, too, was the woman who felt she needed to stay so firmly within the boundaries of societal expectations. When Beryl had careened into her life the previous autumn, she could not have imagined she would find herself offering to pose as an artist's model when not otherwise occupied by tracking down murderers or happily dreaming up adventures for a fictional American cowboy.

Who is this new Edwina? she wondered as she stepped off the gravel path leading to the Japanese-inspired garden and found herself face-to-face with Charles.

"I'm so glad you arrived at precisely this moment," Charles said. He gestured to a stone bench nestled against a cascading maple tree with diminutive burgundy leaves overhanging and softening its rough edges. "The light is simply lovely, and I wish to capture it just as it is now."

Edwina sank onto the bench and leaned back, propping her upper body on her palms. She let out a deep sigh of contentment as she felt a refreshing evening breeze ruffle the edges of her bobbed hair. There was something so delicious about the freedom of no longer fussing about with her tresses but rather allowing them to simply swish about her head without thought.

"Charles, I must apologize for missing our session together earlier. I should have sent a note via one of the servants to let you know not to wait for me," Edwina said.

Charles squinted at her and made some quick dashing motions with a pencil against his sheet of watercolor paper propped against a wooden easel.

"I'm sure you had a good reason. You're not someone I ever think of as thoughtless," Charles said.

"I certainly do have an excuse. But I hope you'll keep it to yourself." Charles nodded and she continued. "Constance threatened to tell Constable Gibbs that if she did not allow us to participate in the investigation she would go over her head and force her to accept our help from someone she happens to know in a position of power."

"Knowing Constable Gibbs, that would not have gone down well at all," Charles said.

"It certainly would not have. Which is why I offered to speak to Constable Gibbs myself immediately and do my best to encourage her to willingly accept our involvement. If I hadn't done so right at that moment, I am afraid that Constance would have gone ahead without me. She was quite worked up about the murder," Edwina said.

"I should think she would be. Maitland Park is not a place one would associate with anything quite so grubby as a violent death. It's bad enough that they expose themselves to speculation by hosting an artists' colony. Constance is right to be concerned," Charles said, squinting at her and making a few more marks upon his paper.

"I think her biggest concern has nothing to do with the reputation of Maitland Park outside of the household but rather something closer to home. She's concerned about losing valuable members of her staff, and no wonder. Servants, of course, hate to be connected with something so unseemly. They're all very snobbish about it," Edwina said.

"I'm sure I wouldn't know. I'm afraid I've little to attract a domestic servant of any sort to my humble abode," Charles said.

Charles was a man of comfortable means, and his home was one that Edwina thought of as tidy and pleasant. But a simple bachelor in possession of a modest home had no real need for full-time household servants. He certainly wouldn't trouble himself to fuss over such things in a wildly competitive market.

Once again, Edwina spared a thought for the excellent Beddoes and her astonishing appearance in their lives. As Edwina sat there, she was enormously relieved to consider that she and Beryl had already thought to stop to purchase a small token of their appreciation for that domestic treasure earlier.

While Edwina well knew that Charles managed to operate his home with an assortment of newfangled gadgets for saving time and energy in performing household tasks, Edwina had no interest in adapting herself to such extreme measures. While she eagerly embraced the modern technology of typewriters and improved photographic equipment, she was not an enthusiast of the telephone, the motorcar, or electrified carpet sweepers. The horrors that were being invented to save labor in the kitchen made her shudder. Apparently visibly, as her movement called Charles's attention.

"I'm going to have to ask you to hold perfectly still, please," Charles said. "You look as though a goose just passed over your grave."

"I was just considering the problem of losing one's servants."

"Why don't you tell me about your investigation instead. I'm sure that will be a far more pleasant topic for one as interested in such things as you," Charles said, giving her a broad smile.

"Now that you mention it, that's one of the reasons I wanted to do the sitting with you. Of course, I wanted to make up for missing our earlier session, but I also had a question I wanted to ask you," Edwina said.

"As long as you are able to do so whilst remaining perfectly still, I'm happy to oblige you," Charles said.

"Hubert told us that he consulted you on the subject of the contract that he had in place with Louis at the time of his death. Is that true?" Edwina asked.

"He did ask me about it and although I don't prefer to offer opinions on legal matters without being formally retained, I felt I could not refuse, as he has been so generous as to host me here at Maitland Park," Charles said. "Is this relevant to the case?"

"It might be. He said that you offered the opinion that the contract would hold up to any challenges from those who would inherit his estate."

"It all seemed very straightforward to me when he showed me the contract. Of course, one can never tell what will happen in the courts for absolute certain, but it doesn't seem to me that there is a good reason why it should be easily broken. And there's nothing to say any heirs would be interested in doing so," Charles said.

"Hubert was very forthcoming about the fact that he felt his end of the bargain was in no way damaged by Louis's untimely death. In fact, he seemed to think that it would make the contract all the more valuable to him and his business concerns," Edwina said. "Could his heirs wish to renegotiate their compensation because of that?"

"I suppose any heirs could try, but they might be equally inclined to simply leave things be. After all, the cigarette card contract is but one part of Louis's estate," Charles said.

"Do you expect he left a fortune to someone?" Edwina asked.

"It depends on what you mean by a fortune. But yes, I would assume he had a healthy bank balance to leave to someone, as well as any unsold works," Charles said. "Those works, and any licenses of them, would be worth a great deal more now that he has died so unexpectedly."

Edwina wondered who stood to inherit Louis's estate and whether or not they would have hastened their receipt of it along. She considered Hubert anew.

"So would you say that Hubert stands to benefit significantly financially from Louis's death?" she asked.

"I expect it will make him a mint. After all, Louis had never before allowed any of his work to be used in such a crassly commercial fashion. It's entirely unprecedented and considering his popularity as an artist in more elite circles, it's astonishing," Charles said.

"Hubert said much the same and also added that since Louis won't be producing any more work that it might make it all the more valuable," Edwina said.

Charles reached for a paintbrush and swished it around in a

container of water before tapping it on the edge and dipping it carefully into a blob of paint.

"I would have to agree with him. In fact, this change in the manner of art production for the cigarette cards made me wonder if it would have any effect on the studio artists like Roger Hazeldine. It might be much more sensible to close down the in-house studio operations and simply make bids for existing artwork instead," Charles said.

Edwina had not considered that the association with Louis might have put Roger or any of the other studio artists' own livelihoods at risk. Being an artist that could support him or herself solely on their art sales was quite an unusual situation. Could Roger have been sufficiently concerned about it to have decided to eliminate the perceived competition?

"Do you really think that's a possibility?" Edwina asked. "Did Hubert say anything to you about eliminating the studio at the cigarette company?"

"No, he didn't say as much, but make no mistake, Hubert Maitland is first and foremost a businessman. Any enthusiasm for art that you see at Maitland Park is entirely down to Ursula. If an art studio were to become a liability, rather than an asset, at Maitland Cigarettes, you can be sure he would ruthlessly hack it out without a second thought."

"But what about all the paintings hung on the walls here at Maitland Park?" Edwina asked. "Surely the family has a history of patronizing the arts."

"From what I've gleaned in conversation with Hubert, and Constance, for that matter, a passion for art died with the previous generations that commissioned it with such frequency. The artists' colony is simply a way that Hubert is indulging his pretty young wife," Charles said.

"Do you think that Roger is aware of that attitude from Hubert?" Edwina asked.

"I would say that if in my short acquaintance with Hubert I have been made aware of it, it would seem impossible that Roger wouldn't be, too. If you're looking for a strong suspect in Louis Langdon Beck's murder, I don't think you could do much better than Roger Hazeldine."

Chapter 29

Beryl was quite sure that Edwina still felt uncomfortable with Roger. The fact that she insisted on Beryl interviewing him on her own about his concerns about his job security clinched it. When Edwina had returned from her modeling session with Charles and had relayed his suspicions about Roger's motives, she had insisted that she had a hankering for some solitude and would go in search of a book in the Maitland Park library to keep her company.

Beryl felt slightly deflated watching her friend head off towards the library on her own. Still, the case took precedence at present and she went off in search of Roger. Knowing his interests, she followed her instincts and headed for the billiards room. He stood alone in the dark wood-paneled game room chalking a cue.

"You're just in time for a game," Roger said. "Why don't you help yourself to a cue off the wall while I rack up a new game," Roger said.

"That is exactly what I was hoping for when I wandered down here," Beryl said. "It's just like old times, isn't it?"

Roger looked at her for a long moment, then shrugged. "Not exactly. But I suppose we can both be glad of that."

He placed the frame over the balls and, when satisfied with their position, removed it and gestured towards the table for Beryl to have the first turn.

Billiards was not her favorite pastime, but she could do a credible job of giving a good enough game to be entertaining for herself and others. She sized up the balance of her selected cue and bent over the table to take her shot. The balls rolled off in her expected directions, sinking two.

"I see you haven't lost your knack for the game," Roger said as she bent over the table once more. Working her way through turn after turn, she finally missed one and stepped back.

"Someone told me that you had spent the first few days of the artists' colony session playing billiards with Louis in the evening," Beryl said. "Or did I hear that incorrectly?"

Roger hesitated before attempting his turn, then sank a ball of his own.

"Whoever told you that was misinformed. Louis Langdon Beck and I did not spend any of our leisure time together," Roger said. "I already admitted how much I disliked the man. You cannot think I would be desperate enough for a game to play with him."

"I should have thought that a little competition on the billiards table would have simply been a reflection of your overall relationship," Beryl said.

Roger missed his next turn and Beryl stepped back up to the table. She wondered if she were getting under Roger's skin and ruining his concentration with her questioning. He had not been so easy to rattle in the past, and for a moment she wondered if he had changed a great deal since last they met. Could he have changed enough to entertain the idea of murdering someone in a fit of rage? Even if he had not, she could not imagine that he would have taken being knocked to the ground right in the center of the village all that well.

"As far as I was concerned, Louis and I did not have a competitive relationship. And to be fair, he probably felt the same."

"Why do you say that?" Beryl asked.

"For my part, I don't think of art as competitive. The more beauty put out into the world the better off we all are."

"And why do you think Louis didn't view you as competition?" Beryl asked.

"It was my impression that Louis Langdon Beck did not feel that there was anyone in the world with whom he competed. He seemed to feel he was absolutely superior to everyone else in every way. From the art that he created, to the money he made, to the women he wooed, he seemed to feel that he was on an entirely different plane of existence than mere mortals such as myself or any of the other artists here this week for that matter," Roger said.

Beryl straightened and gave Roger her full attention. His voice did not betray resentment, but then Roger was a master of keeping his emotions to himself or portraying ones that he did not truly feel. Even for someone such as her who had known him for so long, it could be extremely difficult to tell where he stood on any given subject.

"Is that what you were arguing about in the village the day before he died?" Beryl asked.

"What makes you think we were arguing?" Roger said.

"You don't actually believe that you could get into a physical altercation right on the high street with another man, especially one who ends up murdered the next day, without the entire village talking about it, do you?" Beryl asked.

"I suppose that would be too much to hope. We did indulge in a childish bit of fisticuffs, but that doesn't make me a murderer. Nor does it give you the right to pry into my private conversations," Roger said.

"Putting your hands around someone's neck is hardly a bit of roughhousing. I am doing you the favor of asking you about the fight rather than sending the constable your way to do so. She will be far less likely than I to believe what you say about it. I happen to know that she is very eager to wrap up this case as soon as possible," Beryl said. "We both know you wouldn't like the authorities to poke into your life."

"I suppose you make a good point. If you must know, I told him that considering the types of nonsense he ended up painting, he did not need a model like Tuva to pose for him. I said since clearly he was broke, as he had agreed to license his work to Hubert, he might as well save some money by using rocks or packing crates as subjects instead."

"Why did you throttle him?" Beryl asked.

"He said that even if he were entirely penniless, a model like Tuva would rather pose for a real artist such as himself than she would for a hack like me for a generous wage. He had been making that sort of snide comment ever since we arrived and I finally had had enough," Roger said. "I wish I could say I regret it, but I don't."

"You do know that saying things like that make you seem far more like a suspect in his murder?" Beryl asked.

Roger shrugged. "I can't imagine why telling the truth would make me more likely to be suspected. I didn't like him, and to change my story now would make me seem even more suspicious. I despised him and am not ashamed to admit it," Roger said. "The fact remains he was a tedious and arrogant man, and the world is better off without him."

"I think that what you're stating is an opinion. And it seems as though your opinion was wholly unfavorable. Besides, I find it hard to believe you didn't feel at least slightly threatened by his intrusion into the Maitland Cigarettes art scene," Beryl said.

"Why should I? His involvement with the company was a

one-off situation and had nothing to do with me in the least," Roger said.

"You weren't at all concerned that Hubert was going to dismantle the in-house art studio and begin commissioning works from outside? Or that he might continue purchasing already completed works for licensing instead?" Beryl asked.

"That thought never crossed my mind. There are so many different collectible cigarette cards in demand every year that there is plenty of work for anyone interested in having it. I can't imagine how one man's limited run contract would in any way impact the need for an in-house studio," Roger said.

"Is it really that big of a business?" Beryl asked.

"Let's put it this way, cigarettes are the one thing I can never imagine lessening in popularity. It stands to reason that the cards in the packs will continue to be sought after, at least for my lifetime," Roger said.

"People might say the same thing about Prohibition, but look what's happened to America," Beryl said.

"I can't foresee a future where there are the same sorts of regulations on cigarettes. Or any regulations for that matter. After all, the government implored citizens to send packs to the troops during the war because they were so good at providing health and energy for our boys in the trenches," Roger said. "Besides, what happens in American culture has little to do with the rest of the world."

"Perhaps you're right, but that doesn't mean that there might not be a shifting in the cigarette card industry. Hubert seems to be all business, and he has indicated that he feels the cards with artwork from Louis will be all the more popular following his death. You don't think that might cause him to reconsider his overall business model?" Beryl asked.

"Well, I can tell you one thing, if Louis's death is going to make him all the more popular, it stands to reason that I wouldn't have been the one who killed him. Even if I didn't like him and saw him as competition, I wouldn't want to add any fuel to that fire, now would I?"

Roger flashed her one of his familiar disarming smiles, and Beryl had the feeling she still had no idea how he truly felt about any of it. With pleasure she sank her last ball and won the game.

Chapter 30

Upon returning to the house from her modeling session with Charles, Edwina felt a new respect for artists' models. She had never really given the ins and outs of the job any thought prior to giving a try to it herself. Being required to sit so perfectly still was a sore trial for her. She always thought of herself as quite a composed person, but much to her surprise she found that it had been extraordinarily difficult to remain entirely immobile. She had longed desperately for her knitting or even a seed catalog through which she might peruse.

Instead, she had to sit without even a twitch lest she provoke a criticizing and chastising word from Charles. Not only had she gained some insight into her own proclivity for fidgeting, she had been startled by the commanding presence Charles presented from behind his wooden easel. She had not thought of him in such a way ever before and found herself looking at him with new eyes.

Charles had seemed almost like an entirely new creature as he held a paintbrush in his hand and deftly swept it across his paper. He dipped and dabbed and swooped with such conviction she felt he was almost utterly transformed from the unflappable country solicitor into an artist of depthless passion. She was surprised to find that it made him rather more attractive. The somewhat mousy and always kind man of her long acquaintance seemed replaced by someone with a much bolder spirit.

Now and again he strode forward and made minor alterations to the way in which she sat or tilted her head. Edwina was startled and not entirely repelled by such small intimacies and wondered as she sat with nothing else to distract her if there was more to Charles than she had ever given him credit for.

It was with such thoughts on her mind that she almost tripped over Tuva Dahlberg when she entered the library on the east side of Maitland Park. She always found herself drawn towards libraries whenever she felt at all turbulent in her emotions. There was something so soothing about the notion that any question could be answered between the covers of a book. At least, that's what Edwina liked to tell herself whenever she needed comforting and there was little to be had. In the years of her mother's illness and those of war and loss, she had leaned even more heavily on that belief than ever before.

Perhaps she had more in common with Tuva Dahlberg than just the fact that the two of them had spent some time modeling for an artist. Tuva was curled up on the corner of a sofa, her feet tucked beneath her and a towering stack of books on the table beside her. Edwina could not see the title of the book Tuva was reading, as the spine was placed down in her lap, but she noticed that the other woman was halfway through it—always a good sign that the reading material was meeting with approval by the consumer.

Tuva looked up, and Edwina thought she detected the smallest flicker of displeasure from the other woman's face. Edwina could well understand that. She would have preferred to have the library entirely to herself as well if she could so choose. In fact, she had headed there with just such a thought in mind. But there was no reason not to choose a book or two and retreat to her room.

She could always close the connecting door between her space and that of Beryl's and could expect to have her desire for privacy be respected. Beryl would likely think that she was taking a nap or perhaps, Edwina thought with glee, she might imagine that Edwina was deep in the throes of dreaming up the next part of her adventure novel and should not be disturbed during a spate of creativity.

"You look as though you're enjoying yourself immensely," Edwina said, addressing Tuva. "Don't worry, I won't be here long if you wanted to have the library to yourself."

"You are not bothering me in the least. In fact, I was thinking about heading out in search of some company. As much as I enjoy reading, sometimes it does one good to engage with others and not only to pursue solitary endeavors," Tuva said.

"I know just what you mean. Sometimes I enjoy my own company a little more than is entirely good for me," Edwina said.

"Are you here looking for something to read?" Tuva asked. "Or were you just looking for a quiet place to get away from it all?"

"A little of both, I suppose. I've just been sitting for Charles Jarvis and I must say, the experience was an eye-opening one. You have my admiration for managing to do such a thing for a living," Edwina said.

"It's not quite what people will imagine it to be, is it?" Tuva said, giving Edwina a broad smile.

"It's remarkably strenuous work sitting still and doing absolutely nothing but holding a pose," Edwina said.

"It can be, especially if the artist with whom one is working happens to be of the temperamental sort," Tuva said.

Edwina wondered if Tuva was thinking of any artist in particular. Could Louis have been difficult to work with?

"You sound as though you speak from experience about artists," Edwina said.

"As a matter of fact I do. They are all quite different one from another, and it is important to know how to respond to each of them in a way that makes for a good working relationship," Tuva said.

"I found Charles to be quite changed from his ordinary behavior whilst he was painting," Edwina said. "He seemed bolder and more confident somehow."

Tuva placed her finger in her book as a marker and closed the cover, giving Edwina her full attention. She unfolded her legs from beneath her and placed them neatly on the ornate Oriental rug in front of her.

"Art has the ability to transform not only a blank canvas into something extraordinary but also to transform the heart of the artist. It sounds as though your friend Charles has found a new side to himself. Or maybe just that you have found a new side to him," Tuva said. "The relationship between an artist and the model can be one of tremendous intimacy."

Edwina considered what Tuva had said. She had felt the same way about an empty page rolled into the Remington portable typewriter in front of her. With every word she typed transforming the blank page into an imaginary world of story, she found herself opening to new possibilities, new ideas, and new adventures. No wonder Charles was appearing to be a new version of himself. As his art grew, perhaps that's exactly what was happening with him. Tuva's last statement rang in her ears as well. Was Tuva speaking about Edwina's relationship with Charles, or with her own and the artists for whom she had modeled? How much grief did she feel at the passing of Louis?

"I'm sure that must be quite true. After all, you must have spent countless hours with Louis with nothing to do but sit there and either be silent or to observe him as he worked. Either way, it's not the interaction one has with most other people, is it?" Edwina asked.

"No, it is not. Although, Louis was such a charismatic man that he made a strong impression upon all those he met," Tuva said.

"What will you do now that he has died?" Edwina asked. "Will you continue to offer your services as an artist's model, or do you have some other venture in mind?" Edwina asked.

Truly, she did wonder what would become of the younger woman. After all, from her accent it would be impossible not to notice she was a foreigner. Jobs were extremely difficult for anyone to come by, let alone a woman, and a foreign one at that. She wondered what other skills Tuva might possess that would even allow her to continue to fend for herself in an increasingly desperate world. It didn't bear thinking about and she hoped the best for her.

"I've been giving that a great deal of thought lately. Considering the economic circumstances both here and back home in Sweden, I believe I will accept Spencer Spaulding's offer to model for him."

"How fortunate for you that there was someone who already needed for a model right amongst your acquaintance," Edwina said. She wondered if the coincidence and fortune were too good to be true.

"It's really not that much of a surprise. After all, I modeled for Spencer before Louis managed to lure me away from him."

"I had no idea you had modeled for Spencer. The two of you have not given the impression that you had a prior acquaintance before arriving at Maitland Park," Edwina said.

"I suppose that's because Louis made a point of keeping the two of us apart and I doubt you saw me in Spencer's presence, at least unaccompanied, whilst you've been here," Tuva said.

Edwina thought back on the time she had been in Spencer's company and had to agree that she could not remember the two of them being together, at least not one-on-one.

"Why was Louis so interested in keeping the two of you

apart if he was the one who triumphed in the arrangement?" Edwina asked.

"I suppose it's because Spencer was constantly pestering me to return to him once more. He said that I was his muse and ever since I had left him his work had not been the same. He was quite desperate to have me back," Tuva said.

Edwina wondered how desperate Spencer might have become. After seeing the way that Charles behaved at the easel— mild-mannered Charles whom she had known for years upon years—she could well imagine that someone who came off as so much more impetuous than her dear friend might take matters into his own hands to the extreme when confronted by a loss of inspiration. Spencer looked more and more like a strong suspect in Louis's murder.

"And so you agreed to go back to work for him?" Edwina asked.

Tuva shrugged. "What else could I have done? I need a job and he's offering me one. Besides, I didn't leave him because he and I did not get on well. It's just that Louis had so much more to offer in terms of money and prestige. It was a career move, not a personal recrimination," Tuva said.

"Well, I'm delighted to hear that you've been able to land on your feet despite the setback," Edwina said.

"If there's one thing a dancer knows how to do it's how to land on her feet," Tuva said, getting to hers and giving Edwina a smile before heading out the door of the library.

Chapter 31

Beryl considered Edwina's news that Tuva Dahlberg was returning to model for Spencer Spaulding with a great deal of interest. She could well imagine, from her previous experience with artists, that Spencer would not have taken the loss of his model lightly. It cast an entirely new angle on the investigation, and one she was interested in pursuing immediately.

She also had to wonder about Spencer appearing at the artists' colony if such an invitation would have undoubtably angered Louis. Edwina's insight into the management of guest lists seemed at odds with his inclusion in the artists' colony. She determined to track him down to ask how he came to be there.

Just as it had been easy to find Roger in the billiards room, she was in no way surprised to find Spencer in the smoking room. While she did not have any interest in cigarettes herself, she had been in many smoking rooms over the course of her lifetime. Generally, at least in her youth, tobacco products of all sorts had been the purview of men. But now, young women with bobbed hair and long cigarette holders could easily be found sharing the space with them.

Although Beryl was always glad to see barriers to women's presence and opportunities being removed, she was pleased to find Spencer on his own in the smoking room, leaning back in a comfortable overstuffed chair with a pipe clutched between his teeth and a ring of smoke floating above his head.

Beryl sauntered into the room and stretched out on a sofa nearby as if she intended to stay for a while. He squinted at her as though he were assessing her as the possible subject for one of his paintings. Beryl could imagine him blocking her out on a canvas, creating a series of abstract shapes to represent the contours of her form. She wasn't sure whether or not she approved of his style of painting, but she wasn't about to mention that fact to him, especially if she wanted to pry any information from him.

"May I offer to light a cigarette for you, Miss Helliwell?" he said, looking around as though in search of a lighter.

"Thank you, but I never smoke. Actually, I came in looking for you," Beryl said.

"Really? Why, I am flattered. It's not every day that such an attractive woman hunts me down for a tête-à-tête," Spencer said. He took another puff on his pipe and released another perfectly shaped smoke ring.

"Then today must be your lucky day. I hear that not only are you favored by my attention, but you have received some good news," Beryl said.

"Really? Which news is that?" Spencer said.

"My friend Edwina told me she just heard from Tuva that she has agreed to model for you once more now that Louis no longer has need of her services," Beryl said. "Apparently she is very eager to work closely with you once more."

Beryl observed him closely for his reaction to her words. He had not bothered to change for dinner and had instead remained in his paint-covered smock and grubby trousers. His shoes were in desperate need of polishing and in point of fact she would not have said it would be out of order for him to shampoo his hair.

A wide smile broke out across his face. The mention of Tuva seemed to warm his heart.

"It was only a matter of time before Tuva agreed to return to me. What she ever saw in Louis, I'll never understand," he said.

"Perhaps she was swayed by Louis's money and prestige. Even artists' models need to eat, don't they?" Beryl said.

Spencer bit down on his pipe and took a strong pull before answering. "There's more to the life of a true artist than money and prestige. Surely you know a thing like that. After all, you wouldn't have gone on the adventures for which you are famous with those things in mind, would you?" he asked.

"Certainly not. The money and prestige just followed the pursuit. They were in no way a motivating factor."

Beryl spoke the truth. She had never anticipated that following her dreams would lead to so much interest by the general public. She had simply been determined to set out to do those things that interested her and to do them with zeal. When it had turned out that there were newspaper reporters, photographers, and film directors who were interested in documenting her exploits, she had been as surprised as anyone, perhaps more so. She could well understand how an artist would not be motivated by such things. But could the same be said for a model like Tuva?

"But Tuva is not an artist, is she?" Beryl asked.

"Not a visual artist, no, but she was a performing one. An artist is an artist is an artist, and in the end, she understood the value of what we were trying to develop together," Spencer said. "That's why she could no longer resist my pleas."

"So Louis's death has nothing to do with her decision to return to modeling for you?" Beryl said.

"I suppose if one were a skeptic, one could assume that her decision to say yes coincided with her sudden need for a new employer. Nevertheless, I prefer to think that she had already known the direction she wished to head before such a thing had happened. I think it was fate intervening to bring her back to me, where she belonged," Spencer said.

"You think fate murdered your rival for Tuva's loyalty?" Beryl asked. "I have not ever found it to be so accommodating, myself."

"Why should I not believe it? Fate has guided me to where I should be as an artist over and over again," Spencer said. "Even the disruptions that happened on account of the war have made it possible for me to grow in my abilities as an artist."

While it seemed cavalier to say so, Beryl could understand his point. The world had changed fundamentally since the war had broken out and why changes should occur everywhere but in the artistic realms, she could not possibly say. She did not generally think of artists as benefiting from violence, but she was willing to consider that she might be entirely ignorant of such matters.

"Fate seems to have had a hand in you arriving here at Maitland Park at just the right time, then," Beryl said.

"Yes, I was very fortunate in my invitation here for the artists' colony. Although, perhaps it wasn't just fate after all," Spencer said.

"I understood that Constance was the one who invited you," Beryl said.

"Well, perhaps to say she was convinced to invite me is a more accurate statement. That said, it didn't take much effort on my part to wrangle an invitation. After all, Constance is rather easily charmed," Spencer said. "I find that all unmarried women past a certain age are susceptible to a bit of attention from members of the opposite sex," Spencer said with a knowing wink.

Beryl had not been remotely charmed by the unkempt artist she saw before her and she had not formed the impression that

Constance Maitland was a woman who would be easily flattered under any circumstances. She thought of her as eminently sensible and someone who likely was unmarried despite multiple offers to the contrary. Surely, she was not one to allow clumsy compliments and crumbs of attention to influence her opinions. Still, she needed to know how he had managed to be included.

"How did you succeed in convincing her?" Beryl asked. She tried to keep any recrimination from her voice.

"I made a point to bump into her in Walmsley Parva just before the artists' colony began. I may have implied that Ursula had told me about the event and that I could think of nothing more delightful than spending time with a lady of as much quality as Constance clearly was. I'm sure I laid it on a bit thick when mentioning how much I would enjoy having the opportunity to paint her," Spencer said. "I find that most women fall for that quite easily."

"How lucky for you. Why was it that you were so eager to be included at the colony?" Beryl asked. Was it because he had wanted to put himself in a position to murder Louis?

"I wanted to be near Tuva once more, of course. I just knew that if I could have the chance to speak with her, I would be able to convince her that her true place was with me," he said.

"That was your only reason for wishing to be here at Maitland Park?" Beryl asked. "There was nothing else that drove you to seek an invitation?"

Spencer lowered his pipe and examined the bowl before answering. Beryl couldn't help but wonder if he were concocting a story.

"Why else would I want to be here? It cannot be disputed that the grounds are lovely, and the food is passably edible, but it's not as though most of the company has left me feeling inspired. Luring Tuva back from Louis was the one and only reason I could have possibly wanted to be here."

"So, you didn't come with the intention of harming Louis? For getting your rival out of the way and leaving Tuva with no options other than to return to you as a model?" Beryl asked. "That would have been a far more reliable strategy than hoping to convince her to leave him through some heartfelt appeal, wouldn't it?"

Spencer pulled his pipe from his mouth. "My dear lady, if I had wanted to kill Louis I would have done so in the open and in the presence of witnesses. If I had been so inclined, nothing would have delighted me more than to make rather a large show of it." With that, he stood and strode out the door.

Chapter 32

Constance waylaid Edwina in the main hallway. She was too well bred to overtly betray any signs of worry, but Edwina noticed a deep furrow had appeared between her hostess's brows. Edwina hoped they were not going to have to speak about Constable Gibbs again. She was not sure that she would be able to dissuade a woman as self-possessed and determined as Constance from confronting the police officer.

"I wanted to ask how you and Beryl were getting on with the investigation? The servants are rumbling again about how long the constable has been on the property and how shameful it looks for the occupants of Maitland Park for this to be an ongoing situation," Constance said.

"I cannot say that we have discovered who it is that is responsible for Louis's murder, but I can say that we are zeroing in on a strong suspect," Edwina said.

"And do you feel that you can tell me who that is?" Constance said. "After all, you are not the police, but rather an employee of mine." Constance had allowed a shrill note to creep into her voice, and Edwina could well understand how difficult a position her client found herself in.

It was hard not to take just the slightest bit of offense, however, at being reminded of their relative positions. It was just the sort of situation that her mother would have chided her about should she have been alive. Edwina's mother would have found private enquiry agents to be quite a grubby sort of person and would have told Edwina that she was getting just exactly what she deserved by placing herself in the position of such a lowly form of human being. Edwina pushed the sound of her mother's voice to the back of her mind and instead stood up a little straighter.

"You certainly deserve to be kept informed and have every right to desire expediency in this matter. However, I would not wish for any theories on our part to taint the ability to gather facts from witnesses and those who knew the suspects well," Edwina said.

"I hope I am above shading the facts to suit my preferences. While I would be distraught for any member of the family or staff to be the one responsible for what happened to a guest here at Maitland Park, I hope that I could be relied upon to do the right thing under any circumstance," Constance said.

"I in no way meant to imply that you would purposefully bend the facts to suit your own preferences. But rather am concerned about the reality that any theory can cause distortion of memory and an influence on opinion. Having said that, I can take you into my confidence if that is your wish," Edwina said.

"It most certainly is. After all, I rarely concern myself with the opinions of others," Constance said.

Edwina thought that that was unlikely to be the case. If she had been so separated from concern about others' opinions, she would not have hired Beryl and Edwina in the first place. She certainly would not have bent to the demands of her own cook as regarded the reputation of the estate in the greater society. No, the only opinion Constance was not influenced by seemed to be her own. However, Edwina did not think it would be a savvy business move to point out such a thing to her client.

"Beryl and I have been taking a very close look at Spencer Spaulding. He seems to have had more than one very good reason for wanting Louis out of the way," Edwina said.

"Spencer Spaulding, how extraordinary," Constance said. "Yes, he'll do very nicely."

Edwina didn't much like the sound of that. She had not thought that she was looking for someone who would meet Constance's approval as to who made an acceptable murder suspect in the eyes of the family.

"While I'm sure that you are glad that our suspicions are not leading to a member of your household, do you have a reason in particular that you would not be displeased if it worked to turn out that Spencer was the one responsible for Louis's murder?" Edwina asked.

"I suppose that it would be a bit of getting my own back, you see. To tell the truth, Spencer Spaulding was a bit of a nuisance when he first arrived, and I have to confess he put me in a very awkward position," Constance said.

"How did he do that?" Edwina asked.

"It turns out that he was never actually invited to attend the artists' colony at all," Constance said. "It was really most awkward. He simply appeared with his art paraphernalia and a rather battered-looking valise that I can only assume held what accounts for his wardrobe. The only good thing that came of it was the fact that I was able to reinforce with young Janet Brown why earning one's hostessing badge is of value as an adult."

"You mean to say that you did not actually invite him to Maitland Park?" Edwina asked. A tingle of excitement ran up her spine and lodged itself right below where her bobbed hair swished across the back of her neck.

"I certainly did not. I'd never heard of the man before he arrived on my doorstep, but he seemed to know all about Ursula and myself and the artists' colony. It was only after speaking with Ursula later that I came to realize that she had not invited him, either. But by then it was unfortunately too late to be rid of him," Constance said.

"So you simply allowed him to join the artists' colony despite his deception?" Edwina said.

"What else was one to do? I thought that Ursula simply had not provided me with a complete guest list, or that she had added him as an afterthought and had completely forgotten about it. I had to scramble and inconvenience the butler, Dillings, in order to have a room prepared for him. It's a good thing the staff here are so excellent at keeping everything at the ready for whatever contingency might occur."

"So, you asked Ursula if she had invited him and she denied it?" Edwina asked.

"I was put out enough about the whole incident that I taxed her with it at the next opportunity I had to do so in private. One doesn't air one's private family grievances in front of guests or the servants, and so it took some time before I found myself alone with her," Constance said.

"And she confirmed that she had not invited him?" Edwina asked.

"Yes, she said she'd never thought to do so. In fact, Ursula said she had only ever met him briefly at a gallery opening one or two years prior. She claimed she had absolutely no reason to include him and seemed as baffled about the whole thing as I was," Constance said. "It came to light that she thought that I had invited him."

"And you believed her to be telling you the truth?" Edwina asked.

"Well, of course I did. Why would Ursula have any reason to lie about the matter? Certainly, I had been inconvenienced and placed in an awkward position, but Ursula would not be prompted to lie to me over something so trivial. We don't have that sort of relationship," Constance said.

Edwina wondered if the relationship between the two women was as idyllic as they both claimed. Edwina could well imagine how Constance might feel constantly on edge as to whether or not Ursula might wish to assert her rights as the lady of the household, thus depriving the older, more established woman of her power within the home. And Ursula might feel sidelined and devalued by being relegated to a secondary sort of a role in her own home.

Could it really be that these two women were as mature as they both claimed to be concerning the situation? Did they really play to each of their strengths and admire the other woman for hers in turn? Edwina thought it an unusual situation but acknowledged that it could be the actual truth. After all, she and Beryl generally found it easy to get along with one another despite the fact that they had such very different views on the world and the tactics they preferred to employ in navigating it.

"Was Ursula able to hazard a guess as to why she thought that Spencer would have arrived without an invitation? It seems a very bold sort of a thing to do without a very pressing reason," Edwina said.

"She said something about some scuttlebutt concerning a school of art that Spencer had wanted to establish, one which Louis had derided. She wondered if maybe Spencer was trying to garner support for his position amongst the artists he had somehow heard would be gathered here," Constance said.

"Nothing you are telling me casts Spencer in a less suspicious light concerning the murder," Edwina said. "In fact, the fact that he arrived without an invitation only strengthens the case against him."

"I couldn't agree more. I suggest you inform the constable at once that you have solved the case. I would very much like to announce to Mrs. Morton that she has no reason to leave Maitland Park," Constance said.

With that, Constance inclined her head towards the end of the hallway that led towards the buttery. Edwina could only suppose it was a hint that she should hurry off to do exactly as instructed. As she strode past her client, two thoughts clamored in her mind. The first was that she was no longer sure she wished for Constance to recommend the services of Davenport and Helliwell to her social set. She had no desire to be treated like an undervalued employee.

The second was that Constance had been far more concerned with laying blame on someone who was not connected to the family than she was in arriving at the truth of the matter. Was that because she was so worried about the efficient running of her household, no matter the cost? Or was it because she had something to hide or someone in her family to protect?

Chapter 33

If Beryl had felt uncomfortable with the idea of providing the Girl Guides with a demonstration on the topic of fire starting under difficult conditions, it was nothing compared to the way she felt that morning as she headed towards the campsite. Although she did not say anything to Edwina on the subject, Beryl felt a bit of a prick every time the subject of her inability to cook was mentioned. Before arriving in Walmsley Parva, Beryl had given very little attention to her meals. She knew that she did not have a wide range of recipes in her head or techniques that were more orthodox in nature when it came to which sorts of pans to use and which temperature to set an oven.

All that said, she had managed to keep body and soul together often equipped with nothing more than a can opener, a dependable knife, and a pointed stick. She rather thought she ought to have been offered more credit for her ingenuity and persistence than she had been. Certainly, the things that she prepared were ad hoc and unusual, but that did not necessarily mean that they were the sign of a terrible cook. In fact, she had thought of herself as an innovator. It wasn't until she had seen the looks of horror pass across both Edwina's and, to an even more distressing extent, Simpkins's face that she was aware that her approach to nourishment was not universally enjoyed.

On the few occasions she had decided to marry, she had chosen to enter such a state with men whose standards of living would involve households run by plenty of domestic servants, chiefly an excellent cook. Her mother had insisted upon the same, and Beryl had had no formal training of any sort in the culinary arts. As she headed off to teach a group of eager Girl Guides the craft of campfire cooking, she felt thoroughly uneasy. She had felt less trepidation when once facing down an angry rhinoceros at a watering hole where she had been filling her canteen than she did at the prospect of the obligation in front of her.

Still, she reminded herself, Constance had asked her to be an expert and an expert she would be. She gave herself a little shake and squared her shoulders. A lack of courage had never been one of her faults. As she walked along the well-worn path towards the campsite, she forced herself to move forward with purpose. Rarely did she allow the clamor of dissenting and critical voices of others to fill her thoughts. A fine summer morning in a beautiful wood should not be sullied by any deviation from her normal behavior. The scent of pine needles rose up and filled her nostrils as she crushed them underfoot. Over her head she heard the call of a crow, and then another flitted onto a branch beside it and the two of them peered off intently.

Beryl wondered if her thoughts were turning morbid or even ghoulish as she realized that the crows were facing the general area where Louis's body had been found. Surely there was nothing still there for them to find of interest. While Constable Gibbs might be in over her head with the investigation, she certainly knew how to remove a dead body from a crime scene. There would have been nothing left of Louis for the crows to observe.

As she moved farther along the path, a third crow joined the pair and the calls above her head became raucous. Certainly, the Girl Guides would be willing to wait for an extra moment or two for her to satisfy her curiosity. After all, if she was the expert speaker, there was not much they could do until she arrived. She told herself that she was not simply dragging her feet as a way to delay the inevitable discomfort of interaction with the Girl Guides but rather from the higher calling as a private enquiry agent.

She took the left branching fork in the path that headed towards the clearing in the wood. It was a shame that such a violent act had occurred in so peaceful a setting. She understood intuitively why Louis would have chosen it as a place to paint. There was something so inviting about the open glade appearing unexpectedly amongst the dense trees.

She passed the bush where she had found the knotted rope she believed had been used to murder Louis, and a feeling of coldness crept into the pit of her stomach. There was something particularly creepy about the juxtaposition of the tranquil wood and what she knew had happened to Louis. She suddenly wished she had company other than the trio of crows on the path as she came to the edge of the glade.

There on the ground in the center of the grass lay Cressida. Her arms were crossed over her chest as she lay on her back. Her eyes bulged grotesquely from her head as she stared skyward, lifelessly. Beryl's breath caught in her throat. She looked back over her shoulder but saw no one other than the crows perched on a branch above, watching her every move.

She slowly made her way towards Cressida, taking pains not to disturb the ground around her. She bent and placed her fingers on Cressida's neck, feeling a strong sense of déjà vu as she did so. Once again, as had been the case with Louis, there was no pulse to be felt. And once again, there were signs of strangulation. Beryl gently moved Cressida's Girl Guide neckerchief to the side and noticed a livid bruise below it. Someone had strangled the woman with a piece of her own uniform.

But unlike Louis's, Cressida's body was still disconcertingly warm to the touch. Beryl did her best not to cry out as she realized how little time must have passed since a murderer had left her there, abandoned and lifeless on the ground. Beryl forced herself to take a few deep breaths and to observe the scene around her. Once the official enquiry got under way there would be any number of people trampling the glade. There was not much to see that appeared out of order.

In fact, the only thing visible at a glance was the disturbance in the grass near Cressida's feet and the bits of earth clinging to the heels of her shoes. It was plain to see that Cressida had struggled. She must have put up a tremendous fight as someone stood behind her squeezing the life from her body. The Girl Guides would have to wait. Beryl ran from the glade back towards the house without a look behind her.

Chapter 34

Constable Gibbs appeared anything but pleased at the sudden turn of events in the investigation. Things had been difficult enough with only one murder to solve at Maitland Park. Two murders seemed impossible to resolve as quickly as was necessary. The way she scowled down at Cressida's lifeless body appeared as though she felt it was a personal affront that someone had murdered her as well.

Edwina thought it likely that that was just how Constable Gibbs felt about the matter. After all, her personal life and her position within her brass band were being threatened by any delay to the investigation. Not only that, she had been following a line of enquiry that put Cressida as her primary suspect in the first murder. Her turning up dead herself changed things considerably.

"You don't suppose there are two murderers on the loose here at Maitland Park, do you?" Constable Gibbs asked as she leaned over the body.

"Anything is possible, I suppose, but I would point out that both victims were strangled in a similar manner," Beryl said, pointing to Cressida's neck.

Edwina felt herself involuntarily shudder. There was just something so grotesque about the wholesome and ordinary Girl Guides uniform being turned to such a horrific purpose that made the entire situation all the more disturbing. Edwina thought she would never be able to look at a Girl Guide in uniform the same way again.

"My money had been on Cressida as the perpetrator in Louis Langdon Beck's murder," Constable Gibbs said. She let out a deep sigh as she straightened up and motioned for the ambulance crew to remove the body. "I feel like I'm back to square one." She gave Edwina a morose look, and her shoulders slumped uncharacteristically.

As disturbing as it was to see Cressida's body being lifted onto the canvas stretcher, it was somehow even worse to see all of the fight going out of Constable Gibbs. It was a sight that Edwina had never expected to witness. All through the war years when things had been so grim, when influenza had swept through the village and supplies of all sorts were difficult to come by, Constable Gibbs had provided a kind of normalcy and stability within Walmsley Parva. Edwina felt a tug at her heart and a surprising urge to bolster the police officer's spirits.

"We've had considerable reason to believe that another guest here at Maitland Park is a far stronger suspect," Edwina said, hoping her words would encourage the constable.

"And who might that be?" Constable Gibbs said.

Edwina was pleased to see the constable perk up ever so slightly as she clutched at the possibility that the case might be on its way to a conclusion.

"Spencer Spaulding is our chief suspect," Beryl said.

"The shabbily dressed fellow who shambles about?" Constable Gibbs asked, reaching for a notebook and pulling it from her pocket.

Edwina felt she had been providing the constable with a good influence, as she noticed her fellow investigator thumbing through carefully written notes.

"That would describe him to a T," Beryl said. "There is considerable speculation against him."

"Like what?" Constable Gibbs asked.

"He has more than one very strong motive," Edwina said.

"So did a lot of people, including this victim," Constable Gibbs said, pointing her notebook at Cressida's body. "There hasn't been any shortage of motives."

"Well, for one, Louis Langdon Beck set about discrediting Spencer in the art community. He made a determined effort of it and did so very publicly," Beryl said.

"Well, that certainly seems like something to take note of," Constable Gibbs said, writing in her notebook. "But you said there were a couple of motives."

"It turns out that before she became a model for Louis, Tuva Dahlberg modeled for Spencer. Apparently, Louis lured her away from Spencer with the promises of more money and greater chances of fame as his model," Edwina said.

"As interesting as that is, why would it have come to a head now?" Constable Gibbs asked.

"We aren't sure what would have driven him to take action now instead of previously, but we did discover something else that seemed quite suspicious," Beryl said.

"I'm listening," Constable Gibbs said.

Edwina thought it was quite a pleasant turn of events that Constable Gibbs was encouraging them to participate in the investigation and actually soliciting their opinion rather than doing her best to brush them off and shut them out. As disconcerting as the experience was, Edwina found it rather agreeable.

"It seems that he arrived without any sort of an invitation. He lied to us and said that Constance had invited him, but Constance said that he bluffed his way into the artists' colony by implying that Ursula had included him," Edwina said.

"And Ursula did not do so?" Constable Gibbs asked.

"No, she did not. At least not according to Constance, who

confronted her about forgetting to let her know to expect him. After all, Constance is in charge of the guest lists and all of the arrangements for any people arriving at Maitland Park," Beryl said.

"That does seem suspicious. But I can't see how he had any problem with this latest victim. Can you?" Constable Gibbs said.

The three of them watched as the stretcher bearers headed off along the path through the woods towards the awaiting ambulance parked in the drive in front of the house.

"We had no reason to investigate that question. After all, Beryl just found Cressida's body," Edwina said.

"So I suppose that's what's next on the agenda then, is it?" Constable Gibbs said. Beryl and Edwina exchanged a glance.

"That's who we would speak to if we were leading the investigation," Edwina said.

"Then I suppose that's just what I'll do. If you'll excuse me, I'm going to go track him down," Constable Gibbs said. She snapped her notebook shut, stuffed it back into her pocket, and with a bob of her head to each of them, she hurried after the stretcher bearers.

"What do you think? Do you really believe that Spencer Spaulding might have had something to do with Cressida's death, too?" Edwina asked.

"If he did, we'd best get to the bottom of it before anyone else is killed. I have to tell you it gave me quite a turn to come across Cressida's body here today. I really don't want to discover another one," Beryl said.

Chapter 35

Lunch was a somber affair. Spencer did not appear in the dining room, nor did Constance. Edwina did not know if Constance's absence could be attributed to grief or a sudden excess of work associated with the Girl Guides. Edwina could well imagine Constance's feelings concerning her distant cousin despite the fact that she caused some worry and discomfort. Edwina had had a similar relationship with her own mother. Edwina's mother had been a resolute hypochondriac and spent most of her days demanding to be catered to on account of her ill health.

Edwina was intimately acquainted with the energy it took to cajole and soothe a somewhat unbalanced individual. However, she had come to miss her mother and her persnickety and flustered company in the weeks and months that followed her sudden death. She could well imagine that Constance might feel the same. While Cressida without question seemed to be a troublesome individual, there was no denying that she was an integral part of Constance's life and the lives of others at Maitland Park and would likely be missed.

When she came to think of it, Edwina thought it possible

that Constance was holed up with the cook, once more trying to convince her to remain at Maitland Park. The girl who had waited the table during lunch was visibly shaken. She dropped a cold slice of ham into Roger Hazeldine's lap by accident while waiting upon him, and Edwina could not help but notice that her eyes were rimmed with red as though she had been sobbing. Whether or not her tears had been for Cressida or fear for her own safety, Edwina could not guess.

It was with some relief that she accepted Charles's invitation to join him for some fresh air after lunch. The oppressive atmosphere in the dining room at lunch had been interesting to observe as an investigator but treacherous and tedious as a house guest. He took her companionably by the arm and purposely strode off in the direction of the rose garden. While the season for the best flush of roses was well past, Edwina found she admired the tidy management of the beds. Charles led her to a bench at the far side of the formal parterre and they settled beneath a bower of climbing white roses whose fragrance cascaded down over them generously.

"How are you holding up?" Charles asked her.

"It's rather an unnerving thing, isn't it, to be staying at a place where two murders have occurred?" Edwina said.

"Yes, it is. The other investigations in which you have participated have been far enough from the Beeches so you could feel more at ease. I've almost regretted coming," Charles said.

"You mustn't say that. You've taken such pleasure in increasing your skills. I've been very impressed by all that you've accomplished," Edwina said.

She noted a flush rising on Charles's pale cheeks, but she did not regret discomfiting him. He deserved to be praised for his efforts even if it made him feel slightly uncomfortable to be on the receiving end of her compliment. He reached into his vest pocket and pulled out a pocket sketchbook. He thumbed through the pages and then held it out to her.

"Are these the ones you were doing of me last night in the Japanese garden?" Edwina said.

She was surprised to see that Charles had portrayed her as a far more relaxed and youthful-looking woman than she thought herself to be. Her hair swished coquettishly around her chin, and her hat was perched upon her head at a rakish angle at which she did not remember adjusting it. He had placed a joyous smile upon her face and had surrounded her with luxuriant leaves and rugged boulders. She looked almost like a flower herself nestled amongst them.

"Yes, they are. I thought you might enjoy seeing the fruits of your own labor. I know it wasn't easy for you to sit so still as you did while posing. I'm sure you would have much preferred to have your knitting to use up some of your abundant energy," Charles said, giving her a knowing smile. "Still, I think there is a good likeness even if I do flatter myself in saying so."

"I think you've been a bit generous in your rendering of me," Edwina said.

She flipped from one sketch to the next, wondering what Charles saw in her that she never saw reflected in her mirror at home.

"Not at all. You appear just as I always see you, Edwina," Charles said.

Feeling discomfited by compliments herself, Edwina busied herself in looking through more of the sketchbook. She flipped backwards and saw a sketch of Tuva. The details he had rendered were surprising and exquisite. Edwina always thought of Charles as a watercolorist and had not realized the degree to which his artistic ability and skills had extended to pencil sketches.

"This is really remarkable," she said, pointing to the sketch of Tuva. "I didn't know that you were interested in line drawings."

"There are many things I'm interested in that you have per-

haps not realized," Charles said. "But I would say that drawings like this are a far more recent pursuit than my passion for
watercolors. Spencer encouraged me to try my hand at them
more frequently. He suggested it would increase my confidence
in all aspects of my artistic pursuits and perhaps even my life."

Edwina scrutinized the drawing more carefully. She did not
wish for Charles to be hurt should Spencer Spaulding turn out
to be a murderer. Of course, she could not shield him from the
truth should that come out, but she felt no need to spoil the
pleasant atmosphere by mentioning it before it was necessary.
Instead she chose to admire the intricacy of his sketch.

"You've captured her perfectly, even down to the details of
things like the buttons on her dressing gown. What an eye for
detail you have, Charles," Edwina said. "Perhaps you should
be the one who's working as a private enquiry agent."

"I've always found the details of things to be fascinating. For
me, watercolor is about color and saturation. But with sketching and ink drawings it's more about the lines. I find that by focusing on small details I can really practice my control of the
pencil or the pen."

"I would say that you are coming along really nicely with all
of it and no matter what happens with the investigation I hope
that you will only take good memories of your time here at
Maitland Park with you when you return home," Edwina said,
thinking of Spencer once again.

She spared a thought to how Constable Gibbs might be getting on with her interrogation of the suspect. It might be wise
to head back to the house in order to check in on her. She
handed the sketchbook back to Charles, who replaced it in his
vest.

"I'm sure that it will be just as you suggest. After all, at the
very least, I'll have a painting of you completed when we are all
done, won't I?" he said with a smile.

Chapter 36

One thing was abundantly clear from the outset. Constable Gibbs was more than convinced she had her man. Beryl took one look at Spencer Spaulding, pressed, quite literally, into a corner of the makeshift interrogation room in the Maitland Park buttery, and almost felt sorry for him. Sweat trickled down the side of his beaky nose and he swiped at it with a paint-splattered handkerchief every time Constable Gibbs leaned over the table and jabbed an accusing finger in his face. Edwina sat in a rickety chair next to Beryl, her notebook opened in her lap and her tiny pencil poised intimidatingly above it.

"I must advise you that things look very grim for you, Mr. Spaulding. Very grim indeed," Constable Gibbs said.

"I cannot imagine why that should be. I have done nothing wrong," he said.

Edwina made a quiet tut-tutting noise that Beryl hoped would encourage the artist to come clean. Although, given his lack of attention to his appearance, coming clean was perhaps the wrong choice in words. If anything, he was more disheveled and unkempt than ever and given the close quarters in which they gathered, Beryl thought Spencer could easily do with a bit of a wash. She was used to spending time with people without easy access to the niceties of indoor plumbing, but while she was no snob about such matters, she did prefer to congregate with them out-of-doors.

"I have it on good authority that you not only had two very good reasons to want Louis Langdon Beck out of the way, you also managed to connive entrance into Maitland Park without an invitation at just the same time he planned to be here. You have lied to me and to my colleagues and unless you have a plausible explanation for your presence here, I am going to arrest you for two counts of murder," Constable Gibbs said.

Beryl felt a small thrill pass through her when she heard the constable refer to Edwina and herself as colleagues. She was so surprised by it that she was momentarily distracted from the interview. She must be getting soft, she thought. She rarely let emotions divert her attention from a mission.

"Two counts of murder? You don't mean to say you think I had something to do with what happened to Cressida, do you?" he asked.

"I see no reason to credit the notion that there are two separate murderers running around here at Maitland Park. Even one such criminal beggar's belief," Constable Gibbs said, turning to the other women, who nodded in agreement. Beryl took it as an invitation to chime in.

"It makes sense to me that you would have killed Cressida if she discovered that you were not actually invited to Maitland Park. She was the sort to make accusations, and I can imagine her confronting you with her suspicions," Beryl said.

"And then you strangled her with her own neckerchief," Constable Gibbs said.

Spencer blanched, glanced at the ceiling as if for inspiration, and then cleared his throat.

"I can take your point if I were truly at Maitland Park without an invitation, but the fact of the matter is that I was here with permission," he said.

"From whom?" Edwina asked, using her starchiest voice, the one she usually reserved for errant children and gossipy housemaids.

"Hubert Maitland himself," he said.

Constable Gibbs looked at Edwina as if to confirm that such a thing was unlikely. She arched an eyebrow and Edwina continued the questioning. She flipped back through her notebook and ran her finger along a page filled with her spiky handwriting, pausing for effect.

"Yes, there it is. I wrote down that Hubert Maitland remarked that he had nothing whatsoever to do with guest lists at Maitland Park in general and the artists' colony in particular. Your story does not concur with his," Edwina said.

"I am telling the truth," he said. "Hubert Maitland asked me himself and told me not to let anyone know that he was the one who did so," he said. Another trickle of perspiration raced along the side of Spencer's nose.

"Why would Hubert have any reason to do a thing like that?" Constable Gibbs asked. "It sounds to me like you are just grasping at straws."

Spencer's worried gaze darted from one woman's face to another. He shook his head violently back and forth.

"He wanted our connection to remain a secret. I was here in a professional capacity and one that neither of us wished to have discovered," he said.

"I think you would be best served by telling us about it no matter what Hubert wanted. You don't want to hang for another man's wishes, do you?" Edwina asked.

Spencer shook his head again and his paint-stained hand crept towards his throat.

"Hubert hired me to make copies of the valuable paintings in his collection," he said. "He didn't want anyone in his family to know about it."

"Why would he do that?" Constable Gibbs asked.

"He wanted to sell the originals and pocket the money without anyone being the wiser," he said.

"Are you capable of such a thing?" Edwina asked.

Spencer must have heard the tone of incredulity in her voice because his posture straightened, and he looked as though he were on the offensive for the first time since entering the room.

"I know my reputation, at least here at the colony, is in tatters. But while I presently prefer a more interpretive style of abstract painting, I am actually an accomplished traditional painter as well. I am more than able to turn out a first-rate copy of anything in the Maitland collection," he said.

"How did Hubert know this about you?" Beryl asked.

"He was given my name by someone else I had provided with the same service not too long ago. It is not an uncommon practice amongst the upper classes in these troubled financial times," he said.

"Who was this other person?" Constable Gibbs asked.

"I'd rather not say. While Hubert assured me that he planned to sell the original paintings and pass the copies off as the valuable ones in his own home, I am not certain that was the case with my other clients," Spencer said.

"So, you are admitting to forgery?" Constable Gibbs said.

"I am admitting to having been invited to paint the Maitland collection by Hubert Maitland himself. I cannot see how any probing into my prior artistic endeavors would serve your current investigation," Spencer said.

"As an officer of the law it is my duty to look into cases of wrongdoing," Constable Gibbs said, her voice becoming more strident with each word she spoke.

"I assure you that the sorts of people who hire me think themselves quite above the law," he said. "They would make your life miserable if you tried to look into this matter, I can tell you."

With those final words, he stormed out of the buttery.

Edwina cleared her throat and looked pointedly at the constable. "I believe expedience in your primary investigation is more important than any other concern. I am sure you could follow up at a later date with any other matter if you still see fit," she said.

"Murder does take precedence over any other crime, doesn't it?" Beryl asked. Constable Gibbs pursed her lips before nodding in agreement.

"I suppose the thing to do now would be to confirm or discredit this version of events by questioning Hubert Maitland," Edwina said. She looked over at Beryl, who realized that was not a task for Constable Gibbs, at least not if she wanted to keep her job.

"Do you think Spencer poses a flight risk?" Beryl asked the policewoman. "After all, he has practically admitted to being a career criminal. If I were him, I would try to sneak off as soon as possible."

"I have no intention of leaving him unsupervised until Hubert makes a statement," Constable Gibbs said.

"Then perhaps it would be most expedient if Beryl and I were to question Hubert while you keep an eye on Spencer. We could report back to you very shortly and hopefully rule your suspect in or out," Edwina said.

Beryl thought she saw a look of relief pass over Constable Gibbs's face as she waved them off.

Chapter 37

Hubert Maitland had retreated to his study. Edwina would have recognized it as a gentleman's retreat even if her eyes had been closed. The walnut-paneled, heavily draped room was drenched in the scent of cigarette smoke. She wrinkled her nose at the staleness of it and wondered how Hubert had managed to keep the women in his life from giving the place a good airing out. Her estimation of the vigilance of the Maitland Park staff took a bit of a beating as she considered the layer of dust that settled on every available surface. It seemed that this was the one place the master of Maitland Park truly held sway over all the details.

Beryl seemed to see none of these things as she accepted an offered seat and leaned back in an appallingly shabby wingback chair across from Hubert, who settled himself behind his cluttered mahogany desk. It was the sort of piece of furniture so prized during the Victorian era, and Edwina thought of a similar object back home at the Beeches. Her father had had a private room of his own, she thought for likely similar reasons. No one had been allowed to touch a thing in his office without his express permission, which was something he made a point never to give.

Even after his death Edwina's mother had found it difficult to consider sorting that room out and had left the job to Edwina. Although, truth be told, Edwina's mother had left all unpleasant tasks to Edwina as soon as she was old enough for such a thing to have taken place. She felt rather a kinship with Constance on such matters.

Beryl delivered a pointed look at her as she perched gently on the edge of a wingback chair of her own. They had agreed she would be the one to broach the delicate subject of underhanded dealings with Hubert. Edwina had a way of dealing with self-important individuals that Beryl seemed to be lacking. It was one of the best things about their partnership. Each of them brought strengths and weaknesses, and they valued and recognized them in each other.

Edwina, as competent as she was at asking probing questions without giving offense, wished she had her knitting. There was just something so soothing about feeling a skein of quality wool slipping between one's fingers while attending to life's unpleasantries.

"We are sorry to disturb you, especially considering your bereavement over Cressida, but a matter has come to our attention in the course of our investigation, and that of Constable Gibbs, that we felt needed to be addressed immediately," Edwina said.

"No trouble at all, ladies. One must soldier on despite adversity. How may I help you?" Hubert said.

Edwina thought she saw a flicker of apprehension cross his face. His arms remained uncrossed, but he drummed his fingers on the top of his desk with what could be interpreted as impatience or even nervousness.

"You may or may not be aware that the constable now considers Spencer Spaulding to be her chief suspect in the murders. Until recently, Beryl and I would have concurred with that sentiment," Edwina said.

"Spencer Spaulding, you say? Isn't he one of the artist fellows?" Hubert said.

"Indeed, he is," Beryl said.

"I expect until her death the two of you would have been far more suspicious of my cousin Cressida. As much as I cared for her as one should for a family member, she was a bit off her nut," Hubert said. "You would have to think that since you were hired to soothe her ruffled feathers."

"I'm surprised you knew about that," Edwina said. "Constance had assured us that our true reason for being here was being held in the strictest of confidence," Edwina said.

"Constance is a good sort, but she has never given me credit for being as on top of things as I am. There's very little that goes on at Maitland Park of which I am not ultimately aware," Hubert said.

"Do you mean to imply that you know who murdered Louis and Cressida?" Edwina asked.

"That I do not. If I did, I would certainly have brought such information to the attention of Constable Gibbs," Hubert said.

"We are not as well informed as you seem to be about your home, as would only be right, but some information has recently come to light that we need to discuss with you," Edwina said.

"Go ahead and ask," Hubert said.

"During the interrogation of Spencer Spaulding, he asserted that his presence here at Maitland Park was orchestrated by you and you alone. He claims that you asked him not to reveal that you were the one who invited him to the house. Is that true?" Edwina asked.

"What exactly did he say to you?" Hubert said.

"He said you hired him to create some forgeries," Beryl said.

Edwina shot her a look that was meant to indicate her bluntness was not going to prove an asset in this interrogation. Edwina glanced over at Hubert once more and realized that perhaps Beryl's direct approach was exactly what had been needed. Hubert's face had turned purple, and he was opening and closing his mouth like a fish tossed up on a riverbank. She had a sudden urge to thump him on the back as if he were a small child with a bit of food lodged in his throat. Instead, she waited primly with her hands folded in her lap, trying not to twitch.

"His story was so outrageous we have decided it must be the truth," Edwina said, keeping her eyes firmly fixed on his face. After a moment he leaned back in his chair and nodded slowly.

"I wondered if he would crack under the pressure," Hubert said. "These artistic types are not always made of very stern stuff."

"So, you admit that you hired him to make forgeries of your art collection?" Edwina asked.

"Are you going to need to tell this to anyone else?" Hubert asked.

"Constable Gibbs has already been told, and we of course will have to share with her any information we receive from you. It is not our intention to go broadcasting your private business to others beyond those who most need to know in order to solve this case," Edwina said.

Hubert looked from Edwina's face to Beryl's and then back again before answering.

"The thing you need to understand is that the terms of our father's will made some things rather more difficult than they needed to be. I inherited Maitland Park as had male heirs before me. But my father was a forward-thinking sort of a man and he had a very special place in his heart for his beloved daughter.

He decided to divide his property in a way that he felt acknowledged that fact. While I own Maitland Park, Constance is in possession of all of its contents, at least those that came with the estate."

"So, the paintings you hired Spencer Spaulding to copy in order to replace the originals do not actually belong to you?" Beryl asked.

"No, they do not. They, along with everything else of value here at Maitland Park, belong to Constance. I don't begrudge her any of it, but it has been a confounded nuisance when it comes to managing my affairs," Hubert said.

"Are you in need of money for some reason?" Edwina asked.

"I am. Not to put too fine a point on it, but Maitland Cigarettes is in trouble. When we first started including collectible cigarette cards in our packs, our sales figures went through the roof. But with everyone else doing the same and with my main competitor having secured a government contract to provide soldiers during the war with their brand of cigarettes rather than my own, sales have tapered off."

"So, you needed money from the sale of the paintings to inject into your business?" Beryl asked.

Hubert nodded. "In fact, some of the money was to go to Louis Langdon Beck for the license to use his artwork on our cards. I had hoped it would be worth it, and now with his death I'm sure that it will be," Hubert said.

"Was it going to cost you so very much money to pay Louis for the pictures?" Edwina asked.

"That wasn't the main thing. The money is also for day-to-day operations of both the business and the household. Can you imagine what running a place like Maitland Park costs every year? Honestly, even with the monies from the sale of the paintings, unless something improves at Maitland Cigarettes it will be impossible to continue as things are now," Hubert said.

His shoulders sagged and all of his pomposity drained out of him. Edwina felt quite sorry for him despite the fact that he had engaged in defrauding his sister.

"Whose idea was it to try to buy the rights to the paintings from Louis? If it was so costly to do so, wouldn't your money have been better spent on other pursuits?" Beryl asked.

"It was Ursula's idea. She has had unflagging instincts for such things in the past and I trust her implicitly on all such matters."

Beryl shot Edwina a look. Once again Edwina had to wonder if there was more to the relationship between Ursula and Louis than anyone cared to let on. Had Cressida been the only one who sensed the truth of the matter? Had it gotten her killed?

"How did Ursula come to suggest him?" Edwina asked.

"She has always been involved with the artistic community, so I assumed that she knew him through a gallery opening or some such thing. I'm strictly a businessman and pay no attention to those sorts of events," Hubert said. "It hardly matters, does it? But what does is what you will do with the information. Do you intend to tell my sister?"

"We will share this information with Constable Gibbs. What she decides to do with it will be up to her. One could argue that it's a family matter, but it is even more true that you have confessed to soliciting a theft. The constable may feel she has no choice but to reveal that fact to your sister," Edwina said.

"Hasn't there already been enough trouble?" Hubert said. "Our reputation here at Maitland Park feels as though it's in tatters without adding a sordid family drama to the mess," Hubert said.

"It occurs to me the best course of action would be to get out in front of the story yourself before it's too late. Constance seems like a reasonable woman who has the family's best interests at heart. If I were you, I would go ahead and tell her yourself before she hears from someone else," Edwina said.

"Do you really think that will make a difference?" Hubert asked.

"I think you'll find that she is far more devoted to you than she is to the idea of original paintings hanging on the walls here at Maitland Park," Edwina said.

Chapter 38

As they left Hubert's study, Beryl caught sight of Roger at the far end of the hallway. In a flash she decided that her burden of secrecy had slowed the investigation down for long enough. She wrapped her long fingers around Edwina's upper arm and pulled her along in her wake.

"Where in the world are we going?" Edwina asked.

Beryl did not answer but used her free hand to attract Roger's attention. As they approached him, Beryl thought she could read a question in his gaze.

"Is there somewhere we can talk?" Beryl asked.

She raised an eyebrow at him as if to say the time had come to clear some things up with Edwina.

"Follow me," Roger said, looking over his shoulder before pointing down a hallway that led to another wing of the house.

They followed him to a small room that opened out onto a brick-paved veranda. He pushed open a set of French doors and held them for the ladies to pass through before following out into the open air. Roger pointed at a seating arrangement out in the lawn made up of wicker chairs and tables placed beneath the spreading shade of a leafy oak tree. He inclined his head at Beryl as if to ask if it would suit their purposes, and she nodded before making for it.

"What is going on?" Edwina asked as Beryl led her to a wicker settee.

She waited for Roger to also be seated before turning towards her dearest friend.

"Roger and I have decided there is something that we feel you need to be made aware of," Beryl said. Edwina blanched.

"You don't plan to marry and move away, do you?" Edwina said.

Beryl felt her jaw slacken. While it was true that she and Roger had spent some amount of time together in a manner many people would consider romantic, the notion of marrying him had never crossed her mind. She was quite surprised to think that Edwina would harbor any such expectations of her. She turned her gaze upon Roger. From the look on his face it was clear that he was as surprised as she at the suggestion.

"Most assuredly not. I've no intention of marrying anyone. I've gotten all of that out of my system ages ago," Beryl said.

"Speak for yourself, Beryl," Roger said. "I happen to have a fiancée of my own and considering your attitude on the subject, I'm glad to say it isn't you."

"Then whatever is going on? The two of you have been whispering and keeping things from me ever since we got here," Edwina said.

Beryl kept her eyes firmly fixed on Roger as she spoke.

"After carefully considering the current situation, we feel that there are extenuating circumstances to the usual protocol. The murders have forced our hands. While we will divulge no more than is absolutely necessary, we feel that in order for the investigation to proceed you should be informed as to the true nature of our relationship," Beryl said. "Isn't that right, Roger?"

Surely he must have taken the hint. After a moment's hesitation, Roger nodded.

"I'm very sorry if you've been distressed or misled by what

you have perceived going on here," Roger said. "It was never our intention to cause you strain."

Edwina sank back in her chair as though she were awash with relief. Beryl was truly touched. No one else with whom she had ever spent so much time had seemed so eager for her to remain in their company as had Edwina. In fact, she found that while people were generally eager to meet her in the first place, they had difficulty keeping up with her or maintaining consistent contact over the long run. Certainly, none of her ex-husbands had been able to do so, nor had any of her fellow adventurers.

Perhaps that was one of the reasons she had so determinedly lived the life of a wanderer. It was much easier to be the one doing the leaving than to be the one who had been left. If she were the sort to be moved to tears, she was certain she would have cried. As she was not, she forged ahead despite the inconvenient lump that had inexplicably formed in her throat.

"Roger and I worked together during the war. We cannot go into specifics about what it was that we were doing, but suffice it to say that the activities in which we were engaged were both crucial and secretive. Roger was involved in assuring that no information of a classified nature was making its way into enemy hands through artwork on cigarette trading cards," Beryl said.

"Was that actually a concern?" Edwina asked, leaning forward eagerly.

"You would be surprised at the ingenuity people will display during times of crisis," Roger said. "It was quite an effective way to pass information since the packages of cigarettes were being sent overseas and in such tremendous quantities."

"The modeling that I did for Roger was a cover for us to be able to pass information on the subject back and forth between us," Beryl said. "That is why I pretended not to have remembered much about our earlier connection."

"I understand that I cannot ask for specifics, but it does beg the question whether or not there is any holdover from the war years in the case of these murders," Edwina said.

"That was exactly my concern when I first saw Roger here at the artists' colony. Any undercurrents you saw rippling between us were of an intelligence, rather than romantic, nature," Beryl said.

"I couldn't risk mentioning anything about our previous relationship before I had a chance to run a background check on you, Edwina," Roger said. "I'm very sorry to have put you in any distressing discomfort."

"Does the fact that the two of you are sharing this with me now mean that I have passed muster?" Edwina said.

"It does indeed. But we are expecting that you will be worthy of that trust. As much as people like to tell themselves that the war is behind us, I assure you there is still an awful lot of activity that should give rise to concern both at home and abroad," Roger said.

Beryl wished that he had not made that point to Edwina. While she was perfectly well aware that the armistice had been anything but a decisive event, she knew that Edwina was easily distressed to think war could ever break out again in the future. Beryl saw no reason to agitate her friend unnecessarily and wished that Roger had felt the same before burdening her. Still, Edwina was not a child who needed shielding from life's harsher truths. In some ways she was more aware of them than was Beryl herself despite all of her exposure to the ravages of war.

"Do you think that the murder of either of the victims here at Maitland Park was motivated by something to do with either the war years or some sort of intelligence operation?" Edwina asked.

"That is still to be determined. I have asked for a background check on Louis, as well as on Cressida, but the preliminary information has not revealed any particular connection to ongoing espionage activities," Roger said.

"It certainly is hard to imagine Cressida being involved in

anything with such far-reaching ramifications," Edwina said. "She seemed to be such a domestically oriented sort of person."

"You'd be surprised the people who become involved in supporting things about which they are passionate," Roger said. He gave Beryl a knowing glance and she wondered if he was thinking about a woman the both of them had known in Belgium years before.

"What about Louis? As a figure of some notoriety, could he have been in the same position as Beryl to move about and promote a cause?" Edwina asked.

"Louis has never turned up in any investigation that I know of so far until his murder. Artists are always on the edge of society, so I suppose it's possible that he was involved with some things that would be worthy of a bit of a raised eyebrow from an ordinary citizen but might not do the same from someone such as him," Roger said. "It might be the perfect cover. Beryl here has acted in a similar fashion, haven't you?" He turned to Beryl.

"There is a great deal of latitude in being someone who is outside the expected parameters of society. It extends to both artists and adventurers, and I found it easy to explain away any unusual behavior on my part. People are always willing to accept that outrageous people may be doing things just because they delight in doing them rather than for any sort of methodical or strategic reason," Beryl said.

Edwina looked at her as if seeing a side of her for the first time. Beryl did not think her friend underestimated her and had always suspected Edwina remained taciturn on the war years out of courtesy rather than a lack of curiosity. Still, it was somewhat gratifying to see Edwina appraising her through a new set of eyes. Beryl, of course, would not brag about her contributions to the war effort, but she realized that she wished for her friend to esteem her as much for her brain as for her bravery.

"Could any of this be connected with Maitland Cigarettes? Could there have been someone involved in operations there during the war who was passing information they should not have done?" Edwina asked.

"Maitland Cigarettes was of real interest to the intelligence community. I assure you we had the entire operation under extreme scrutiny. With both Ursula and myself stationed there we kept a very close eye on things," Roger said.

"Ursula Maitland also worked for the intelligence community?" Edwina asked.

"Yes, she was sent there to help pass disinformation through the coded messages included on the cigarette cards. In fact, we continue to work together monitoring things as they unfold even now," Roger said. "Of course, that information needs to be kept strictly to yourself."

"Are you here at the artists' colony because of something to do with your intelligence work?" Edwina asked.

"No, if you can believe it. I am truly an artist at heart, and Ursula is someone who enjoys supporting emerging artists, as well as those who are far more established. The artists' colony simply is an artists' colony—nothing more, nothing less. At least as far as I know. If you want more answers, you'll have to ask Ursula herself. Since there is nothing more that I am legally able to share with you, I'm going to get back to my painting."

Chapter 39

Beryl had just leaned in towards the mirror at the dressing table to touch up her scarlet lipstick when she heard a tentative knock on the bedroom door. She returned the lipstick to the table before turning and asking the visitor to enter. The door creaked open slowly and young Janet Brown peeked her head around through the crack.

"Am I disturbing you, Miss Helliwell?" Janet asked.

"Certainly not. Come on in. You can keep me company while I freshen up my face," Beryl said.

"Are you sure it's no trouble?" Janet asked her, as she shut the door behind her and crossed the room so slowly Beryl wondered if the child had developed a case of early-onset rheumatism.

"None whatsoever. And despite what the late lamented Cressida might have thought on the subject, I see no reason why an adventurous woman with outdoor skills should not also present herself with as much attention to her appearance as possible," Beryl said. She smiled at Janet and gestured towards the chair in the corner nearby as she reached for her lipstick once more. "So what brings you to see me?"

Janet looked down at her lap for a moment before taking a deep breath. "I need to ask your advice about a missing button."

"I've only been asked to assist with the more outdoorsy pursuits as concerns the Girl Guides. If you want advice on how to reattach buttons, you should speak with Constance or even with my dear friend Edwina. I never was one to have mastered the home arts," Beryl said.

"All the Girl Guides are taught how to sew on buttons. It's one of our earliest badges. That's not why I'm here," Janet said.

"Well, then what does bring you?" Beryl asked, placing her lipstick back on the dressing table and swiveling her body to face Janet.

"There's something I know I shouldn't have done, and it's been nagging at me and gnawing away at my conscience ever since," Janet said.

Beryl looked the girl in the face and was surprised to see Janet's lower lip wobbling and her eyes shimmering with unshed tears. Could Janet have had something to do with the murders? Beryl had no sentimental belief that children were inherently innocent, but she would have been quite surprised to learn that Janet had such a capacity for violence. She seemed altogether simpler than that. Not simple in a mentally deficient way but more in an uncomplicated and unlikely to behave in a premeditated manner or with the calculating and cunning required to keep such a crime, or crimes for that matter, to herself afterwards.

"It's always best to get such things off one's chest, I find," Beryl said. "I'm sure you'll feel better once you tell me what's on your mind."

Janet nodded and one of the tears escaped and slipped down her cheek, making a long, damp track against her freckled skin. "I found a button in the glade at the same time that I found Louis's body and I decided to keep it," Janet said.

"You took a piece of evidence from the crime scene and never thought to mention it to anyone?" Beryl asked.

Janet nodded again, and the tears spilled out and rolled down her cheeks with abandon. Her shoulders began to shake, and Beryl wished she had the habit of keeping a fresh pocket handkerchief handy to give out to all and sundry like Edwina always seemed to do. Fortunately, Janet seemed prepared to take care of her own needs. She dug through her pocket and withdrew a small square of white linen, which she dabbed over her face before proceeding to speak.

"I know it was very wrong of me to take it, but I didn't think it had any bearing on the case and I just wanted something to remember Louis by. Cressida was right when she accused me of having developed an enormous crush on him. When I saw him just lying there and knew that I would never see him again, I just felt like I needed something to remember him by."

"Do you think the button belonged to Louis?" Beryl asked. "Did you remove it from an article of his clothing?"

"No, it was just lying on the grass nearby. In fact, it pressed into my knee when I knelt next to him to see if he was still alive. It felt like a sign. At least that's what I told myself when I decided to take it without telling anyone I had found it," Janet said.

"But you don't think the button was ripped off of his clothing in the struggle?" Beryl asked.

"No, I don't. It didn't look like something I had seen on his clothing before. It wasn't his style at all," Janet said. "As surprised as I was to discover him like that, the whole situation made a strong impression upon me and I cannot shake the memory of how he looked from my mind. None of it tallies with the button I found."

"Can you describe the button to me?" Beryl asked.

"It was brass and ornately embossed with swirls and small flowers. It was quite a pretty little thing, really," Janet said.

"And you never thought to tell anyone about it until now?" Beryl asked.

"That's just it, you see. I did tell someone about it," Janet said. A fresh set of tears spilled down her cheeks and she began to sob in earnest.

Beryl felt completely at a loss with such a display of youthful emotion. She waited for the noise to subside before continuing her questioning. Once Janet had deftly blown her nose, Beryl continued. "Janet, you need to tell me who you told about the button," Beryl said.

"I told Cressida. At first I tried to forget about it by hiding it in Constance's button box. But it didn't make me feel any better. I couldn't take the guilty feeling anymore of having taken it without telling Constable Gibbs. So, I showed it to her," Janet said.

Beryl felt a familiar tingly feeling creeping up the back of her neck as she always did when closing in on an important clue in a case.

"What did Cressida do when you showed it to her?" Beryl asked.

"She told me that I had been very wrong to take it, but that she was glad I had trusted her with it once my conscience got the better of me. She told me not to give it any more thought and that she would take care of the whole thing," Janet said.

"Did she ever speak of it again?" Beryl asked.

Janet shook her head. "She didn't and I didn't bring it up. But I can't help but wonder about the timing."

"The timing of what?" Beryl asked. The tingly feeling grew even stronger as sensations raced up and down her spine.

"It was only a few hours later that Cressida was found dead. I can't help but wonder if the button had anything to do with what happened to her," Janet said.

Beryl did not wish to be subjected to another spate of tears, but she also did not want Janet to leave the room giving any sign of extreme distress. Such a thing might cause questions and leave her vulnerable to whomever had killed both Louis and Cressida.

"You did the right thing by coming to see me. It's important that you don't give this any more thought. I've made many foolish decisions when following my heart, so I understand why you took the button, but it's important that you leave all the rest of this to the adults. This isn't something for you to concern yourself with any further. Do you understand?"

"Do you think I'm in danger?" Janet asked. "If I'm right about Cressida being murdered because of the button, might someone feel concerned about me knowing about it, too?"

"There's nothing to say that the button has anything to do with Cressida's murder, so please stop worrying yourself about it. However, in the interest of your safety, I think it would be best if you kept what you know about it to yourself until this case is solved. You can rely on me not to share this information with anyone other than Miss Davenport and Constable Gibbs. Do I have your word that you will not mention it to anyone else yourself?" Beryl asked.

"After what happened to Cressida, I'm certainly not going to say something to anyone else. In fact, it was all I could do to come and tell you about it," Janet said. "I just kept hearing Cressida's voice in my head telling me that the right thing to do was to tell the truth and reflect well on the Girl Guides." Janet stood and, without another word left the room.

In a flash, Beryl slipped her feet back into her satin slippers. She needed to find Edwina and in a hurry.

Chapter 40

From the look on Beryl's face Edwina knew her friend had learned something of vital importance to the case. Beryl had tracked her down to the Japanese garden, where she was once more posing for Charles. She had swept in and with her usual display of charm had managed to extract Edwina from the obligation without leaving Charles feeling disappointed.

At least it did not seem that he was. He mentioned that he was armed with enough sketches to proceed without her company, at least for the time being, and waved her away absentmindedly as though he had already dismissed her presence from his thoughts. Edwina hurried along the gravel path away from the Japanese garden and waited for enough distance between the two women and Charles before prompting Beryl to speak.

Beryl recounted her conversation with Janet in vivid detail. Edwina felt a prickling of enthusiasm that she always associated with the pieces of a case falling into place.

"What a foolish child that Janet is," Edwina said. "If she had brought that button to the police instead of Cressida, and had done so immediately, Cressida might never have been murdered."

"My thoughts exactly, but I did not say so to poor Janet. The girl is eaten alive with guilt about it all. I'm not sure she will ever entirely recover," Beryl said.

Edwina thought it likely that Janet would end up being just fine. The young were so capable of moving on. Look at the way the younger generation had thrown itself into pursuing lives of wanton pleasures. Not that she blamed them for wanting to distance themselves from the horrors of war. They just seemed to be so exuberant about it with the dancing and the drinking and their general zest for life.

Come to think of it, Beryl was a bit like the younger generation in her enthusiastic embrace of all things that pushed the edge of societal norms. No, if Janet turned out to be anything like those young people who were only slightly older than herself, Edwina thought there was no reason to worry about her future state of mind.

Still, something about the whole thing tickled at the edge of her brain.

"Describe the button to me once more," Edwina said.

"Janet said that it was of medium size and made of brass. She mentioned that the surface was embossed with flowers and swirls. Does that ring any bells for you?" Beryl asked.

"I know that there's something about it that sounds familiar, but I shall have to think on it a bit. I'll let you know when I bring it to mind," Edwina said.

"Well, see if you can't hurry the process up a bit. I have a feeling that it's going to be most important to solving this case. And you know that Constable Gibbs is desperate for it to be wrapped up before tomorrow," Beryl said.

"These things can't be hurried. Just leave me on my own to think for a while. I'll let you know what I come up with," Edwina said.

Beryl agreed and made some mention of being pressured into helping out with the Girl Guides, especially now that Cressida was no longer able to do so. Edwina wandered, lost in thought, back towards the house and mounted the stairs to the second floor and her awaiting typewriter. She settled herself in front of the gleaming machine and rolled a piece of typewriter paper under the bar.

She had always found that when she tried to concentrate directly on something that eluded her memory it slipped away from her grasp invariably. But if she allowed her thoughts to wander elsewhere, the memories came to the surface and poked at her like Crumpet needing a walk just as she had taken off her outdoor clothing and settled into her dressing gown and slippers for the night.

Sure enough, halfway into an exciting scene involving cattle rustlers and her heroic cowboy protagonist, her fingers froze over the clattering keys. Charles's sketchbook. She jumped from her seat without bothering to tidy up her work area. She opened the door to her room, poked her head out, and looked back and forth down the hall.

She made her way several doors down and having decided she would come up with an excuse should the need arise, rapped purposely on the door in front of her. When no one answered from within she tried the knob, which turned smoothly in her small hand. She pressed it open cautiously and poked her head around the edge of the door, sweeping her gaze across the room before her.

Tuva Dahlberg was nowhere in sight. Edwina closed the door behind her quietly and crossed to a large maple wardrobe and opened the door. Tuva had a great number of items of clothing stuffed inside it. Many of the things were not what one would consider day-to-day streetwear. Tuva's wardrobe included costumes of all sorts. Historical dress and that of other cultures, like a silk jacket and loose pair of trousers one might find worn by a woman in China, as well as a dancing costume from the Middle East that brought a furious blush to Edwina's spinster cheeks. As she looked carefully for items that contained more buttons than beads, she honed in on the items she sought.

A blue dressing gown, of summer weight, hung at the far right of the wardrobe. Edwina's heart beat faster in her chest as she held it close and looked at the buttons running up the front, as well as those attached to the cuffs. They were made of brass and ornately embossed with flowers and swirls. Edwina leaned in and squinted carefully at each of the buttonholes and lined them up with the matching buttons. None seemed to be missing.

Feeling slightly defeated, Edwina took a deep breath and reconsidered what that might mean. She carefully inspected each of the buttons, paying attention to the way each was attached to the fabric beneath. The seven buttons running up the front of the dressing gown were all secured with a great deal of skill and precision. She checked the one on the left cuff and then the one on the right.

Edwina turned it over carefully and looked at the stitching holding the buttons onto the garment. The attempt at attaching the one on the right cuff was nowhere near as expertly managed as the other eight buttons. And upon an even closer inspection it became clear that the color of thread was not the same, either. Rather than it being the same dark blue used to attach the first eight buttons, it was of a dusty black shade. If Edwina had to guess, she would have said that the person who had sewn that button to the dressing gown was still learning how to do so and had not yet mastered the skill.

Not only was the thread slightly different, but as she ran her finger over it and then felt the others, she noticed how much more firmly it was attached to the garment. The other eight buttons demonstrated a slight amount of give when she ran her hand over them as though they had been subject to frequent manipulation as they were moved in and out of their button-holes. The button on the right cuff held so firmly it did not move in the slightest as she attempted to waggle it back and forth. There was only one person to ask about such a thing. She needed to find Constance.

Chapter 41

As she had each of the last few times Edwina had encountered her, Constance appeared extremely harried. Edwina knew that if they did not wrap up the case soon, it would not just be Constable Gibbs who was going to be distressed. Constance Maitland was in a prime position to do the reputation of Davenport and Helliwell Private Enquiry Agency a great deal of harm should she so choose. From the thunderous look on her face as Edwina approached, she suspected it was likely that that would be exactly the choice Constance would be inclined to make unless something altered, and soon, to change her opinion.

"Please tell me you have some good news concerning the investigation," Constance said.

"I think it's safe to say that I'm following a very strong lead," Edwina said.

"Your last strong lead seems to have gone absolutely nowhere," Constance said. "Not only is my staff continuing to be up in arms over the state of affairs here, but now I have Cressida's funeral to arrange as well. When do you think you will have gotten to the bottom of this?"

"Hopefully very soon. That's why I've come to speak with you. I have a question," Edwina said.

"Can you guarantee that the investigation will be wrapped up before Cressida's funeral? I don't think I can face such a thing with a black cloud hanging over Maitland Park and what remains of the family."

"I can't guarantee anything, I'm afraid, but your cooperation with my question will go a long way to resolving it, I expect," Edwina said.

"I'll do my best to answer, but please be brief," Constance said. "I'm expected to be with the Girl Guides almost constantly now that Cressida is no longer able to assist me with those tasks."

"My question involves the Girl Guides. Have you had any girls who have earned their sewing badges recently? Or are at least working towards them by practicing sewing on buttons?" Edwina asked.

"That's exactly the sort of thing that Cressida always took care of. I know she kept detailed notes about how each of the girls was progressing towards badges so that she could award them appropriately. I suppose that's just one more thing that I will need to add to my plate now that she's no longer able to shoulder that task," Constance said.

Constance's tone sounded peevish to Edwina, but she knew that people displayed their grief in many different sorts of ways. Perhaps her hostess was less irritated with Cressida and simply wanted to keep her emotions private. Edwina herself made it a point of pride not to have made a fuss about her own grief in front of others when each of her parents and her brother had died. There was something so unseemly about laying one's self bare in such a vulnerable way that she found exceedingly distasteful. The only person who had actually seen her shedding tears over the various members of her family had been Simpkins. Somehow, he happened to appear whenever she had tucked herself away for a good cry.

"If anyone can manage all these things deftly, I'm sure it's you, Constance," Edwina said. "Do you think it would be possible for me to take a look at Cressida's notes? I could do so on my own since you are so busy."

"She would have kept them in her room along with the badges. Go ahead on up and take a look for yourself at anything you think will assist with the investigation. Whatever you need to get this finished is fine with me," Constance said, turning her back and hurrying away towards a housemaid, who looked to be loafing and chatting with one of the grooms rather than going about applying the duster in her hand to its purpose.

Edwina hurried up the stairs and located Cressida's bedroom in a wing of the house far removed from the rooms where she and Beryl had been placed. Inside the large, airy room, Edwina felt filled with sadness. Cressida had a photo of Hubert and Constance framed in a little silver frame on her dressing table, but no other personal memorabilia were displayed. On the dressing table lay a hairbrush and a dish of hairpins. There was a distinct lack of clutter or personal imprint on the room, and Edwina wondered if it had already been cleared out or if Cressida had simply not had much in the way of personal possessions to leave behind her.

As she glanced around the spare-looking room, she spotted a writing desk tucked up in an alcove. In the top right drawer of the writing desk Edwina found a blue leather-bound notebook. She opened it and set about deciphering Cressida's system of note taking as concerned the Girl Guides. It took some doing. Cressida had been verbose in life and continued to be so on the page. She took painstaking care to record all details of the Girl Guides and their progress towards their badges, as well as any other information concerning day-to-day operations of the group.

The book was organized by the name of the Girl Guide

rather than by date or even by subject matter, such as sewing skills or campsite cooking. After some time, she came upon an entry that mentioned that a guide named Sylvia had been working towards her sewing badge and had asked Cressida to inspect her work on reattaching a button. It was the last entry listing any such task as far as Edwina could tell.

The next thing on her to-do list would be to track down Sylvia and ask if she had been the one who had reattached the button to Tuva's dressing gown and, if so, when she had made the repair. Edwina decided to take the notebook with her rather than leave it in Cressida's room. It might be important as evidence, and she would not want whomever was responsible for Cressida's death to have the opportunity to get ahold of it.

Chapter 42

There was something about the way that Roger had mentioned Ursula's involvement that made Beryl wonder if there was more to the young lady of the house than first met the eye. Beryl could not help but feel as though the intelligence community might very well play a part in the mystery surrounding the murders. After all, she wondered, was it too much of a coincidence for at least three people who had been involved in intelligence work during the war to have converged upon the same country house?

Certainly, her own reasons for being there had nothing to do with her war years other than the ways in which they had prepared her for work as a private enquiry agent. And she supposed that it was possible that Ursula and Roger could be accounted for by dint of their continuing connection through Roger's employment at Maitland Cigarette Company. But why was he still there after the end of the war? Was there still concern about enemy agents using the company to pass secrets to the nation's enemies? Yes, Beryl thought, it would be best to make further inquiries just in order to cover all the bases.

She found Ursula in the drawing room arranging a vase of Oriental lilies. Beryl rarely paid attention to flowers other than in an abstract sort of way, but she had once had an admirer who had sent her a steady onslaught of the heady and stately flowers complete with reams of poetry he had written explaining how he felt she compared with their regal beauty. Ursula turned and looked at her as she entered the room, and Beryl thought a guarded look flitted across her face.

"You've come upon me caught up in an act of unabashed domesticity. I hope you shan't hold it against me," Ursula said, giving the vase a final tweak before placing it on the mantelpiece beside a ticking clock.

"Why ever should I hold something like that against you? I happen to benefit enormously from other women's desire to perform household tasks and to make the creature comforts available for the rest of us," Beryl said.

"I suppose it's because I rather pride myself on being a modern woman who leaves such things to others, but there's just something about arranging the flowers that I can't seem to resist. While I am not a visual artist like the others here at the colony, I do have an eye for what is beautiful and this is my way of contributing," Ursula said.

"Hubert was telling us earlier today about his reliance on your understanding of what makes for appealing art," Beryl said. "He was waxing effusive on your knack for helping to choose the right images for the cigarette cards as one of the reasons that the company has been holding its own against competitors," Beryl said.

If Hubert did not wish to share with his wife that his company was in financial difficulty, she certainly would not be the one to do so.

"Hubert is rather inclined to be effusive with his praise. I think he's still somewhat surprised to find himself married after all these years of bachelorhood and the novelty of it has not worn off. He's almost embarrassingly indulgent of me," Ursula said. She gestured towards a set of chairs near the fireplace and after Beryl had seated herself, sat into one, too.

"I expect you are well worth the praise he's heaped upon your head. After all, you convinced Louis to allow his art to be used on your cigarette cards and he'd never before entered such a crass commercial arrangement. I remember distinctly that being mentioned by both Roger Hazeldine and Spencer Spaulding," Beryl said.

"Well, I suppose that really was rather a coup now that you come to mention it. Hubert was quite pleased when I managed to secure Louis's promise of the license," Ursula said. "But I'm sure that Hubert doesn't need me to run his business effectively." Ursula waved her hand up over her head as if to dismiss the entire idea as nonsense.

"It seems to me that you must have had quite a persuasive argument in order to convince him to make that deal. It's not as though Louis was in need of money or more acclaim," Beryl said.

"Are you implying that I behaved in some way that was inappropriate?" Ursula asked. "I know that Cressida had many insinuating and insulting things to say about my morals, but I assure you, I used no such feminine charms to convince Louis to agree to license his work to Maitland Cigarettes."

Beryl did not have as keen a knack for ferreting out lies as Edwina, but she did have a very strong sense of the currents that ran between people. As soon as she had laid eyes on Ursula and Louis, she had had no sense the two of them were romantically entangled. If she had to lay money on Ursula spending time away from her husband in ways he would not approve, she would have placed her bet on a connection between Ursula and Roger.

No, there was nothing unseemly, at least in a romantic sense, between Ursula and Louis that would explain why he would have bent to her wishes. If it was not that, then what might have caused him to break with his past behaviors in terms of his art? Beryl decided to take another tack.

"I have no illusions that you were romantically involved with Louis. Cressida suffered from an overheated imagination and I'm sure it was very troublesome for you. She did, however, seem to have been someone who had a finely tuned ability to pick up on subtle currents that ran unsaid between people. She just didn't know how to interpret what she saw," Beryl said. "I have to wonder if that's what got her killed."

Ursula crossed her arms over her chest, then lifted her chin slightly. She might not have been born into the same sort of society as the Maitlands, but she certainly had learned how to adopt their strategies when it came to dealing with any unpleasantness in life. The haughty arch of her brow implied she felt entirely affronted that someone might suggest she had taken part in any kind of wrongdoing. Gone was the lighthearted ingénue who flitted about Maitland Park pacifying artists and complimenting work in order to smooth ruffled feathers.

"You certainly cannot be accusing me of murdering Cressida. She was a person to be pitied, but not to be feared. I found her to be a pathetic inconvenience at the worst of times and a sort of benign family pet at the best."

"I'm not suggesting that you killed her, or Louis, either, for that matter. But I am saying that Cressida picked up on something between you and Louis that others missed. Roger mentioned that you were involved in the intelligence service during the war, and it strikes me that a man who has enough money and no emotional attachment to explain it might be influenced by the desire to keep a secret. Who better than an intelligence agent to know about secrets and how best to leverage them?" Beryl said.

"I assume that you're saying this having some degree of experience with such matters yourself," Ursula said. "I'm not the only one that Roger has spoken of in confidence."

"I see that we understand each other entirely. I have an

obligation not to reveal anything concerning your intelligence work or the secrets you keep unless they have a direct bearing upon the murders here at Maitland Park. But I will continue to pursue this as thoroughly as I need to, using whatever means necessary. It would be in your best interest to share anything relevant with me and avoid me poking my nose into things that might prove embarrassing for you or for His Majesty's government," Beryl said.

Ursula took a deep breath and sagged back against her chair. She looked ten years older, and Beryl found herself feeling quite sorry for the younger woman. The war years had taken so much out of so many and Beryl always felt that those who were the young adults at the time were the hardest hit. They had never had access to the same levels of optimism about the future that her generation had enjoyed.

"What I'd like you to know is that I've never done anything like this before," Ursula said. "And I need your assurance that you will not say anything to my husband."

Beryl nodded. "As I said, if I am able to keep your secret I most assuredly will do so. I understand firsthand the value of such a promise."

Ursula gave her a long look and then continued.

"You're correct that Louis was not a man who would be easily persuaded to enter into any sort of agreement with Maitland Cigarettes. He was quite arrogant about the fact that he was both a commercial and critical success. He liked to pretend he was above such things, but the fact of the matter was his reputation was his bread and butter."

"And you had some way to threaten that?" Beryl asked.

"Part of my work for the intelligence community during the war involved keeping tabs on artists who had interests in the United Kingdom. Louis was already well known before war broke out, and his paintings were collected and admired. He made a great show of being supportive of this nation's interests during the hostilities," she said.

"You make it sound as though that was a pretense," Beryl said.

"That's exactly what it was. While Louis was here in England throughout the war years donating paintings for fundraisers for injured soldiers and being a mouthpiece for our causes, in reality his loyalties lay elsewhere," Ursula said.

"And where might that have been?" Beryl asked.

"Louis was very concerned that should Russia be on the winning side of things, his native country of Sweden would be under threat of invasion by them. He felt that it was in Sweden's best interest to side with the Germans because that was the way to side against Russia," Ursula said.

"But he never said so publicly?" Beryl asked.

"No, it was a closely guarded secret. He had only a few people with whom he entrusted his true views, and one of them happened to be a double agent who served as my source," Ursula said. "I've had Louis under observation for quite some time. You know as well as I do that the Great War was not a war to end all wars and we may find ourselves in similar difficulties once again and not so far into the future as one would hope."

It was a sobering thought and one that Beryl did not like to dwell upon, but she wholeheartedly agreed with Ursula. She had not entirely given up her own observation of those people she had been taxed with keeping tabs upon during the war years. Her network of informants left her feeling unsettled on the subject of global peace for the future.

Rumblings and grumblings from Germany left her feeling a low hum of anxiety whenever she let her thoughts turn that way. She could well imagine why Ursula would have continued to keep her eye on a man like Louis, whose hidden agenda could prove very damaging for England's future given his widespread appeal and clout.

"I'm assuming that you blackmailed him with this information in order to coerce him into allowing his art to be presented on the cigarette cards," Beryl said.

"That's correct. I'm not proud of it, but when I became aware of the financial difficulties Hubert was having with the company, I felt desperate to do something to assist him," Ursula said.

"So, you know about the troubles that he's having?" Beryl asked.

"I work at the office and as I said, I have ways of knowing things that the average person doesn't. Hubert, of course, has no idea that I'm aware of our precarious financial position. I'm afraid that while he loves me, he does not completely understand who I am," Ursula said.

Beryl thought that extremely likely. A man like Hubert Maitland would prefer that life continue as he had always assumed that it would. She was not sure what Ursula saw in him, but such was the way of love. Who could understand any of it? Hubert was the sort of man her parents had wanted her to marry, and the thought of spending her youth shackled to someone with so little imagination had been a sore trial to her. Still, she had done her duty and was rewarded by her first husband's swift demise, thankfully prior to the conception of any children.

"So you told him that you would expose his secret disloyalty to the British government if he did not grant a license to Maitland Cigarettes for the use of his artwork?" Beryl asked.

"That's exactly what I did. We needed something very different and unique in order to bolster sales. That contract that the competitor received for shipping cigarettes to soldiers has had a very prolonged and profound effect on our own sales figures. Once soldiers began smoking a certain brand of cigarettes during highly stressful conditions like the trenches, you can bet that they continued to purchase that same brand when they returned home," Ursula said. "It was destroying Hubert's business, and I wasn't about to stand idly by and let that happen if there was something I could do about it."

Beryl had to wonder if there was anything else that Ursula would be willing to do in order to protect her husband. Was there some way that Louis had been planning to withdraw from the agreement? If so, it would have been in Hubert's best interest to kill him before he could do so. And given the way that his death would increase the value of his artwork, she had to think it made Ursula a very strong suspect indeed.

Not only that, but Beryl knew firsthand the sort of cold-bloodedness and nerves of steel it took to perform as an intelligence agent. Ursula would have had the temperament necessary to follow through with not only strangling Louis but also carrying on as though she had nothing whatsoever to do with it.

"Thank you for your candor. I hope when the truth of all this comes out you won't turn out to be the person who is responsible for either of the murders. The intelligence service benefits from women like you and as you say, we may need you again before long," Beryl said, getting to her feet. "But if you were responsible, I won't hesitate to bring such matters to the authorities."

"I would expect nothing less of you," Ursula said.

Chapter 43

With some help from Constance, Edwina was able to single out Sylvia, the Girl Guide who had been actively working on achieving her sewing badge. The girl's eyes widened, and the color drained from her face when Edwina asked to speak with her on her own. After soothing her by reassuring her that she would be fulfilling her duty as a Girl Guide by telling the truth and offering to be of assistance, she calmed down and fixed her attention on Edwina and her questions.

Edwina led her to a quiet spot a little way away from the rest of the Girl Guides who were involved in constructing a litter to carry an injured person over rough terrain. Edwina could tell from the quick glances she sent at the others that Sylvia was eager to get back to the activity, so she decided to make her interrogation as brief as possible.

"Sylvia, I understand that you were working on earning your sewing badge while you've been here this week. Is that correct?" Edwina asked.

"That's right. I've been practicing with all sorts of repairs. You wouldn't believe the number of rips and tears that happen to garments when you're camping. I've been able to practice on a lot of the uniforms of my friends," Sylvia said. She pointed to one of the girls in the near distance.

"But you don't just practice on the other Girl Guides, is that right? Do you sometimes do repairs for other clothing items as well?" Edwina asked.

Sylvia looked uncertain, as though she had been caught doing something wrong. Edwina gave her a warm smile and nodded at her as if to encourage her to open up about her activities.

"Yes, I do. One of the tenants of the Girl Guides is to look for ways to be helpful every day. So, when I see ways to be useful to others I go ahead and take care of them," Sylvia said. Her gaze returned once more to the group of girls using rough twine to secure branches together to assemble the litter.

"Do you remember sewing a button onto a blue dressing gown as one of your good deeds?" Edwina asked. The girl gazed skyward as if searching her memory. "It would have belonged to someone other than a Girl Guide."

Sylvia snapped her fingers and looked Edwina in the face. "Yes, I sewed a brass button back onto one. It was a shank button and not one I had practiced on very often before, so I was glad to see it," Sylvia said.

Edwina felt a tremor of excitement rush through her, fluttering along through her stomach and then her upper back. She kept her voice even in order not to worry Sylvia and cause her to withhold information or become scattered in her recollections.

"Do you remember where you found the dressing gown and to whom it belonged?" Edwina asked.

"I spotted it thrown over the back of a lounging chair near the main house. I was headed to the kitchen garden to help pick fruit for the jam making when I noticed it. There was a button missing from the sleeve, which was easy to notice because the sun was reflecting off of the brass. I've been paying special attention to little things like that since I've been trying to earn my badge," Sylvia said.

"Do you remember when this happened?" Edwina asked.

Sylvia looked at the sky once more before nodding slowly. "It was the day after that famous artist was killed."

"When you saw it, what did you do exactly with it?"

"I picked it up and took it back to the camp. Cressida always kept a biscuit tin with extra buttons and thread and needles and things so that we could make repairs and could practice earning our badges. I rooted through the box looking for a match and wasn't at all expecting to find something that was particularly suitable. The buttons on it were rather distinctive. But luckily someone must've found the button because there was an exact match right there in amongst the rest of them. I stitched it back on and before I returned it to the chair where I had found it, I showed my work to Cressida so that she could make a note of it for my badge."

"And you're sure about when you did this?" Edwina asked.

"Absolutely. I remember because I had to hurry to return the dressing gown to where I had found it before it was time to begin making the campfire for dinner. Your friend Miss Helliwell was supposed to be giving us a demonstration and I didn't want to miss it," Sylvia said.

"Did you see who the gown belonged to when you returned it? Was anyone about?" Edwina asked.

"I didn't see anyone at all. And it didn't take all that long for me to sew the button back on. Probably whoever owned it hadn't missed it at all before I returned it. What I do know is that it wasn't there when I next went by to get something else from the kitchen garden," Sylvia said.

"When was that?" Edwina asked.

"It was later that evening but before it was time to turn in. One of my friends was feeling a little sick to her stomach after dinner and I went to the garden to collect some peppermint for some tea for her," Sylvia said. "I'm working on my first-aid badge, too."

Sylvia looked at the group of girls fashioning a litter once more and began to shift back and forth from one foot to the other. "Did you have anything else you needed to ask me?" Sylvia asked.

"No, that's everything. You've been very helpful. But, Sylvia, I need you to promise me that you won't mention this to anyone. It's your duty to help the authorities in the case of wrongdoing and this most assuredly is such an instance. Do I have your word?" Edwina asked.

"I promise. My lips are sealed," Sylvia said before bouncing back towards the group and looking as though she had not a care in the world. Edwina fervently hoped that Sylvia would remain so carefree and that the investigation would in no way taint her or hurt her. But there was only one way to assure that no one else was harmed at Maitland Park. Edwina hurried away in search of Beryl. The pieces of the puzzle were finally all coming together.

Chapter 44

Beryl and Edwina had agreed to meet back in their adjoining rooms to share what they had discovered before including Constable Gibbs in their assessments. Beryl had arrived first and found she felt like a tight knot of excitement coiled and ready to spring. She paced the room with the pent-up energy of a tiger in a cage.

When Edwina finally appeared, she had almost resolved to go and look for her friend. It had begun to worry her that she had not arrived, and Beryl had started to be concerned that Edwina might have fallen victim to the same fate as had Louis and Cressida. It was with a great deal of relief she saw her diminutive friend hurry into the room, a look of triumph upon her face.

"You won't believe what I have to tell you," Edwina said, hurrying through the connecting doorway and perching on the edge of Beryl's bed.

"I have much to share with you as well," Beryl said. "Why don't you go first?"

"The button that Janet found from the crime scene definitely belonged to Tuva, and a Girl Guide sewed it back on prior to Cressida's death. I think that Tuva was somehow involved with what happened to Louis and Cressida confronted her with it," Edwina said.

Beryl thought back to her conversation with Ursula and a sneaking suspicion began to gather in her mind. She didn't have all the facts, but she knew without a doubt that the two of them needed to speak with Tuva immediately. On their way to confront her they stopped in at the buttery and suggested Constable Gibbs might want to accompany them. The police officer readily agreed, and they went in search of the former dancer, whom they found curled up on the sofa library.

"We need to speak with you for a moment, Tuva," Edwina said. Tuva laid her book aside and turned her attention towards them. The three newcomers took seats close by with Constable Gibbs positioned between Tuva and the door. As Beryl looked at the younger woman, she found it hard to believe that she might be facing a double murderer, but it was not the most incredible thing she had encountered in her time investigating nefarious deeds.

She could feel the tension in the room crackling like the air before a summer storm. Edwina sat unusually upright and at the very edge of her chair. She had removed her notebook from her pocket and tapped upon a blank page with her tiny pencil. Tuva seemed the most relaxed of all the occupants of the room. Her hands sat neatly folded in her lap, and her demeanor was decidedly languid. Perhaps it was her experience as an artist's model that allowed her to remain so still when confronted by faces of authority in a murder enquiry.

"Tuva, do you own a light blue dressing gown?" Constable Gibbs asked.

"Yes, I do. Is that a crime?" Tuva asked.

"And do you remember if it was missing a button recently?" Constable Gibbs said.

Tuva shrugged. "Such matters never interest me much. My appearance is no longer something I concern myself with to any great extent, as I'm sure you can understand," Tuva said, holding a scarred hand to the damaged part of her face.

"I have it on good authority that the button from the right cuff of your dressing gown was discovered in the glade where Louis Langdon Beck was murdered by the girl who found his body," Edwina said.

"Is that right? I still don't see what that has to do with me," Tuva said.

"You don't think it odd that you came to be missing a button in the very same spot that Louis was murdered? I suggest that you lost it in the act of killing him," Constable Gibbs said.

"I don't believe you're going to be able to prove any such thing. I was in that glade over and over, and I could have lost that button at any time," Tuva said.

Edwina leaned slightly forward as she copied something into her notebook. "I'm afraid that's not true. My friend Charles had made a sketch of you wearing it after you had finished up modeling for Louis the evening before he died. In the sketch the button is intact," she said.

Tuva's eyes narrowed slightly. "I don't think that that would prove much of anything other than the fact that a button from my dressing gown appeared in the glade. Someone could have removed it and placed it near the body to implicate me. That girl, Janet, may well have killed him. Girls that age can be quite unbalanced by their emotions, especially if they feel they have been slighted by the objects of their affections."

Beryl was surprised to hear Tuva implicating the child. While it was true that Janet was leaving girlhood behind, there was still something particularly nasty about trying to blame such a horrific crime on one so young.

"There's a record of one of the Girl Guides reattaching the button to your garment. It was included in Cressida's notes on the progress of the children towards earning their badges. We believe that not only did you murder Louis, you also killed Cressida when she confronted you with the evidence concerning the button," Beryl said.

"Button or no button, this is preposterous. After all, why in the world would I want to murder Louis? He was my employer and without his patronage I risked what little financial security I had. In this economy that is certainly not something anyone would want to do," Tuva said.

"It's come to our attention that you might have had a very personal reason for killing Louis," Beryl said. "I believe you discovered he was behind the bombing at the café where you were injured and where your dance career so tragically was ended."

Tuva's eyes widened slightly. She looked as though she was about to protest.

"Your injuries at the café are a matter of public record. In fact, you kept clippings of them in your own scrapbook, did you not?" Edwina asked. "What was less well known was that Louis, despite his public persona supporting neutrality, was an active agitator in an effort to convince the Swedish people to support the German interests during the war."

Tuva leaned back even farther into the depths of the sofa as though all the fight had gone out of her. "It certainly was not a matter of public knowledge. As well as I thought I knew the man, I had no idea until the night before he died."

"How did you come to find out?" Beryl asked.

"I overheard a conversation between Louis and Ursula that night. He had already told me he had reconsidered his decision to allow Maitland Cigarettes to use his work on their cards. He said he was going to try to convince Ursula to allow him to back out of the agreement. Because I felt that it involved my business interests, I made a point to secretly follow him when he went to speak with Ursula," Tuva said.

"But Ursula didn't agree to allow him to back out, did she?" Beryl said.

"No, she certainly did not. She told him that if he withdrew his permission she would inform the authorities that he was responsible for the bombing at the Swedish café. We had always been led to believe that it was an act of aggression by the English who did not want foreigners in London during the war years. The violence that occurred there stirred up considerable animosity towards the English just as it was designed to do. If it were to come out that Louis had been behind the violence, not only would his reputation internationally have been destroyed, he would have faced criminal charges as well here in England," Tuva said.

"Then what happened?" Constable Gibbs asked.

"I realized that he was the one who was responsible for ending my dancing career. When the bomb went off, I was so badly injured I could no longer perform as I had once done. And even if my legs had not been damaged, can you imagine any ballet troupe in the world wanting the prima ballerina to perform with her face so covered in scars?" Tuva asked.

"So, you killed him because he ruined your career?" Constable Gibbs asked.

"That was one of the reasons. The other was that several of my closest friends were killed in the blast. It seemed only fair that Louis should pay with his own life for what he had done," she said.

"And what about Cressida? Did she deserve to die, too?" Edwina asked.

"I felt terrible about that, but I couldn't have her exposing my secret. Besides, she was a very unhappy woman and it's likely that I did her quite a favor. With her paranoid delusions it's a wonder she was not already committed to a mental institution," Tuva said.

Beryl heard Edwina gasp. There was something so cold

about Tuva's overall attitude of nonchalance about her responsibility in the matter.

"I'm going to have to ask you to come with me now," Constable Gibbs said.

Tuva nodded and gently placed her two feet on the floor in front of her. She rose with a dancer's grace and held her head high as she made her way towards the constable. Beryl thought she could well imagine Tuva onstage once more. Over Tuva's head Constable Gibbs flashed both Beryl and Edwina a grateful nod. With any luck she would be well on her way to join her bandmates before the passage of too many more hours. Beryl realized she would feel grateful to leave Maitland Park and head back to the comfort of the Beeches herself.

Chapter 45

All seemed once more right with the world, Edwina thought to herself as she looked around the parlor. In the short time she and Beryl had been away from home, Beddoes had done a thorough and remarkable job of cleaning the entire house. The windows sparkled, the draperies were freshly laundered, and the floors shown with a subtle luster from properly applied wax. Beddoes herself seemed cheered by her efforts and had even managed to interact with Beryl in a far less prickly way than was her habit.

Edwina thought it likely the two had benefited from some time apart. Simpkins, however, seemed to be extremely grateful to see them. As was Crumpet. Edwina had been quite heartbroken to have to leave her little companion behind but as was always the case with dogs, he did not seem to be holding a grudge.

Simpkins had made quite a fuss over them when they had returned, churning out meal after delicious meal for their benefit. He had declared Edwina to look rather peaked and expressed no surprise that the murderer had turned out to be a foreigner.

Beryl had managed not to take offense at his remarks and had declared his culinary offerings a triumph.

After a few days of blessed mundanity, Charles telephoned to ask if he might pay them a call. She found she was looking forward to seeing him and wondered what his visit might be about. He had implied that he had something he wished to show them. At the appointed time Crumpet pricked up his ears and leapt from his basket near Edwina's desk in the morning room. She followed him down the hall and opened the front door. There, on the front steps, stood Charles, a large brown-paper-wrapped parcel held under his arm.

"What have you got there, Charles?" Beryl asked as she joined them a moment later.

"See for yourself," he said, placing the object in Edwina's hands. She carried it to the front parlor, where she placed it upon the table they used for playing bridge. Simpkins appeared at the sound of the commotion, as he so often did. Edwina had never met anyone quite so nosy as he, except for Prudence Rathbone, that was. However, he happened to have a pocket-knife handy to help with the twine knotted securely around the paper wrapping. She slipped her slim fingers beneath the flaps and pulled away the heavy brown wrapping.

"What do you think? Do you like it?" Charles asked with a tinge of nervousness in his voice. Edwina could not quite believe what she saw. A beautifully framed watercolor lay in front of her. Beryl pressed in close and peered over her shoulder.

"Why, that's us," Beryl said. "Look how well he's captured your hat." She extended a long finger towards the painting. Charles had indeed done a remarkable job of expressing exactly the way Edwina wore her hat, pushed back slightly on her head to allow herself to see whatever life might be sending her way. In her hand he had painted her trusty notebook. Crumpet stood near to her in a playful pose of readiness for adventure.

"I see he's done a good job with you as well," Edwina said, gesturing towards the figure of Beryl.

"Is that a pistol?" Simpkins asked.

It most certainly was a pistol. In the background sat the motorcar. The colors and the lines on the watercolor were bolder than anything Edwina had seen Charles paint before. Anyone in the village would be able to tell it was the two of them. She was absolutely enchanted by the rakish tilt of her hat and the boldness with which he had rendered the figures. She felt as though someone were finally seeing her the way she wished to see herself. A little flutter filled her chest as she looked down at it and she ordered herself not to cry.

"Do you like it?" asked Charles once more. Edwina nodded.

"I call it *Intrepid Sleuths*," Charles said. "I'm so glad you're pleased with it."

"Why wouldn't we be?" Beryl said. "It's wonderful, don't you think, Ed?"

"I don't believe I've ever received a nicer gift. I know just where to put it," Edwina said.

With that, she carried the painting to the morning room with her friends following in her wake. She took down the heavy oil painting of a mallard duck that had hung across from the desk where she worked on her novel. She handed the watercolor back to Charles, and he reached up to carefully place it on the awaiting nail.

"I think that's just exactly the inspiration I'll need for whatever I choose to get up to next," Edwina said as she sat back down to her typewriter and rolled a new sheet under the bar.